RIDE THE
TRAIL OF DEATH

A Novel

KENNETH L. KIESER

La Frontera Publishing

RIDE THE TRAIL OF DEATH
A Novel
Copyright© 2007 Kenneth L. Kieser

Cover Illustration © 2004 L.D. Edgar,
All Rights Reserved, Used with Permission.

Cover design, book design and typesetting by
Yvonne Vermillion and Magic Graphix

Copy edited by Matti L. Harris

Printed and bound in the United States of America
First edition

Publisher's Cataloging-in-Publication
(Provided by Quality Books, Inc.)

Kieser, Kenneth L.
  Ride the trail of death : a novel / Kenneth L.
Kieser.
    p. cm.
  LCCN 2007933640
  ISBN-13: 978-0-9785634-1-7
  ISBN-10: 0-9785634-1-7

  1. Murder--Fiction. 2. Redemption--Fiction.
3. Dakota Territory--Fiction. 4. Historical fiction,
American. 5. Western stories.   I. Title.

PS3611.I395R53 2007   813'.6
                  QBI07-600207

Published by La Frontera Publishing
(307) 778-4752 • www.lafronterapublishing.com

WHAT OTHERS ARE SAYING ABOUT *RIDE THE TRAIL OF DEATH...*

"Kenneth L. Kieser weaves fiction and history into a spirited tale of the Lakota Sioux and Black Hills gold hunters, of murder, vengeance, and redemption."
– Elmer Kelton, author of over 40 novels including *Texas Showdown*

"An historically accurate tale rich in character development, action and perhaps, most importantly, the power of redemption. Kenneth Kieser knows Deadwood and the Dakotas and *Ride the Trail of Death* glows with realistic energy."
– Cotton Smith, President, Western Writers of America

"Kenneth Kieser blends a wonderful mix of historical research with great story telling as we follow the tragic trail of Birch Rose from boyhood to manhood in his quest to find his family's killers and avenge his own past."
– Thadd Turner, author *Wild Bill Hickok: Deadwood City – End of Trail*

"If you like Westerns, you're going to love this book. Author Kenneth Kieser matches dogged historical research with a real reverence for what the West was in fact. A solid read."
– Andrew R. Cline, Ph.D., Assistant Professor of Journalism, Missouri State University

This book is dedicated to Cathy Kieser
for her love, patience, ideas and understanding.
Love,
Kenneth L. Kieser
03-21-07

Debts of Gratitude

I want to thank God who makes all things possible, Cathy Boehm, Wayne West, Don Vaughn, Bob Keefe, Andy and Lola Cline, the Deadwood Chamber of Commerce, the Adams Museum in Deadwood, S.D., Jerry Bryant, LaDonne Kieser, Rodney Kieser, Ronnie Pike, Darrel Pike, the Olathe Kansas Library, the Deadwood Library, the Custer Chamber of Commerce, "Doc" O'Meara, Jud Cooney, the remarkable Matti Harris, the just as remarkable Mike Harris, the Mahaffie Stagecoach Stop and Farm, the Kansas City Library, Charley Green, Holly Kieser, Lisa Snuggs, Sharon Rushton, Mable and Milo Rose, Lawrence Taylor, my uncle Vinton Pike who showed me appreciation for a good horse, and many others.

RAND, MCNALLY & CO.'S
Indexed Map
of
BLACK HILLS

McNally & Co.'s Map
—OF THE—
RTHERN PORTION
—OF THE—

Black Hills

Comprising the following Mining Districts:

LOST DISTRICT, consisting of Deadwood Creek, with its tributaries,
WHITE WOOD DISTRICT, from its headwaters to mouth of Split Tail Creek,
CAPE HORN DISTRICT, from the Southern boundary of White Wood District to Foot Hills,
GOLD RUN, BOULDER, SAND AND BEAR GULCHES DISTRICTS,

And all Prominent

Gold and Silver Quartz Lodes.

COMPILED FROM ACTUAL SURVEY AND OBSERVATION BY GEO. HENCKEL, U. S. DEPUTY SURVEYOR.

===== 1877. =====

COPYRIGHT SECURED.

SCALE OF MILES

Wall Map of the Black Hills, size, 40 x 46, with Fine Illustrations, mounted on rollers. Sent on receipt of $3.00

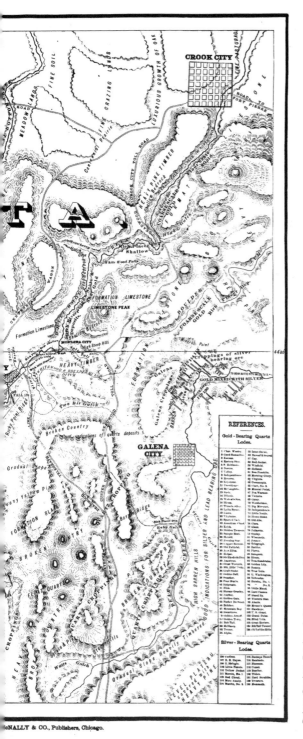

An 1877 map of the Black Hills, Dakota Territory, showing mining districts. Map courtesy of the Adams Museum, Deadwood, SD

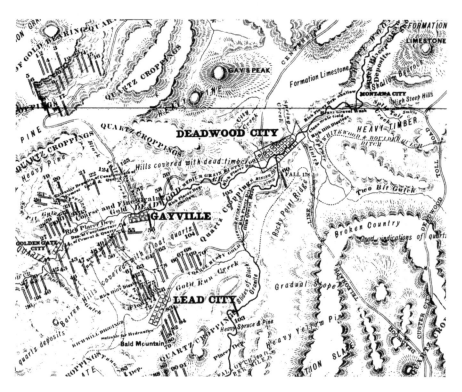

Enlarged section of the map showing Deadwood City, Deadwood Creek, and nearby mining towns. Map courtesy of the Adams Museum, Deadwood, SD

A team of oxen and two tandem freight wagons are shown posing for their photo on Main Street in Deadwood, circa 1876. Photo courtesy of the Adams Museum, Deadwood, SD

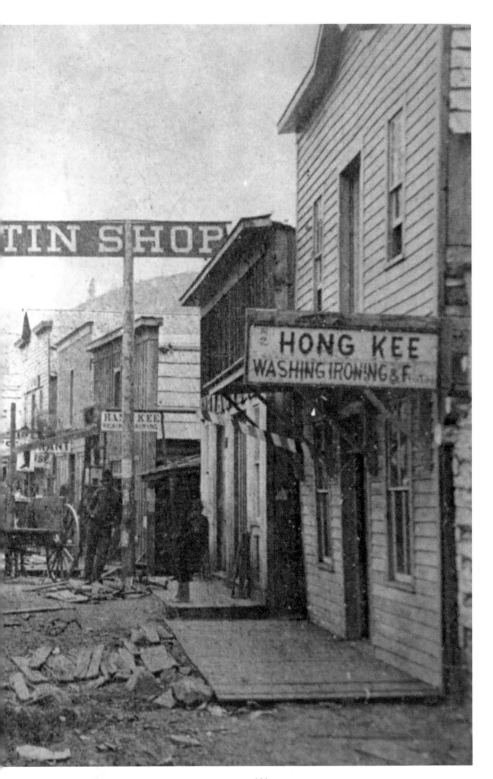

(photo page x)

Main Street, Deadwood, circa 1877. The lure of gold has increased Deadwood's population and spurred business growth. Note indicators of growing prosperity; the tailor shop sign in the foreground on the right, and part of a bank sign on the left side of the street. Photo courtesy of the Adams Museum, Deadwood, SD

(photo page xii)

Deadwood's Chinatown in lower Main Street—what was known as the Badlands—and a little further in, a sign advertising the Oyster Bay Restaurant and Lunch Counter, circa 1877. Photo courtesy of the Adams Museum, Deadwood, SD

Main Street, Deadwood, possibly circa 1876. The tent on the right is the corner of Main Street and Lee. The photo is one-half of a stereoscope photograph. The view is toward the north part of Deadwood and shows many miners and adventurers posing for this photo, taken by JS Morrow, photographer. Photo courtesy of the Adams Museum, Deadwood, SD

FOREWORD

Black Hills gold was discovered during the Custer Expedition by Horatio Ross and other miners along French Creek in 1874. Prospectors eagerly moved into the area in 1875, but were quickly evicted by the Army and escorted to Fort Laramie for their own protection. The Army removed the first group, knowing the kind of welcome they would receive from the Lakota, but the miners returned, determined to strike it rich after more gold was discovered.

The town of Custer City, founded by the Gordon miners party, came into existence on French Creek about this time. The huge group shared a case of gold fever, the disease that has broken many good men. The government attempted to purchase the Black Hills from the Lakota tribes who would never turn loose of their sacred grounds.

The Lakota soon found their hills filled with a great number of white people, an invasion that did not set well with the good people of the Lakota, Dakota and Nakota tribes. These groups were commonly called Sioux, an Ojibway word meaning little snake or enemy, so called by the white man's newspapers. This noble race suddenly had unwanted pale-skinned men and occasionally women in their backyard and too often in their front yard. They did not want this white invasion in their beloved black hills that they called Paha Sapa. The miners decided to push on for the gold, and the Army set out on a campaign to protect the determined whites who were invading the equally determined Lakota.

The Lakota people suffered many insults and deaths in the 1876-1877 period. Notably, the United States government issued an ultimatum stating, "All Sioux who are not on the Great Sioux Reservation will be considered hostile." Unaware of this proclamation, many Lakota were killed while trying to survive the harsh winter. The Lakota were forced to take their stand as warriors against impossible odds.

The great chief, Tatanka-Iyotanka, commonly called Sitting Bull, held a council to unite forces. During this council, the chief had his famous vision of soldiers falling into the Lakota camp like grasshoppers. The Lakota Nation knew their backs were pinned against a wall, making war an easy decision.

Remarkably, no major deposits of gold were ever found in the Custer area. Only the determined discovered just enough color to whet every prospector's appetite. When gold was discovered in the Deadwood area, word of this new strike turned Custer into a ghost town overnight—the population dropped from 10,000 residents to 12 in only a few hours.

About this time, Elizabeth Young Hicklin Rose, my widowed great, great, great grandmother, bravely loaded her four children—Sarah, Bird, Oliver and my great, great grandfather, Francis Marion Rose—on wagons and moved from Custer to Deadwood. During the trip, Lakota raided their camp one dark night and stole the horses. The family walked out of the Black Hills to an undisclosed location, possibly a stage relay station or perhaps a mining camp, purchased more horses and continued the trip.

My family legend stubbornly contends that Elizabeth was the second white woman in Deadwood, though some historians may disagree. She and the boys set up a livery stable and food tent for hungry miners, and business was good. My great, great uncle Bird Rose sold newspapers on the streets of Deadwood while my great, great grandfather prospected, apparently without success. The following year Lakota braves raided the Rose livery stable and drove off their stock, leaving my great, great grandfather Francis for dead.

Thankfully, he survived, or you would not be reading this book.

Deadwood Gulch, so called because of the tangle of fallen dead wood in the area, quickly became a fledgling town started with tents and shanties in 1876. The first gold strikes quickly made Deadwood a rough-looking town with only a few solid wooden buildings and many basic shacks, tents, and several log cabins. Progress was not surprising, considering that gold production in 1876 netted approximately $1,500,000, a considerable amount in a day when a dollar was still worth a dollar.

The Abbott-Downing Gold Wagon was built to move gold shipments from Deadwood to Fort Pierre's steamboat landing in 1876. The wagon weighted over 3,000 pounds and was pulled by oxen. The wagon and escorts made 20 miles a day on the 186-mile trip. Many robberies occurred during this period, increasing the need for larger groups of armed guards.

The beginnings of a real town eventually developed as solid businesses including a general store, a hardware store, livery stables, food tents, and legitimate hotels rose literally from the muck and mire. But, the so-called "good people" would never raise a family in this town filled with whorehouses, opium dens, over 70 saloons, and other places of iniquity when men out numbered women 200 to one.

The Lakota light cavalry was all but defeated by 1877. Most Lakota were on reservations, but history shows that some small bands continued to roam the plains, constantly dodging Army patrols who would have attacked. My fictional character, Black Moon, is a good example of a Lakota that wanted to fight on; no doubt there were others like him.

Deadwood was wide open during this period when gamblers, prostitutes and fortune hunters ran the town. Murder was common, and all forms of crooked schemes took mining fortunes on a weekly basis. A man would work long, hard hours in his mine for a sizable poke, only to be killed and robbed.

The town decided that a sheriff was needed.

Seth Bullock was nominated as sheriff by the territorial governor in 1877. Bullock only wanted to live in peace, work in his hardware store, and invest in ranch lands, but he accepted the nomination to become sheriff and quiet a dangerous town.

According to history, Seth Bullock ironically never had to draw his gun while arresting tough men in a town sick with gold fever. He was very handy with a six-shooter, but preferred to leave it holstered and physically crack heads. With his piercing eyes and shaving brush mustache, the 6'6", 240-pound sheriff had a stare that intimidated even the most crazy, tough, or drunk troublemakers.

Back shooters, common in all lawless towns, were one of Deadwood's biggest problems for law enforcement. Cowardly men (or men with common sense, depending on your point of view) reasoned, why face a man in the street who will likely kill you when you can shoot him in the back?

Bullock knew of this dangerous mentality and learned to be more careful than most. Some claimed he had eyes in the back of his head. This instinct kept him alive in a town where many would have loved to shoot him down.

On September 1, 1889, my great, great uncle Bird Rose made a small headline in *The Black Hills Daily Times* with the following passage: "Word comes from the Belle Fourche, announcing the death of Bird Rose while en route to Pierre with a bunch of horses. No particulars are obtainable at present and we are not able to verify the report. The report is that he was killed."

The September 3, 1889 edition brought uncle Bird back to life with the quick quote, "The death of Bird Rose was incorrect. The death of a relative in Colorado gave rise to the report."

Historical accounts were not always accurate in those days, and historians agree that some printed history considered factual throughout the years may indeed be fictionalized. So sit back, imagine what might have been and enjoy this account of fictional deeds from several lifetimes ago when the hunter often became the hunted and those willing to kill without question survived.

Kenneth L. Kieser,
February 6, 2007

PART
ONE

-→≫══◑ ⊂══→-

CUSTER, DAKOTA TERRITORY
August 7, 1877

Birch Rose opened the large loft door of his father's livery stable, inhaled a deep stream of fresh mountain air and took a long look at the approaching clouds that topped distant hills.

Rain, he thought, we could use it. Damned hot lately, maybe a shower will cool things off.

The tall, dark haired 18-year-old stretched his broad shoulders and 170-pound frame before looking down the main street of Custer, a town surrounded by the pristine Black Hills. The once busy street was empty after the miners and businessmen left for the strike in Deadwood, abandoning Custer like rats leaving a sinking ship. He could see vacant buildings and flattened out spaces between buildings where tents once stood, housing hard-working miners. Ruts in the road from wagons hauling supplies and men's lives out of town cut deep.

Working around his father's livery stable and blacksmith shop built up Birch's upper body, a fact not lost on most girls and even some women. He raised his muscular, well-tanned arms and took another deep breath, catching a hint of wood smoke from the nearby mercantile, a reminder that he was hungry.

He looked across the area to make sure his mother was not in the area before spitting a long stream of green chewing tobacco out the window. She had forbidden him to chew, and she made him polish his teeth morning and night with baking soda. He stretched again and surveyed the area.

Man, this place is really quiet now that the miners all moved out, he thought.

As Birch rubbed his thin beard with hopes of new growth, he caught a slight movement from the corner of his left eye. He turned to see two shadows sneaking along the side of Rex Sherman's mercantile, a drab, weather-beaten building that boldly advertised in white paint, "Sherman's—The Best Mercantile In Custer." It was, in fact, the only mercantile in Custer. Sherman had seen to that.

3

Looks like my brothers are sneaking up on something with that Apache rock sling I made for them, Birch thought. That was a big mistake. I hear about it every time they do something wrong with that damned thing. Maybe I shouldn't have made the sling for Bud, but dad made one for me and I got pretty good too. I hit bull frogs back in Arkansas with mine.

Birch glanced down the yard to see a white object waddling towards the boys, and he groaned.

Rex Sherman's white goose. Oh no, the boys are bushwhacking his old goose with their rock slinger, he thought.

He suddenly had to smile at the drama that was taking place across the yard. The goose, who had a habit of nipping both boys on the back of their legs and butts when they weren't looking, continued moving towards a foul situation. Birch watched, partly fascinated and partly wondering if he should stop this ambush.

The goose continued moving closer to the nine-year-old Bud, who was kneeling down with his rock sling in a menacing fashion. The goose stopped and stretched his neck, "her-honkkk, her-honkkk."

"That damned old goose sure is loud," eight-year-old Benny said while covering his ears. "Hate that stupid old bird."

"Give me a smooth creek rock, Benny." Bud whispered.

"Here's the black one. Use it. It's my favorite."

Bud grinned and slipped the rock into a leather patch with two longer strips of cord, his favorite possession.

Birch stood just inside the hayloft door, quietly talking the boys through their hunt. The goose had walked within 10 yards of the hunters who were cocked, ready and primed.

"Alright Bud, the goose will soon turn and you'll have a wide butt shot," Birch whispered. "Now draw back your creek rock and wait for your shot."

The goose took another step, made two interesting circles like a wild turkey, and then turned away from the boys like Birch had predicted. Bud could only see goose tail and felt the moment of truth that hunters live for.

Bud spun the rock slinger around his head a couple of times, and then let the smooth creek rock fly through the air like a well-placed bullet. The rock flew straight and struck almost dead center with a resounding "THUMP" that Birch could hear across the yard.

4

The flabbergasted goose yelped a high-pitched "ONKKK" and started running across the yard and past the outhouse, flapping his wings while making several more stressful high-pitched goose squawks.

The weather-beaten outhouse door slammed opened, and a rotund Rex Sherman stood there, pulling his black suit pants up and glaring straight at Bud and Benny, who were jumping up and down in celebration for a well-placed shot. His face was redder than usual, and his short-clipped red hair gave evidence why the miners referred to him as Pumpkin Head.

His attention shifted to the right for a second as a white goose feather gently floated past in the light breeze, almost touching his face. His eyes crossed while watching the feather.

Sherman had observed the entire incident through a crack in the door and was not going to let these two get away with their dirty deed. Birch saw Sherman and quickly ducked back behind the old livery stable's loft door.

"Hey, whadda mean shooting my goose?"

A look of fear crossed the boy's faces.

"Let's get out of here Benny!" Bud said. "Old Pumpkin Head is going to get us and maybe cook and eat us!"

Both frightened boys took off towards the safety of home as fast as their skinny legs could carry them.

Sherman chased after them as quickly as his overweight frame would go.

"Stop you little varmints, get back here! Stop now or I'll whip you good when I catch you!"

Sherman chased Bud and Benny past the livery stable where a thick glob of hay flew out of the loft, covering the angry storeowner like snow over a big rock.

He paused to stare up at the loft where Birch stood with intense blue eyes glaring straight at him. He instantly knew better than to start a confrontation with this well-muscled young man. Sherman decided to continue after the two little boys, who by now had run down a short street and to the family's pine-log cabin where they found sanctuary under their beds. Birch had a good laugh to himself as he watched Sherman try to run after his brothers.

Sherman soon arrived at the family's cabin. He banged on the door, but quickly gave up when he realized the boys had thrown

5

an iron bar to block all intruders. Then he slowly walked around the cabin, peering in the dingy windows and frightening the boys who thought "ol' Pumpkin Head" looked like a monster, especially at that moment.

Suddenly, the enraged storeowner turned his ankle on a smooth rock the size of a cannon ball that the boys had found in the creek. With a yelp of pain, he finally gave up on catching the children and decided to try another ploy.

He limped down to the lone food tent that was owned and operated by the boys' mother, Susan, who was frying ham, bacon, eggs, and potatoes for several of the few remaining hungry miners. He stepped into the old Army tent, frowning across the group of miners sitting at rough-lumber tables, ignored the "Hi Pumpkin Head" greetings and saw the unsuspecting woman.

"Those two boys of yours, they shot my goose!" the angry store owner shouted at Susan, who stood starring at the red-faced man with her mouth open in astonishment. "They hit my damned ole goose in the butt with a rock, the goose that I am fattening for Christmas, and I don't want the meat bruised or the goose stressed out. Then your older son covered me with hay."

By now several miners had busted out with deep hearty laughs that made the storeowner even madder and his red face even brighter.

"I want that goose to be good and fat, not scraggly and nervous. A nervous goose doesn't taste good like a fat goose. You better tell your boys to stop shooting my goose, and that big boy better never throw hay on me again, or I'll, I'll, well, it just better not happen!"

He was out of breath from chasing the boys and from yelling; his red face and the spittle flying from his lips had the miners almost rolling on the dirt floor with laughter.

The storeowner turned and limped back down the rutted street while stepping gingerly on his sore ankle and trying to shake hay out of his shirt.

Susan watched with her mouth still open, not believing what she'd just heard. Her bright blue eyes held a dark tint as she glared at the now distant storeowner waddling down the street much like his goose. He had wisely made a timely departure before her half-Irish temper had kicked in like an exploding volcano.

The miners were mostly fed and leaving, or sitting and talking, so she decided to look further into this "goose matter."

"Shing-Lee, please take care of the food for a while. I have to see about something," Susan told her Chinese employee, who spoke broken English. "I have to go talk to my boys about a goose."

"A goose, oh I like roast goose, maybe some for me too?" Shing-Lee asked.

Susan shook her head in frustration and headed towards home with a very angry expression.

"Roast goose indeed," she muttered. "I'm going to roast my boys' goose."

Back at the cabin, Bud and Benny had crawled from under their beds, satisfied that Sherman was gone. Both boys wore faded bib overalls just like their grandpa back in Arkansas, and their dirty faces were often the victims of spit baths on a cloth from their mother, an act they both hated. The rock sling was well-stored in the oversized back pocket of Bud's overalls, and one pant leg was rolled up to avoid contact with a nasty skinned knee from the day before while he was snooping around an old fish-filled creek up in the hills.

The boys finally decided it was safe to leave, and they opened the cabin door to face an angry mother. Her blue eyes glared straight through them.

"Alright boys, why did you shoot the goose?" she whispered in a voice that lacked her usual patience.

"The goose pinched my bottom yesterday," Benny said in a low voice as tears appeared in his blue eyes. "So me and Bud decided to shoot that damned old goose."

"You watch your mouth young man, or I'll scrape your teeth with lye soap!"

"But mommy, Birch says that and you never yell at him," Benny pleaded.

"All I can say is, wait and see what your father has to say about this. I am going to let him deal with this goose incident. Now hand it over."

Bud pulled the rock sling out of his back pocket and took one last look at it while handing it to his mother—who glared at the boys like a cougar starring at a rabbit—before slamming the cabin door and stomping back to work.

That afternoon their father, Jack Rose, pulled his team of mules and his red and green painted wagon loaded with burlap bags of oats in front of the livery stable.

"Birch," he yelled, deciding that the boy had either gone home or had gone over to visit the doctor's pretty daughter, Sarah. Jack took a long look through the stable and found what he had expected. The boy had shoveled a fair amount of hay into the wooden troughs and had cleaned each stall, which once reeked with horse and mule manure, wet hay, and other nasty stuff associated with a stable.

Jack was proud of his oldest son who sometimes worked like two men. Birch worked with some complaint, but only an understandable amount expected for a boy his age. He was unloading the wagon when a commotion started up the street.

What now, he wondered.

He soon saw Susan pulling Bud and Benny by their ears to the old stable, followed closely by a smirking Birch. He could not help but notice how their mother looked exceptionally attractive when she was angry, her straw-colored hair and slender shape looked beautiful in the morning light.

Not bad for a woman in her early 40s, he thought.

"I want you to punish these boys," Susan said in a low, dangerous voice. "Do you know what they did?"

"I know what they likely will not do anymore. They'll likely never hear again now that you almost pulled their ears off."

The two boys giggled and were rewarded by a sharp yank on their already sore ears.

"Now listen Jack. I was yelled at by old man Sherman in my tent today because of these two. Birch watched the whole thing, but he did nothing to stop them, and then he kicked hay on Sherman's head from the loft of Sherman's own stable. Do I have to remind you that we are renting the stable and cabin from him?"

Jack was not overly fond of Sherman because of his constant attempts to sell Jack things he didn't need. The last time they had spoken, Sherman had studied Jack's work pants and made mention of how worn they were, a comment that was not well taken. Jack also resented Sherman's obsession with collecting the rent at the exact moment it was due.

Truthfully, Jack did not like the man at all.

"What did you do boys?" Jack asked, half-intrigued to hear their answer.

"We shot Mr. Sherman's damned ol' goose with a creek rock," Benny answered. "An' we shot him right in his fat old rear end."

"Oh no, you shot Mr. Sherman in the rear?" Jack asked.

"No daddy, only the damned ol' goose, not ol' Pumpkin Head" Benny answered while Bud stood by with a look that said he was expecting the worst. Birch started snickering, but immediately stopped when he noticed the deadly look on his mother's face.

"Alright Birch, why did you kick hay on the old man?"

"He was chasing the boys and yelling at them," Birch quietly explained. "I just wanted to slow him down."

"I see," Jack calmly answered while stuffing his pipe with rolling tobacco from a tin that he had purchased two days before at Sherman's mercantile.

"Well, what are you going to do about it?" Susan asked in an indignant voice.

Jack looked at his younger boys' pitiful faces and at Susan's burning eyes. Then, he did the worst thing possible: he burst out laughing.

"Sounds like you made a darned good shot boys," he said.

"It was, pa," Birch said, "just like we showed them."

"You stay with your father, all of you," Susan exploded in a loud voice. "I'm going home. Jack, you might consider taking the boys camping for the night, or maybe for the next year or two!"

Jack watched Susan stomp back to the cabin, her hands rolled in tight fists and her back stiff and ramrod straight. She occasionally tripped over dirt clods that had been raised when the army of miners moved to Deadwood. He had been happy to bring his family to this old gold camp, at first in search of gold. He soon discovered that panning for gold like the thousands of other miners in the region would never pay as well as a good stable and a food kitchen.

The Roses had made good money from the two businesses, and some of the earnings had been stashed away for a better life back east. The boys would go to a good school after enough money was made.

Jack and Birch finished unloading the oats while Bud and Benny played in the hayloft. They finished working an hour later and decided it might be safe to go home. He put his big, rough hands on the younger boys' shoulders as they started walking on the same road that Susan had stumbled down earlier.

"Now boys, tell me all about that damned ole goose. Did it squawk when you hit it?"

9

THE DECISION
August 9, 1877

Jack Rose was a stoutly built man who stood slightly under six feet and weighed 180 pounds. His dark brown hair was streaked with gray, and the wrinkles on his face gave evidence of a hard life.

Most men who moved to the dirty gold camps in search of fortune did not last long. Some died, maybe from a case of claim jumpers, lead poisoning, pox or some stupid accident, without ever seeing their precious loved ones again. Others simply packed their bags and went back—homesick and defeated. Jack knew this was a tough area for the boys, but he had not wanted to leave them back in Arkansas with their grandparents. He had not wanted to leave his wife behind either. He depended on his family.

Susan had calmed down. She regretted losing her temper and made the boys' favorite dinner: pancakes with strawberry jam spread on top.

I can't stop thinking about Old Pumpkin Head's expression, especially after the hay bath, she thought. That must have been something to see.

She wanted a final look at her angels' sleeping faces. Susan slipped into the back room to make sure they were well covered; nights in the Black Hills tended to be chilly, even in August.

Birch stepped outside after dinner for an evening walk in the cool air, a reprieve from that day's heat. Jack and Susan knew he would wander somewhere close to Sarah's house, exactly where they would expect an 18-year-old boy to be. The girls tended to be fond of Birch, whose blue eyes pierced right through their hearts, and his thick, brown hair was always neatly combed—unlike the other boys.

Susan and Jack sat at the kitchen table, sipping coffee and talking quietly to avoid waking the two younger boys. The Rose family had bigger problems than the trouble with Sherman and his goose.

"Jack, we need to face facts. The miners aren't coming back, and things aren't going to get any better here. What are we going to do?" Susan asked.

"I would love to pack up and go home," Jack answered. "But we have to finish what we started. We came here to get enough money for a new life for us and the boys. Birch is getting older. Soon he'll be married with kids of his own. I would like for him to have a fair poke to start with."

"I know darling, and I agree, but I'm tired of moving. I only wish the miners had hit it big here instead of 60 miles away across those rough hills," Susan whispered, almost crying after a very long day. "I really don't want to move again."

"I know, dear, neither do I, but how else will we survive if we don't follow the miners? I promise that we will look for a permanent home after Deadwood."

Jack reached his arm over her shoulder, pulling her close. He kissed his wife, the woman who had saved him from a life of violence against carpetbaggers and the like after the Civil War. He started to kiss her again when the cabin door creaked open. Birch walked through the door, smiled at his parents, and settled in bed.

"Do you think we have too many kids?" Jack asked.

"Sometimes." Susan returned his grin and gave him a long kiss.

The following morning, Susan woke first and slipped several pieces of well-seasoned oak into the old cook stove. Supply wagons sometimes brought better burning wood into the area where conifers, willows, and aspens were plentiful. They would do in a pinch, but would not burn as well or hold a fire as long as oak or hickory. Jack and his boys woke to the smell of bacon and eggs sizzling with coffee's fragrance drifting through the cabin.

Jack is probably right, Susan thought. But I have a beautiful garden here, and there was talk of building a schoolhouse before everyone moved out, something the boys need badly besides my home teaching. I'll move when Jack says it's time, but I hate to leave.

Jack wrangled some trading of furniture they could not take and acquired two additional red mules with white faces and two narrow but sturdy freight wagons, a requirement for negotiating the old trails and passages that ran through the Black Hills. Horses were fine on the prairie with the reasonably flat ground, but here granite outcropping slipped down in places to make a rough path.

11

"The trip could take just over a week," Jack told Susan. "We will have to keep watch for danger by critters, robbers, or Lakota. They all are around and would love to take everything we've got, that is except for the animals that only want to eat us. We have guns and plenty of ammunition," Jack quietly said. "You, Birch, and I are all good shots and anyone in their right minds will not stay around long when we start shooting. We will just have to be alert."

Later, Birch carried an anvil out to the wagon. He loved to help his father, who had some remarkable stories about his service as a Confederate officer in the Civil War. Jack had received numerous decorations for his bravery in battle. But he never really talked about the battles with his sons. Just camp life. Men he'd met and fought with. Places he'd seen. He hesitated to tell his son about the men he had killed, some during the war and some before and after. Jack Rose never backed down from trouble.

I just wish he would tell me more, Birch thought.

Birch and Jack started loading up the livery stable supplies on a big wagon. The necessities were quickly packed, except for one rough-looking item behind the barn.

"Dad, what about our knife plank?" Birch asked.

Jack paused, considering the rough plank of wood. Finally, he smiled.

"Yeah, bring it son, we'll fit it in somewhere, but watch out for splinters. Seems we cut it up a good deal."

"Bet I can out throw you right now, best of ten tosses."

"No, we have to get moving. We'll have plenty of time to cut up that old slat in Deadwood."

They had spent many hours throwing Jack's knife at the plank. The knife was made in an Arkansas forge from the finest steel and showed little damage from hundreds of throws.

Jack had learned to throw a pig sticker in the army from a Texan named Jim Howard. They practiced with the knife during the many boring hours that always preceded the horror and anguish of battles, each man trying to top the other like two old men playing horse shoes.

"A man who passed by last week said he fought in the war and he had heard of you. He told me some stuff." Birch suddenly said.

"What did you hear, boy?" Jack asked warily.

Birch didn't answer right away. He lifted the knife plank onto the wagon and secured it in place beside the kitchen table between several pieces of burlap. Finally, he spoke, and his voice was quiet.

"I heard how you killed men with a gun and knife. That right?"

Jack sighed. He rested his eyes on the knife plank, as if remembering every time he'd thrown the blade. There were too many cuts to be counted.

Beside him, he sensed Birch shift his weight. He could feel Birch's sharp eyes piercing him.

"Yes, I killed," Jack's words came slowly, "but only because I had to for survival. I am and will always be against killing. But I would rather kill than be killed. Maybe I'm glad you heard about what I did in the war. It's time you understand that the need to survive can bring out the worst in a man, the killer side of him. I hope you will never have to kill, but this is rough country and I want you to remember that those who are willing to kill live and those who hesitate die. I want you to live long and give your mother and me lots of grandkids." He paused and smiled, "that is, after you're married."

Jack rubbed the top of his son's head and walked away.

Birch took in all of the details and decided that it would be foolish to ask more questions. His dad had spoken to him like an adult and that was enough.

THE TRAIL BETWEEN CUSTER AND DEADWOOD
August 10, 1877

A curious, unsettled feeling permeated the beautiful Black Hills.

The evening air felt cool, and yet it was still warm enough for comfort. Long hills covered with tall pines and big boulders made the area cozy. Soon the night sky would be filled with stars that the warriors, their ancestors and generations before them had pondered before sleep took over.

Eight Lakota warriors made makeshift beds out of what was available, mostly grass and leaves.

Black Moon, who stood a head higher than most warriors, and his best friend Red Pony had drawn six young men off a Reservation. They all wanted to follow in their ancestor's footsteps instead of living under the white man's thumb, or as the white man called it, under his protection.

Black Moon and Red Pony had been close friends since early childhood, sharing both the good and the bad times that had fallen on their people. Both had watched their families murdered over the years, and revenge became a shared lance.

Black Moon looked at Red Pony across a small campfire that was quickly burning down to glowing embers. Both men's faces showed worry.

As the campfire's sparks slipped over their heads, they were serenaded by an occasional popping of wet, burning wood. The younger warriors were never allowed to sit at their mentor's campfire. They sat back wrapped in blankets, watching and listening to the men whom they respected.

"I once wanted to raise a family and live in peace with mother earth," Black Moon said to his friend. "That was before fire tore across our country. Our sacred Paha Sapa may be lost. Crazy Horse surrendered and even Red Cloud acts like an old woman under the white man's laws and protection, protection from what, them?"

Red Pony added wood to the fire from a pile the younger warriors had gathered. Lakota knew better than to make a big fire in a world full of enemies, red and white. He glanced around the camp at this pack of young men who wanted to learn and fight. He and Black Moon had reached 25 years and seemed like old men to the teenagers; the youngest was just 15 and the oldest barely 18.

"My heart sank," he said, "when their General Miles defeated that small bunch of Minneconjou; my cousin died in that fight. Even Tatanka is gone, slaughtered and skinned by white men, his flesh left to rot and become food for the trickster. Now only a few of us are here to face these white men."

"We must train the few who are still free," Black Moon said, his eyes blazing in the campfire light. "Those who are not old women cowering in fear with the very people who have made them their favorite animals to be trained and fed. We must fight a good fight my friend. Our ancestors will know and their hearts will soar."

14

Black Moon stood up without another word, looked at his friend who nodded in agreement, and moved away to rest.

The young Lakota warriors in their camp wanted to be like the great Black Moon, who at that moment only wanted to sleep. He stretched out his tall, lanky body several feet from the others, took one last look at the stars, closed his tired, pitch-black eyes and quickly drifted off. The horrors returned.

"Here father, try my arrow and see how it flies," a young Black Moon said to his father, Buffalo Calf, who stepped outside his tepee.

Buffalo Calf drew a well-crafted arrow back on the gut string of his old bow. Black Moon moved beside his father to see a line of U.S. Cavalry charging straight at them on black horses and shooting bullets that splattered Buffalo Calf's blood on mother earth while the mortally wounded warrior tried to release his arrow. The riders quickly arrived, ignored Black Moon, and ran down his father with thundering horse's hooves.

Black Moon turned to see his mother and sister standing there, looking at Buffalo Calf, who was stretched out on the ground with his eyes wide open.

"Mother run!" Black Moon shouted.

The soldiers raced towards Black Moon's mother and sister, stopping their horses just before trampling the frightened women. Then, a big man with auburn hair on his face pulled out a pistol as Black Moon tried to run towards the soldier, but he found his feet would not move. The boy could only stand there as the white man pulled the trigger while laughing a loud, hideous laugh.

Black Moon watched in horror as the bullets pierced both women's foreheads, ending their lives immediately. His family lay on the ground in a pool of blood that spread across the grass, growing wider.

Then the soldiers changed into a pack of snarling wolves that moved forward to eat his family's flesh while he could only helplessly watch. His feet were still frozen to the ground as they moved closer and closer.

The others heard Black Moon grunting and moaning in his troubled sleep and knew he had witnessed his family's murder once again. The dream was a curse he could not escape.

"The great warrior is dreaming again," a young man whispered to Red Pony. "Do you think his nightmares will ever end?"

"Only the spirit world can end his suffering," Red Pony answered. "For some reason, they are letting him keep this dream as a reminder. They are using him as their well-honed spear to continue this fight against our enemies."

"Maybe," the first warrior answered before rolling over to sleep a little more.

Red Pony listened to the warrior's troubled sounds like he had on so many other raids. He shook Black Moon, who sat up with his eyes wide and sweat covering his face.

"Wake up my friend," Red Pony said. "You were dreaming again, and it is time to rise anyway. We have work to do."

Black Moon stood and stretched before walking over and delivering a well-placed kick on the rear of a young brave who rolled down the hill. The young man jumped to his feet and looked to Black Moon for orders. Then the young warrior glanced at the eastern horizon, fixing his eyes on the orange glow that filtered through a group of low clouds.

A gift for my eyes from the Great Spirit, he thought. This must be the day when I will kill my first enemy, maybe a big soldier who has fought many battles. Then Black Moon will look at me like a man.

A FATEFUL MOVE
August 12, 1877

"We'll that's it. The furniture and supplies for setting up our kitchen and livery stable are loaded," Jack said. "I settled up the rent with Rex Sherman on the livery stable and cabin, and he agreed to store our remaining furniture. Birch and I will bring the wagons back for the other stuff next spring. We're blessed with clear skies and warm days, good conditions for traveling."

"Do you think we have enough money to set up both businesses before winter?" Susan asked.

Jack took a long look at his wife and noticed the tightness in her jaw and the worry lines around her pretty blue eyes that all three of her sons had inherited.

16

"We had better, dear. I'm sure those miners are getting sick of their own cooking. They need one of your homemade meals. I've heard several say that you are a beautiful woman who reminds them of better times. I think you look pretty good myself," he said while patting her on the butt.

"Stop that Jack," she said. "The boys don't need to see you doing that."

"It's alright mama, you spank us too sometimes," Benny said. "You just spank us harder than daddy spanks you."

Jack and Birch took a long walk around Custer the evening before they pulled out. The once busy town now looked deserted except for a hound dog sleeping on the mercantile front porch. He stopped in front of an old lodge where he had played poker with several ranchers and miners many evenings. An empty whiskey bottle leaned against the building, a jug he had personally shared with two miners before they left.

Sherman's old goose made a long "her-honkkkk" somewhere behind the old building. Jack grinned and lightly punched Birch on his right shoulder in a playful manner. The boy grinned at his dad and punched him back, an act of affection that was not lost on Jack as he looked off into the ancient Black Hills.

"Ready to move, son?" Jack asked.

"Yes pa, guess I am, don't see any reason to stay here, except maybe for Sarah."

"You were getting fond of her, weren't you boy?"

"Yes sir, maybe too fond."

Jack turned to look at his son. "Something you need to tell me, Birch?"

"No sir. We weren't that fond of each other, sort of, well, you know, a little smooching."

Jack nodded, relieved. "Well listen son, forget about her now. I'll need your help looking after ma and the boys. You are a man now and capable of a man's responsibilities. Think you can handle one of the teams over them rough hills?"

"You bet pa, I'll be fine."

"Great, we will get underway tomorrow morning and remember son, I know you can do it."

"Count on it pa."

The next morning, Jack gathered the family around for a prayer.

"Our most kind and gracious heavenly father, thank you for this remarkable family. Please give us good traveling weather and a safe journey. In Jesus' name I pray, amen."

Everyone loaded up in the wagon and Jack slapped leather to the rear mule's behind. The team started up and everyone jerked forward. The boys laughed with delight as Susan gave Jack a very sexy smile. Birch stirred up his mules while thinking about the girl he was leaving behind. Benny took a long look for another peek at the goose, but he was gone, probably hiding. Hope his butt is still sore, the young man thought.

Birch took a long look at Sherman's Mercantile and laughed as they slowly moved past. Bud and Benny had insisted on riding with their big brother, and they sat scrunched up against him on the narrow wagon seat.

Progress was slow and bumpy over the hilly trails of rocks and washed out ditches. A miner's map showed the route that would eventually lead the family to their new home. The Black Hills trail would challenge the capable mules that were long bodied and even longer winded.

The first nights were fun for Bud and Benny, who thought camping in the Black Hills was an adventure where they might see injuns or wild critters, especially on the first evening when they stopped in a field of grass alongside the trial.

"Look dad," Birch said, "you and I hunted deer in that part of the Black Hills. Look at those granite outcroppings washed white from the bad weather, and the endless pine and cedar groves that grow on the hills, thick as hair on a dog. I like those occasional stands of aspens and white-barked birch trees. They really add to the color of this place."

"You're right boy," Jack answered. "I wish we were hunting instead of packing the family across these damn rough hills."

"Where do you want to start the fire?" Birch asked.

"The wind is out of the west, so start it somewhere east of the wagon and not too far away. You know boy, I lived around campfires for three years during the war. I hated it. But this is different with my family. Mom, set that cast iron Dutch oven out and we'll try some of that good stew you made before we left Custer. Boy, get the fire going, and I'll scoop out some coals to set the big pot on. We'll use the little grill for coffee. Bud and Benny, get a move on and help your brother pickup some kindling. I'm hungry."

18

Susan's cooking was excellent as always, and later that evening they all said goodnight before rolling up in their blankets beside the fire that had finally burned down. The boys listened to a great horned owl hooting somewhere down the hill.

Something heavy moved several yards in front of the camp, and Jack feared a bear might smell the food, so he loaded his old muzzleloader and laid it close by for an easy reach.

Morning came, and the family got under way after some of Susan's pancakes were devoured. The first few days saw little trouble and a good advance into the unpredictable hills, but misfortune found the Rose family about 40 miles out of Custer on the fifth night.

TRAGEDY FOR THE ROSE FAMILY
August 17, 1877

"**D**o you smell that food Black Moon?" Red Pony asked. "I think we should see what is cooking. It has to be better than this old dried deer meat."

"Yes, my friend," Black Moon answered. "I already instructed one of the young men to sneak in and grab that pan of food off the coals while we get the mules. I just hope these young ones can do this quietly enough to not wake everyone until we are ready."

One of the young Lakota slipped past the sleeping family that was rolled up in old Army blankets a few feet from the fire. He quietly took the Dutch oven full of white beans that sat on a grate positioned a few inches over glowing coals. Black Moon and some of the others moved just outside the camp without a sound.

Suddenly, each man jumped on a mule and galloped away with the prized animals that would serve as transportation and food. The family woke to yelling and whooping mixed with the sounds of hooves heading east.

"Stay put," Jack told Susan as he left his old Army blanket and ran towards the melee with his knife and the old Civil War musket he had carried at Bull Run before catching a Yankee's pumpkin ball in his left shoulder.

"Bud and Benny, come over here," she said, tightly pressing both boys against her to shelter them.

The first Lakota warrior turned to see Jack, changed direction, and charged. Jack stood his ground, slipped the knife in his hand and flipped it underhanded into the brave's chest. The Lakota hit the ground, stone dead.

A second brave bored in at full speed, making a loud war whoop that frightened Susan and the boys. Jack raised his old rifle to shoot. The family watched in horror as Jack was shot in the chest by the Lakota leader, Black Moon.

Birch watched this horrible scene with hot tears running down his cheeks. He ran towards his father's rifle and looked up to see the elated warrior jump off the mule, slip a sharp knife from its sheath and easily take Jack's scalp. Black Moon held the scalp up high and made a high-pitched yell that sent chills down the shocked family's spines. Birch grabbed the rifle, took careful aim, and squeezed the trigger like his father had shown him. There was a "click."

The rifle misfired.

Birch looked at the faulty firearm in total disbelief that quickly turned to horror. He knew that the warrior who had killed his father could turn and shoot him, happy to end his life.

I'm going to die, he thought. We're all going to die.

He continued fighting with the gun, cocking the hammer again to get the percussion cap to fire, but without success. The cap wouldn't fire, and he couldn't reach his father's possibles bag for a new cap.

The warrior leaped on the mule, spun towards Birch, held up the scalp and yelled in broken English learned from a trapper, "I am Lakota, Black Moon. Can you not see that I took this enemy in battle? Now part of his soul belongs to me. Leave our land. You are not wanted here. I let you live to tell others who come here to stay away. I, Black Moon, have spoken."

Birch starred at the warrior, hoping to remember his face while still fumbling with the old firearm for a shot. For the first time in his short, 18 years of life he wanted to kill another man, and he vowed that this murderer, Black Moon, would die. But the Lakota had turned the mule away, yelling into the night, whooping and hollering as the mule carried him over the ridge.

Birch turned to look at his dad, who was losing a lot of blood out of his chest. Jack's mouth was open, and he was trying to speak. Only a gurgling sound came as a stream of blood slipped from the corner of his mouth.

"Jack," Susan screamed in a voice so full of anguish that Birch would hear it for many years afterwards. She cautiously raised Jack's body as he fought to live. Gently, she cradled her beloved husband's head in her lap, stroking his face with trembling fingers while sobs made her body quiver.

"Take it easy honey," she said softly. "Stay with me, it is not time for you to go yet. I won't allow it, now stay with me. Oh baby, please, don't go now. We are supposed to grow old together. Please honey."

Jack tried again to talk, but did not have enough life left for final words.

And then, he was gone.

Birch did not understand how the Lakota's rights were violated through treaty violations and brutality, nor did he care while pulling his father's knife out of the dead warrior's chest. He only knew that his father had died at the hands of this vicious Black Moon.

Birch vowed again that he would find the murderer and take an eye for an eye, words his mother had read from the Bible. He spent the rest of that morning digging his father's grave while Susan prepared Jack's body for its final resting-place. She laid her right hand on Jack's face, then reached down and softly kissed his forehead. Her quivering hands washed his face over and over again as the tears rolled down her well-tanned cheeks. She slipped a cloth over his head where the Lakota had cut his scalp and then tried to dust off his clothing. Birch paused from digging and took a long, concerned look at his mother.

Benny and Bud sat against a tree. Neither boy spoke as they stared at the hole Birch was digging. Birch could tell they were trying not to cry as they sat shoulder to shoulder, finding strength in the closeness, each pretending not to notice when the other wiped his nose and eyes on his shirtsleeves.

The soft soil dug up easily except for an occasional root that had to be cut and the occasional rock that had to be removed. Finally the job was finished, and Susan helped Birch slip Jack into the well-dug hole.

The family stood around the grave, crying and starring at the bundle that had been their father and husband. On his chest, Susan laid a small bundle of dried flowers from her garden in

21

Custer. His family sang a couple of hymns and prayed for the salvation of his soul. Then Birch tried to say a few words, but he had trouble speaking.

"His grave will be lost forever in this maze of hills and pines," Birch observed. "What a magnificent cemetery for this great man who we already miss. Dad fought in the war and survived many conflicts even after the fighting was over. He was a good husband, father and friend. We will never forget you, and we will always miss you dad."

Birch could say no more, and tears ran down everyone's cheeks, marking the soil where Jack would rest forever.

They turned and walked back to the wagons, trying to comfort each other. Susan's legs buckled in a moment of grief, and Birch caught her with surprising strength. They stepped back into camp and sat around the bed of dying coals, with arms around each other. A horrible silence filled the camp as each starred at the embers, trying to make sense of what had happened.

BIRCH MAKES A HARD DECISION
August 18, 1877

Birch did not sleep that night. Visions of his father's death haunted him and worse, he had to decide how to save his family. The following morning he argued with his mother after breakfast.

"I don't see that we've a choice," Birch said. "We don't have mules, no one is expecting us in Deadwood, and help will only come if I bring it back."

"Alright, I understand that, but we've already lost your father," Susan said with tears running down her cheek. "I don't want to lose you too—I couldn't take that. I only wish that we had gone back to Arkansas—he would still be alive."

"But we didn't mom, and now I have to get help or we will never get out of here."

"Then we should all go together."

"I might have 20 or 30 miles of rough walking—the boys could never manage that walk and I'm not sure that you could either. Besides, who knows what I might find on the path? The miners had safety in numbers, but we're all alone. I might have a chance to slip by any Lakota, but it would be impossible with all of us. Carrying enough food is another problem, but you can feed and take care of the boys here at camp. Wild animals are another thing to think about."

"Alright," Susan interrupted, "I understand your point, and you are probably right. I can shoot, but show Bud and Benny how to use the guns so maybe we can scare off trouble. I still can't believe that your father is gone...and you are leaving."

"I'll be back, mom, and with help so we can continue on to Deadwood and run both businesses. Dad taught me a lot about the livery stable business. We'll be fine. We will earn enough money to move somewhere, maybe St. Louis. Haven't you always wanted to go there?"

"Just come back to us."

Birch packed a canteen, some jerked beef, several hard biscuits, and a piece of hard candy Bud had given him yesterday afternoon. He walked over and put his arm around his brothers' shoulders. They were heartbroken, but both would have to grow up fast in this dangerous country. Birch spent some time teaching them to use the musket. Bud glanced up at Birch and tried to look and sound brave.

"Benny and I will keep the musket to protect mom," Bud said. "Thanks for showing us how to use dad's gun. Maybe I will shoot that damned old injun who killed dad."

They have plenty of food and water, Birch thought. They shouldn't have a problem unless the same bunch of Lakota or another roving band returns.

Birch looked at Bud, who was holding his dad's old musket. "Don't worry, Birch. We can take care of mom. You just bring back help and hurry." Bud said.

Birch knew better, realizing that the boys were too young. Susan was a good enough shot, but not against men who knew how to shoot. There was no doubt that Birch had to send back help soon as possible, but that would take a lot of luck without a horse or mule.

"I'm afraid they might come back and murder us too," Susan told Birch out of earshot of the boys while stroking his thick brown hair. "We're counting on you, son. You have to make it. We have your father's old guns, some ammunition and plenty of food, but I'm afraid that we'll not be much of a match for another band of Indians or even wild animals, so please hurry."

Birch only heard half of her desperate words while remembering the furious face of the Lakota who killed his father. His new friends, hate and revenge, would travel with him for a long time, time that would make that hate turn to obsession.

Birch turned his father's sheaf over and over, pausing to take another look at the knife. He had always wanted the slender fighting-style knife with a cold, black handle, but certainly not like this. The well-sharpened weapon that he would have treasured under different circumstances was a grim reminder of his father who had used the knife bravely before his death.

He slipped the sheaf under his left flannel shirtsleeve, strapping on the forearm harness, an uncomfortable device he thought. The added knife made an annoying weight that Jack had long ago gotten used to. Birch adjusted the sheaf's straps to fit his smaller arms instead of Jack's thick, shorter forearms. He slowly buttoned the sleeve and looked down at his arm. This hidden knife felt strange, but it made him feel more dangerous than he had ever felt.

He turned away and walked down the trail before another word could be spoken. More talking would just be a waste of precious time in a dangerous land.

BLACK MOON'S DEPARTURE
August 18, 1877

Black Moon and Red Pony argued over who would take the mules back several miles to a small village in the east where old men, women and children were trying to survive. Black Moon finally gave up and led the string out early that morning just before daylight. People in the village would welcome the mule meat that could be dried after some was prepared for a celebration of this gift of survival. Red Pony would stay and lead the young warriors further along the trail, looking for other white men who came to Paha Sapa seeking the yellow metal.

"Mule meat," Black Moon had grumbled to Red Pony before he rode out. "I remember when buffalo filled the bellies of our people. These white killers rode in and slaughtered our buffalo and now our people eat mule."

"Mule is not that bad old friend," Red Pony answered. "I miss buffalo, too, but Tatanka is gone and we must live on."

"Yes, the old times are gone forever, just another reason to fight."

"You, my brother, take care," Red Pony said. "I have lost most of my family and friends. You are my last brother, even though our mothers were different. We have endured much together, but I fear a snare is closing around our necks."

"Be careful and don't go to the spirit world yet." Black Moon spoke. "We have been defeated until most of our people have given up and settled on the reservation. But now it is time for us to carry on the fight. For now, live and be well, my brother. I will be back, Red Pony. Teach these young fools so they don't die before my return. I'll see you soon."

Red Pony watched Black Moon ride away before he reached into his buckskin bag for a piece of dried venison and felt a foreign object. He pulled out the knife wrapped in oiled deer skin and turned it over and over in his hands—Black Moon's favorite knife with a well-polished handle and good steel from the white man's world. He turned the beautiful knife over and over in his hands, feeling more invincible than ever before.

He must have slipped it there when I was talking to the young ones, Red Pony thought. I think my brother pulled a quick one on me. I will return his kindness when he least expects it. He is a crafty one, that Black Moon.

Red Pony silently motioned to the young braves. They quietly moved single file through the pine forest filled with huge, white rocks. The older brave led the silent procession and thought about the days when he and Black Moon had chased children around the camp, pretending to shoot imaginary white people who had moved onto their land, uninvited. He remembered when Black Moon had bartered on his behalf for the lovely Fawn Woman who was to be his wife before the soldiers attacked their village and killed his lovely lady. Black Moon had stood beside him on that day too, when she traveled to the spirit world and was gone from this earth.

Red Pony and his braves stepped down the hill in silence, each hoping to find their enemy so they could take blood and hopefully a scalp. Each man was positioned at different areas on the trail where danger might approach from any direction.

STAYING ALIVE
August 18, 1877

Birch was gone, and Susan had never felt so alone. She knew Birch was capable in the woods; Jack had seen to that. She only hoped and prayed that help would come before the Lakotas returned.

The Lakota, I mustn't think about them or what to do if they come back, she thought. I pray to God that was not my last sight of Birch. I am alone with two little boys and what I do will decide if they live to be old. God, Jack, I wish you were here to tell me what to do. I hope sending Birch out was a good decision.

"Mom, you said we can't go anyplace, but I got to go to poop," Benny pleaded. "Bud can go with me. He is a big boy now."

"Oh Benny," Susan replied. "Come on, I'll take you over behind that bush. Let me get the rifle first."

"O.K. Mom, just don't look."

"I won't dear, now hurry up," Susan said while trying not to sound impatient.

"Do you think an injun would get me while I am going mom?" Benny asked from behind the bush.

"No dear, even they wouldn't attack while a boy is going, even they aren't that bad."

"No, but what if a critter or a big, fat rattlesnake bites me on my butt, mom, then what will we do?"

"Hurry up, Benny, nothing is going to bother you," Susan answered while trying not to panic.

Benny finally finished and stepped from behind his natural outhouse. Susan tried to help tuck in his shirt but the eight-year-old boy refused help and did it himself in a sloppy fashion.

"Hey mom, shouldn't we have a plan if the injuns attack?" Bud asked after Benny walked over and sat beside him. "How am I going to protect you until we find Birch?"

"If they come, Bud, and we can't stop them, then you run over into those woods by the big boulder when I tell you to," Susan said. "Then, no matter what happens, you and Benny hide where no one will ever find you."

"Where can we hide, mom?" Bud asked.

"You find a good spot where no one would think to look," She said. "No matter what, I want you to protect Benny and yourself. I want you to grow up and tell your kids about me and your dad, do you understand, Bud?"

"Yes, mom," Bud answered, not totally understanding what she was trying to say.

Try not to think about Birch or Jack, she said to herself. Think about cooking my boys' breakfast in the morning. Be strong for them. Panicking in this horrible situation would only make things worse. I have to be strong—the strongest I have ever been. Our very survival depends on it.

She settled in to sleep after the boys drifted off—an almost impossible venture. She closed her eyes only to see Jack dying on the ground, or Birch walking down that horrible path and out of sight.

THE TRAIL OF DEATH
August 18, 1877

Thought I heard something, Birch thought towards evening. Must be my imagination. Got to keep my head clear. Just walking can be dangerous, might trip over things like white rocks and pine tree limbs. Is someone watching me?

Birch paused to listen, but the trail was quiet. He continued walking along the trail.

Thinking about dad and the good times helps, he thought. How he always laughed when I stuck my throwing knife in the wood beam and how well he took care of other men's stock in his livery stable and how he looked at mom and us.

Birch could not forget that horrible expression on his dad's face just before he died. He couldn't forget the way it felt to help mom wrap and sew up his dad's body in an old Army blanket before slipping it in a dark hole and shoveling the dirt over the remains. He had watched the blanket-covered body disappear with each shovel full of black soil, and he could not forget the shovel of dirt that had covered his last view of the old blanket. After that, filling in the hole was easier, just a job to be finished.

His sorrow quickly turned to hate and revenge—emotions he was not used to. He had been angry, but never like this.

SQUAAAAAKKKK! A red-tailed hawk brought Birch back to the present with a loud scream meant to attract a mate.

Then the path became quiet again, and his mind wandered to bad thoughts.

I can't stop thinking about that spirit stuff the old miners talked about, especially that one dark night when that wrinkled-faced miner, Ol' Ike, spoke of such matters.

Shadows from a kerosene lantern in the back of their livery stable had made Ike's face look evil as he squinted his one good eye, spit a stream of tobacco juice and said, "Yep boy, there is some evil doings in them-there hills. Indian spirits, ol' trappers' ghosts and even some critters leave haints that travel on a dark night. Ah don't know what they air looking fer an ah don't want to know. Ah jest know they air up to no good."

Ol' Ike disappeared in the hills sometime after that, never to be seen again.

Birch thought about that and felt a chill, wondering what had happened to Ol' Ike.

Certain areas of the path seemed darker now than others. Birch tried to stay on parts of the path still lit by the day's remaining sunlight.

The unknown made his situation twice as bad, and he looked over his shoulder several times to make sure someone or something was not ready to grab him. Then he started thinking too much.

Am I being watched? Maybe my imagination? How do you fight a spirit? Wonder if Lakota spirits will attack me. Damn, wish dad was alive. Wonder where his spirit is. Wonder if somehow he is walking with me.

This last thought brought comfort, but he was too exhausted to stay focused.

28

Great, it's getting dark and here I am alone with dead spirits and live Lakota on this damned, dark hill. Hell with the Lakota— they can only kill me, but who knows what a spirit might do? Damn that Ol' Ike. Wish I'd never talked to him.

Birch sat down and slowly looked around, hoping not to see whatever had taken Ol' Ike. He tried not to think about the skillet full of bacon and potatoes his mother would be frying about then. A swallow of water and the jerked meat tasted good as he savored the meat juice in his mouth before swallowing. He finished the meat strip, had another shot of water, and leaned against a thick pine tree while the cool evening air made him scrunch down into his dad's old Confederate jacket. He started feeling much warmer as his body heat mixed with the thick wool material.

The stars are barely visible through the trees, he thought. Wonder if dad is there. Guess he is somewhere up there, probably wondering about us. Damn sure wish he was here now.

He took a long look at the stars until his eyes grew heavy and darkness took over the mentally and physically exhausted young man. The timber became his refuge as he dozed off into a deep sleep.

Birch dreamed about his dad most of the night. Jack was talking about things that did not make sense, saying something about the horses and his wife's comb and something about the boys' wings. He calmly mentioned the mules being stolen and something about Indians coming. Suddenly he looked at Birch and said in a strangely calm voice, "Wake up, son, you're in danger."

Birch woke to stare straight into the face of a Lakota, one of Black Moon's young warriors. The brave had happened upon the sleeping boy and was moving in to cut his throat. The man spoke softly to calm the boy before ending his days on mother earth, as if reassuring him that all was well.

Birch didn't know what to think of this dangerous-looking man with the soft voice, except that he couldn't be more than Birch's age and that he looked scary with the sinister strips of black and white paint on his face. The knife in his right hand continued to move closer to his throat. Birch could see the dull metal and bone handle; the blade's edge was sharp and clean, probably stolen from a trapper. Sinews in the warrior's wrist seemed strained as he tightly squeezed the bone handle.

The horrible fear of dying filled Birch's mind with blind panic as the Lakota's left hand touched his shoulder for leverage. Birch's right hand slipped out his father's old knife. The handle popped out of the sheaf like his father had taught him and into his left hand. The Lakota did not seem to notice this deadly movement and continued slowly positioning for the kill, clearly savoring the moment. There was a great deal of satisfaction in taking an enemy's life, and he would celebrate this victory with Black Moon when he returned.

I can't believe this is happening, Birch thought. Everything seemed to be happening in slow motion. Sleeping just seconds before talking to dad, and now this man is going to kill me.

Instinctively, Birch lunged straight up in a death strike of his own, driving his dad's blade straight up under the Lakota's chin. The surprised man's eyes bugged out, and he seemed to gurgle something as blood spurted from his opened throat. He collapsed on top of Birch, who rolled sideways to shed the dead body that was emptying blood all over his shirt. His mind flooded with dozens of thoughts.

Is this the Lakota who killed dad, he wondered. Feel sick to my stomach and that damned warm feel of blood... I think I'm going to throw up. Got to wipe this blood off my hands, but it don't seem to come off very easy.

He looked down at the dead Lakota and wretched, suddenly realizing that he had just taken a human life.

Birch leaned against a tree to think this out. He took control of himself and started checking the Lakota's personal belongings. He took the warrior's knife and a necklace with a good-sized turquoise-colored rock the brave had traded a pony for, tucking both into his belt.

Got to move quickly, he thought. Got to get help for mom and the boys. Another bloodthirsty Indian could find mom and the boys, got to move quicker, got to be careful. That damned spirit world doesn't seem so frightening now.

Birch moved two more miles before the shocking sight of his next enemy became visible in the morning haze. Birch saw him first and quietly slipped behind a large pine tree. He immediately knew that the surroundings were too thin to evade this warrior. Birch would have to kill him.

The young warrior was starring down the trail, possibly watching for the brave Birch had killed.

Jack had taught him on hunting trips how to be quiet in the woods, training that came in handy while sneaking close to the

30

tall Lakota. A sense of power suddenly flushed through Birch; he could kill this man who unknowingly was at his mercy. He felt a new sense of power, to be in control of an enemy.

Birch was almost close enough to strike, when the brave turned his head slightly to the right. Birch froze and waited, not daring to take a breath.

He has to see me, Birch thought. Got to do something, maybe swipe at his throat with my knife. No, can't move, or he'll hear me. I could throw it, maybe hit him under a rib, then I'll jump forward, grab my knife and finish it. He is still looking, like maybe he is getting ready to jump on me. Damn it, I'm going to die!

Suddenly the brave looked forward again and starred down the trail. Whatever he was thinking was his last thought as Birch slipped behind him and slid the razor-sharp knife across his throat. Once again the horrible gurgling sound filled the air. Only then did Birch realize that the crotch of his pants was wet.

He wondered if the two dead Lakota were part of the bunch that took their mules and killed his father.

Killing is the key to staying alive on this path, Birch thought. Killing and moving quietly are all that matter right now so I can get back to mom. Seems easier now to take a life—almost kind of a game. I hope I find Black Moon. He will be the easiest to kill.

DEATH WALKS THE PATH
August 20, 1877

Birch was still moving two days later. His father's wood lore training paid off as stealth was required when moving in close enough to shoot a deer with the old muzzleloader. Neither Birch nor Jack could have realized at the time that this training would eventually save Birch's life now and many times after throughout the years. Death walked that path for the next several hours as the young man managed to kill two more Lakota.

He finally figured that removing his shoes made his movement quieter through the pine timber, and he learned even more quickly that the price of walking barefoot in this forest was painful pine

31

needles and an occasional cactus spine in his feet. He endured this pain without a whimper, but with some loss of blood. He solved the problem by taking a dead brave's moccasins, which fit snugly but were good enough and extremely quiet when moving through pine timber. He walked up on one more young brave and cut his throat, producing the sounds, feelings, and smells that continued to make him gag.

Birch's fortunes changed when Red Pony rode past on one of Jack's old mules. This mule had broken away from the others on the night of the raid, and Red Pony had found the mule wandering in the woods. He hadn't planned on delivering the mule to the village himself, but as he rode in search of his younger braves he found the woods to be strangely quiet and empty.

Something, he thought, is not right.

Birch became bolder than he should have at the sight of a mule he had tended to many times. Besides, he needed that mule.

"Howdy," Birch said to the shocked warrior.

Startled, Red Pony easily slid off the mule and drove his knife into Birch's shoulder, a quick upper body twist by Birch had stopped the knife from entering his chest. Burning pain jumped up the boy's arm as nerves sent shock waves, and blood poured from the wound. The pain was excruciating, but he knew life would end without a good fight.

The older Lakota had leaned into the boy during his knife thrust, exposing his chest and providing an easy target. Birch's knife drove deep into Red Pony's heart, drawing a scream and lots of blood. He collapsed, never to rise again.

Painfully, Birch caught and mounted the mule while losing a lot of blood. He knew that time was running out for himself and his family.

Got to make Deadwood. Got to save my family, he thought while trying not to pass out. Got to tell someone, even if I die doing it.

"Come on, let's go," he said while kicking the old mule and hanging on with his failing strength.

Only luck made him gallop his mule past an old prospector that the other miners called Cookie, who was wandering the trail with his donkey, Ginger.

The old prospector made a remarkable lunge and grabbed the leather strap tied around the mule's neck. Birch's passage any sooner or any later would have meant missing the old man who was leaving the path for higher ground and a stream hopefully choked full of gold nuggets—if only he could find one. Birch would have missed his turn to Deadwood, if not for Cookie, because he was almost delirious.

"Damn boy, what buzz saw did you run into?" he asked Birch while looking at his bloody shirt, partly Lakota blood.

"My ma and brothers, still out there," he feebly said, weak from the loss of blood. "We buried pa there before I walked for help."

"What ye saying boy, is yer kin still out there?"

"Back up the trail," Birch pointed before passing out.

"Here boy," Cookie said. "I'm taking you to the sawbones in Deadwood. You've lost way too much blood."

Cookie opened Birch's shirt and looked at the wound. He stuffed a dirty old kerchief deep into the wound, deep enough to stop most of the bleeding.

He continued talking to Birch down the five-mile grade to Deadwood, even though the stricken young man could not hear a word. Finally they reached the muddy street and Doc Crebb's office, where someone helped the old man carry Birch to a waiting bed.

A BLACK DAY
August 20, 1877

Black Moon cut over a steep hill of broken pines from a past storm and looked down on the spot where he left Red Pony and the young braves. He knew they planned to move east, and he decided to follow from the original spot. Red Pony figured this and left signs with rocks and sticks that showed Black Moon he was on the right track.

He quietly moved down the trail for several hours before finding the first body. He examined the young brave and quickly moved on, trying not to think that Red Pony may have met the same fate.

I only see one white man's footprints, Black Moon thought. One white man is not going to defeat Red Pony. I will find him, and we will dine on mule meat that the camp sent. He could be several miles from here now. I will move faster.

Black Moon picked up his pace and soon found another dead Lakota, then another. Eventually he found five slain warriors, but not Red Pony, and he started feeling deep panic like when his family was killed. He moved faster down the path with reckless abandon in search of his friend.

Let my enemies hear me coming, he thought. That will save me the trouble of finding the monster that is killing my brothers.

Towards dark, Black Moon spotted a pile of something alongside the path. He realized that the pile was a dead Lakota as he broke into a run. He pulled the body over and looked into the dead face of Red Pony.

"YEEEEEEHAAAAAAAA," he screamed in absolute grief, the sound filtering through the Black Hills and a nearby valley, spooking critters several miles away. He hugged his friend and felt the clotted blood give way, soaking his chest and making his pain more intolerable. He wept uncontrollably for his only friend, releasing years of anguish and anger.

Hours later he stood, raised up his arms and looked up where many felt their ancestors danced among the stars.

"Now my friend," he whispered. "You are Wakan, part of the sacred ghost people. Please guide me on my quest as my brother here on mother earth."

He starred up for a moment and then dropped back down to sit with his friend one last time.

The following morning he tended to his friend's body before moving on down the trail. Red Pony's eyes would not shut, so he gave up trying and covered the body with rocks before setting off to the village where mule meat was being savored during the evening meal. Old men and women from the camp would come back and care for the six bodies for Black Moon who felt a dark rage that meant many whites would soon die. He had to find answers from the Great Spirit to understand why his world was ending. He had to find answers that only his ancestors could provide.

34

BROTHERS LOST
August 20, 1877

Dawn broke as dark eyes starred down at Susan and her boys from a distant pine knoll. The Mexican bandit, know as Rico, sharpened his 10-inch drop point knife on a well-worn whet stone. He breathed harder while studying the camp, feeling the excitement of an easy kill.

His gang, positioned on a hill 100 yards away, kept their distance. They thought their leader was damned strange, especially before a kill. He never blinked, but just starred and sharpened his knife. The other men hated the sound of his slow, deliberate strokes across the whet stone. They knew better than to make comments, knowing that Rico would never hesitate to kill them too. They were a gang of outlaws with nothing to lose; each man hoped to steal enough money to leave the territory and considered Rico their ticket out.

One of the men changed positions and kicked a round stone that rolled down the hill, crashing and banging into other rocks and vegetation. Rico gave the man a deadly glare.

Susan had stayed awake all night, wondering what to do, and mourning over Jack. The crashing stone made her sit up and look at the ridge with Jack's spyglass. She saw a man next to a tree, then two and knew danger would soon be in camp. Susan wanted to run, but decided to stop the men or at least slow them down while her boys escaped. Bud and Benny were looking at the ridge when Susan motioned to them.

"My darlings, crawl into the woods behind that old boulder where you can't be seen," She said in a soft voice. "I will try to give you time to escape. Find Birch. Now go my darlings and remember that mommy will always love you. No matter what happens, go and don't look back."

Both boys quickly crawled behind the log and into heavy cover where Bud cut his arm on a sharp stick.

"Ow!" He whispered.

"Forget it. Come on, Bud!" Benny hissed. Bud laid the wound on his white shirt, causing frightening bloodstains. He scrambled after his brother. The men who were moving down the ridge did not see their escape; they were focused on the covered-up body in camp that was female. They would find the boys later.

Susan planned to fight off the intruders like any good mother protecting her young. She started to panic and then remembered what Jack had told her about how he stayed alive in the Civil War: "The element of surprise saved me many times." She cocked back the hammer on his pistol and waited, hoping to surprise this vermin.

Rico and his gang preferred easy victims. The men, who badly needed shaves and baths, moved towards the camp from behind a nearby granite boulder that stood over a high cropping of rocks and pine trees. The slender, yet muscular Rico barely stood 5'8 and weighted 120 pounds soaking wet. But his deep, dark eyes showed a fire that would never be consumed.

His black mustache met sideburns that would have been thicker had he not chosen to trim them nightly, a habit his gang found annoying on the trail. Rico considered himself a ladies man and had to keep up all appearances.

Two more rough looking men, Hawson and Taylor, both dressed in old buffalo coats, were experienced hunters who knew how to move quietly through the timber. They stayed on the hill and tended to the horses while figuring that Rico, Casey, and Murray could handle one woman and her kids.

Rico finally slipped out of the brush while signaling two other cutthroats, Casey and Murray, to be quiet and follow. They crept behind another boulder and eased into open ground where Susan's blanket-covered form became visible. Rico took slow, deliberate steps while slowly slipping his knife from side to side, and his deep breathing increased.

The gang moved closer, but stopped with only enough time to stare as Susan sat up, pointed her pistol at Rico, and fired. The bullet propelled his black hat in the air, making a neat hole. Murray fell down and peered from behind a tree while Casey dropped down to see what would happen next. They wanted this woman alive if possible to explore her charms, but now Rico was too angry to care.

"Shoot the bitch," he growled.

Both boys lay on their bellies and watched through the underbrush as the men aimed their pistols at Susan. She tried to cock the hammer back for another shot, and they started shooting.

The boys watched in horror as several shots were fired into Susan's body. Bud realized she was dead and knew they had to get away.

"Kill the kids," Rico ordered as he picked up his hat.

Rico had lost track of the boys before overrunning the camp, and the hardened men looked through the brush for the young witnesses, but without success. Casey had come close; his horse's left front hoof had kicked the hollow log where the boys were hidden about 30 yards from camp. Finally, the men gave up.

"Rico, I couldn't find them," Casey said. "They somehow got away."

Rico did not tolerate failure in his men. He gave orders and expected them to be carried out, without exception. So it was not surprising to anyone when he walked over and dropped Casey with a well-placed roundhouse punch on the chin.

Casey was knocked half-silly as he fell back on the old campfire, dredging up some burning coals, but had the presence of mind to roll out of the burning spot that was scorching his back. He looked up at Rico's drawn knife.

"Do you realize what this means, my friends?" Rico yelled. "This fool has let escape the only humans alive who might identify us for killing their sainted mother. So why should I not kill this worm who brings me this bad news? Why should I not cut his worthless throat? You are all lucky to ride with Rico. Why can't you just listen and do what I say?"

Rico started moving closer to the panicking Casey. The other gang members grabbed Rico's arm, twisted the knife away, and tried to talk him down. Each man had learned how to deal with Rico's mood swings. "His face changes like the seasons," Casey had said one night in camp. "The trick is staying out of his way when winter returns."

The boys watched this scary man continue to throw a fit and decided to hide deeper in the scrub before the murderers found them.

Soon Rico calmed down and walked over to help Casey up.

"My friends, now we must move quickly to Deadwood in case someone finds those boys," Rico said quietly. "Then we will know, and they can be silenced forever with bullets or perhaps with our knives cutting their worthless little throats. Yes, that's it, we will cut their little throats and then no one will know that we killed their sainted madre."

Rico started laughing, first quietly and then quite loudly while swinging his knife at imaginary victims. The others looked at each other without a word and continued looking through the campsite for anything worthwhile.

The boys returned to camp an hour after the men rode out.

Bud walked in first and shook his mother once. Then he covered her with a blanket so Benny wouldn't see the horrible damage done by several bullets. He closed his eyes and tried to fight off the anguish of his family's death and the morbid fear that this could happen to them.

Got to stay strong for Benny, he thought. Got to move now, while we still can. Those men will kill us if we don't move quickly and maybe find Birch.

He wrapped his cut with an old rag, then changed his bloody shirt for a clean one. The men had scattered the family's possessions around, but they missed several pieces of jerked meat. Jack's old canteen had survived, and Bud filled it with water from the barrel that also had somehow survived.

"What about mom? Should we bury her like Birch buried dad?" Benny asked.

"There's no time. What if they come back? We got to find Birch now that mom and dad are dead," Bud said while trying hard to be brave. The words settled in on both boys, and they started crying uncontrollably.

"I'm scared Bud," Benny said. "Those men might find us too, or some damned ol' injun."

"Yeah, I don't feel very good either," Bud answered, too tired and scared to sound brave. "But we have some jerked meat and water. We'll walk out of here and find Birch. He'll know what to do. Just wish mom hadn't taken my rock thrower. I wonder where she put it."

"How are we gonna find Birch?" Benny asked.

"We'll start walking to Deadwood," Bud said.

The sight of his mother had been too much, but he tried to revive his bravery for Benny. He was not sorry to start walking down the trail, even though the thought of the unknown that lay ahead was the scariest feeling he had known in his short life.

The first day both boys walked in the same direction where Birch had disappeared.

That seems like a million years ago, Bud thought. I know we can find him. I heard mom say to follow the trail where the miners walked, pretty easy to see which way to go.

That evening, they held each other to stay warm and lay down in a pile of old, soggy leaves. Bud waited until Benny was asleep before rising to take one last look around, before trying to sleep too, but he couldn't sleep. An overwhelming sadness and sense of responsibility kept him awake, well into the night. Normal forest night sounds vibrated through his ears.

Could be bears or mountain lions prowling around and maybe some pesky injun, he thought. I'm scared and wish Birch would come around to get us. I don't want to die, and Benny don't neither.

"Dear God," Bud whispered. "Please let us be saved from this horrible place where we are alone. Please don't let us get ate by a bear or some other critter and please don't let the bad guys who killed mom or some injun kill us too. Please let Birch find us and take us home, wherever that is now. And God, could we please have something to eat, been a while and we both can't find anything fit to eat here in these hills. In Jesus' name I pray, amen."

Bud immediately felt better. He rolled over and fell asleep.

The following morning Bud awoke to look up at a big Lakota warrior who had his bow drawn back. He could just see the arrow with a slate broad head that was pointed straight at him.

He is going to shoot us, the boy thought in sheer terror. Suddenly a deep voice spoke loudly in a language Bud did not understand.

Another big Lakota stepped forward and grabbed a boy in each arm. Bud looked up at the warrior's face painted with white and black paint, and he closed his eyes.

The big man called Red Hawk threw the kicking Benny to the warrior nearest him while keeping a firm grasp on Bud.

Bud looked at the warrior's face again, not realizing how fate had turned in his favor. The man was not Black Moon, bent on killing every white person, but Red Hawk, a kind man who had discovered Susan's body and had followed the boys' tracks from the camp. He felt sorry for the boys, knowing only too well what it was like to lose family to stupid violent acts.

Suddenly he lifted Bud well over his head and said something in Lakota. Bud's breath caught in his chest, and he prepared for the worst. In fact, Red Hawk was giving thanks to the Great Spirit for two fine healthy boys.

Neither Bud nor Benny could have realized just how safe they were at that moment after becoming wards of a very powerful warrior. Soon they rode down the path in single file, each boy riding behind a Lakota brave.

PART
TWO

-+≒⊙⊂≕+-

DEADWOOD
August 29, 1877

Deadwood was full of life. Miners led their mules down the street while the clinking of a blacksmith's hammer on steel could be heard in the distance. The smell of wood burning in cook stoves filled the air as the clicking of metal could be heard from passing teams of mules. A long row of older wooden buildings and tents lined the streets of gold, so-called by a New York newspaper. Many considered Deadwood to be their land of promise.

A dandy from back east would have called Deadwood a dirty little town with mud streets, partly from rain, but more likely from mule and horse manure or urine that was hard not to step in while walking across the street.

The region's gold strike turned the small town of Deadwood Gulch into a very busy place. Hammering nails could be heard on any given day as buildings pushed out old tents and shanties that had been quickly constructed by miners and others who endured severe hardships while trying to get rich. The lure of gold was an age-old sickness that had invaded the Black Hills.

Most in town looked like dirty miners or cowpunchers, but the new buildings brought in a new class of well-dressed men and women who wanted the dirty men's gold, some by honest means and others by deceit or even robbery in its most sophisticated form. Bankers and loan sharks called it high interest charges—legal and easier than sticking a gun in an honest man's ribs.

Seth Bullock stepped up to the Nuttall & Mann's Number 10 Saloon door and took a long look around the room. Oil lamps hung over dirty tables scattered throughout the long, narrow hall. An old piano sat against the wall just past the bar. The last piano player had been accidentally shot during a squabble between two ranchers. He survived but left the territory.

Several drunken miners glanced at Bullock's glaring dark intense eyes set deep in a tanned, well lined face and quickly looked away. The 6'6" newly-elected sheriff towered over everyone, and no one doubted that he was quite capable of cleaning every man out of the room. And yet, no one had seen him lift a finger; his reputation was enough. He finally stepped into the bar after satisfying himself that everyone in the room was harmless.

The tired sheriff had dropped by for a drink after being gone for more than a week in search of a cattle thief. He did not like this bar where Wild Bill Hickok had been murdered.

That sneaking dog Jack McCall snuck up and shot him in the head. I would have loved to bust a cap on that pig, he thought.

He glanced at the table where Wild Bill had held black aces and eights, the winning hand that would become known as the "Dead-Man's Hand."

I don't like walking in these doors, he thought. Damned good place to hear what's going on in the area, though. God, look at these vultures. Wild Bill's death didn't hurt business here. Damned vultures.

The Number 10 Saloon was so named because it sat directly over the Number 10 claim that never produced as a gold mine. The dimly lit establishment had always pulled in a fair share of gamblers, miners, and a few low-rent prostitutes. The prettier women worked in better paying places throughout Deadwood.

Seth sat down at the end of a homemade wood slat bar where he could watch the door and those already drinking or playing poker.

"Hey Seth," Harry the bartender asked. "Did you hear the news?"

"What news?" Seth returned while looking around the bar, not seeming very interested.

"That old drunk Cookie brought in some kid off the trail from Custer."

"Yeah, I heard."

"Well, your deputy Mason led a search party to go looking after the boy's family several days ago and guess what? The boy's ma had been murdered—shot several times—and the kid's two younger brothers were never found. They buried his ma near a fresh grave where they figured his pa was laid. Her body was too far gone to bring back, and besides, some critters had found her. But here is the strange part. The men that raided their camp rode shod horses. They were likely all white men."

"Why hadn't I heard about this?" the now attentive Bullock demanded. "I only heard that they brought the kid in."

"Well, that's not all," Harry countered. "Mason's search party found what was left of six dead injuns between where Cookie found the kid and where they found the family's camp. That 18-year-old told Doc Crebbs that he killed them all with only a knife. Here, look at this paper."

Seth soaked in that news for a minute, before glancing at the newspaper. A headline in the *Deadwood Pioneer* stated in big, black letters, "Young Man Survives the Trail of Death."

The trail of death, Bullock thought. Where in the hell is that?

He tipped a shot of whiskey, slapped a coin on the bar, and without saying a word walked outside still carrying the newspaper.

Inside the bar, Harry picked up the coin and dropped it in an old, sectioned tin box used to keep track of money. He was used to this kind of behavior from the highly intelligent sheriff who seemed to spend a lot of time thinking by himself.

DOC CREBBS' PLACE
August 29, 1877

Main Street in Deadwood was busy that afternoon, partly because more freight wagons appeared daily in the growing town. Miners of all ages led their mules through the mud; most walked with everything they owned on their back or in their hands.

Bullock decided that it was time to meet this kid. He glanced up at Al Swearengen's Gem Theatre where several ladies of questionable character stood looking out of the windows of the notorious establishment where anything could happen—and often did. Most wore bright-colored clothes on the street side and nothing below the window—a fact that they made sure every man understood and thought about.

Swearengen, a stocky, well-dressed, gentleman with a thick, black mustache, stood on a lower balcony. He wore suits from back east, quite a contrast to most of his poorly dressed customers. He smiled at the big lawman, gave a sarcastic wave, then turned and walked back into his office to make sure no one was stealing his profits from the popular gambling operation downstairs.

Bullock allowed the Gem Theatre to stay open because the town needed successful businesses, but he never turned his back on Swearengen. He knew better.

Bullock walked down where several boards were stacked across the muddy street. He took special effort in choosing each step to keep his beautifully shined brown boots clean, while particularly watching out for the stinking horse or mule shit that was everywhere, including splattered on the boards.

Guess I can't fault them for that, he thought, but got to watch where I step. Took forever to shine these damned boots.

Seth knew that meeting the kid was not going to be a pleasant experience.

This boy could be crying his eyes out, he thought, and who could blame him? Can't help but feel sorry for the poor little bastard, but six Lakota with a knife? Just who is this kid?

He knocked on Doc Crebbs' door, an unusual door made in St. Louis that had a big oval window covered by a lace curtain. It was an adornment that Bullock found peculiar for a man living alone. Truth be known, everyone in Deadwood found the doctor to be a little different when in fact, he was considered stylish back east.

Doctor Crebbs answered the door of his modest shack. Bullock looked at the old man, slightly amused by the spectacles that framed his beady brown eyes and adorned the tip of his thin nose. His head was covered with long gray hair that was never quite properly concealed by a brown derby. His store-bought black suit cost more than the house he lived in. The smell of bourbon from his own private stock that adorned his breath daily in the afternoon and every night brought out different opinions. The best drunks in town considered his daily medication a fine stock, but Bullock considered him to be "nothing but a whiskey-soaked Yankee who happened to be a good doctor."

The town committee brought Crebbs in from back east with the promise of fine living quarters, the best medical supplies available and a good salary. So far none of this had happened, but the community needed a good doctor, so he stayed and besides, he came from plenty of old money. Crebbs did his job, but he was not happy about it or almost anything, a fact well reflected in his mood changes—grouchy and grouchier.

"Hey doc," Seth said. "How's the boy?"

"I'm fine, thanks for asking," the doctor grumbled.

"You didn't get stabbed, damn it. Why should I ask about you?"

"Wait until you're my age. Hell, you aren't even half my age, you young fool. The boy is doing fine. He's in the other room with Cookie, and I don't want to talk with you any longer."

Seth, half-amused, watched the doc stomp away.

Grouchy old fart, he thought. But he is a decent doctor. Guess I'd better get this over with.

Birch heard a light knock on the wooden door, but he ignored it.

I don't want to talk, he thought. Especially to that grouchy old bastard, constantly asking stupid questions, poking and prodding me. Cookie's alright, but I don't want to see him either. I just want to be alone. Guess I should sleep, but I really don't want to. Keep seeing my family in those damned dreams.

Bullock decided to step in the room without an invitation. Birch looked up at the huge sheriff.

"What do you want?" He asked.

"I only want to talk," Seth softly answered.

Normally, the big sheriff sounded gruff, but he decided that an easy approach was important. This kid had been through more than most men would suffer in a lifetime. Yet, he noticed that Birch did not seem to be suffering. If anything, he seemed strangely calm and collected. The broad-shouldered kid just laid there with a deadly confident look in his eyes.

Those eyes, Bullock thought. Stern, blue eyes. A killer's eyes that look straight through me and well beyond. The eyes of someone who's seen too much in a short lifetime. That young man has learned on the trail that killing is not so hard, a lesson some never get the chance to learn.

"You've been through a lot young man," Seth continued. "Just thought I'd stop by to see how you're making it."

"Guess I'm alright, considering."

"Can I get you anything?"

"No, I'm fine."

"Well, sorry about your family."

"What about my family," Birch snapped back. "Are they alright?"

Bullock glanced at Cookie, who was sitting quietly off in the corner. He was looking down at the floor.

47

"Well, I thought you had been told," Bullock said. "Your ma is dead, and the search crew couldn't find anyone else. They buried her beside another grave. Your pa?"

"Yeah, we buried him after an injun killed him," Birch answered while trying to be strong in front of both men.

"You had two brothers I understand? They were never found, just a bloody shirt that would fit a boy."

"Could be a critter found them boys," Cookie said. "Maybe a bear or big cat dun drug them off and ate them, or some damned injun might have got them."

Bullock quickly gave the old miner a dirty look that immediately shut him up, and Cookie looked back down at the floor.

"Dead. Ma is dead," Birch said as if trying to understand the words. "How?"

"Shot, and we will find who did it and hang them, son," Bullock said, only half believing his own words. He knew the killers could be anywhere in this big territory. "Now you rest and I'll go arrange another search party to look for your brothers. What are their names?"

"Bud and Benny," he said before turning away from both men. "God, they're all gone." He muttered.

"When you get better, I want you to stop by my office. I want to talk to you some more."

Birch didn't answer.

"Good," Bullock responded. "I'll see you then."

Bullock motioned to Cookie and both men stepped out the door.

Cookie turned towards his favorite bar while Bullock walked down the street, thinking.

Those eyes, those intense eyes. Definitely a killer's eyes, I think.

Bullock's mood was becoming darker as the day progressed. He did not like surprises, and this kid showing up fell in that category. His best deputy, a man only known as Jed, made the mistake of stepping through the door of Bullock's office. Jed had been taken and raised first by the Cheyenne and then by a white rancher after the Army rescued him when he was a boy, making him extremely valuable to Bullock as someone who understood both worlds.

"Where in the hell have you been?" Bullock growled.

"I rode out towards the trail alone to look for any survivors," the calm Jed answered.

"Damn it, what trail? Are you talking about this Trail of Death the newspapers are writing about? Just where is this damned place supposed to be?"

"The trail is between Custer and Deadwood through the hills," Jed answered. "Lakota believe that the spirit world made the trail before man walked mother earth. Only Lakota and other tribes used the trail until white trappers and the Army came. Then the miners, at first a few and then thousands of them when the gold strike came. They really beat up the trail and made it wider. I found where the boy's family died and where the boy fought his fights; he moved down that path with the spirit of a bear in a foul mood. I found signs of fighting and blood in several places."

"So that's it, the family is dead and the boy is here safe after killing several Lakota and in self defense, quite a story," Bullock growled.

"Yep, quite a story," Jed muttered while walking outside. "That is one lucky kid."

Lucky alright, Bullock mused. Extremely lucky or is he that damned good?

BLACK MOON'S VISION
September 1, 1877

Black Moon had walked away from Red Pony's body feeling numb and hollow. The angry warrior had become a despondent man.

Seeking answers, Black Moon rode his pony for several days and nights through the sea of prairie grass and deeper into the Black Hills. Nothing made sense.

He rode northeast of the Black Hills to Bear Butte, a sacred place that overlooked the plains.

When he could ride no farther, Black Moon walked the lower paths before climbing to the top and then to the edge of a cliff. Crazy Horse had set up his sweat lodge here and so had other great leaders. This holy place was rich with flowing energy.

Black Moon made an offering of an old cotton shirt and some tobacco—all that he owned. He wrapped up the tobacco in the cotton and laid it down as an offering to the Great Spirit, then sat cross-legged, looking out across the open space. He prayed and then started meditating.

He sat in this sacred spot, hoping for an answer, and soon the spirit world felt the strength of Black Moon's prayers and granted him a vision.

He saw faceless men in soldier suits covering the plains; their faces were round, white spaces. They were moving towards him, pushing away elk and deer as birds and butterflies flew from their path. Prairie grass was stripped from where their feet touched and the great sea of grass became barren. They left buffalo and Lakota bones behind them, turning white on the sun-bleached plains.

Then Black Moon saw a buffalo, two wolves, and a golden eagle blocking the soldier's path. They stared straight at the unholy mob and did not waver; they would be defeated by shear numbers, but they would not back down.

Then he saw his spirit helper, a maiden. She waved and smiled at him from a distance and drew closer. She did not walk or run; she just moved closer. He reached to her and felt the soft fox furs she wore. He looked into her face as she turned her head and then looked back at him, a beautiful face.

He awoke from his vision, sweating, tears running down his cheeks. He wanted to stay with her, and then he suddenly felt weak from lack of food and water. He tried to stand up and fell almost into the lap of a very stern-faced shaman who sat next to a medicine man. Both had been summoned to join him.

The shaman said a prayer and touched Black Moon's forehead; his hunger was gone and his strength returned. Then he was strong enough for his vision quest. He helped the shaman construct a sweat lodge of bent willow branches; the dome frame was then covered by deer and antelope skin. The sweat lodge would purify him before they engaged in a dance for the spirits of those murdered.

A healthy fire soon created the glowing orange coals that would heat the smooth rocks in their sweat lodge. All three men stripped down to only a brief garment and stepped into the lodge as Black Moon occasionally poured water on the rocks. The heat was intense, and he felt an outer layer of skin peeling loose from his shoulders.

"Black Moon," the shaman spoke. "I will tend to the fire. Close your eyes and go find your spirit helper. She will guide you to the truth. You have to find answers before continuing your quest. Then we will dance in honor of our dead.

Black Moon closed his eyes in darkness and the heat, and soon he saw a light that opened up into a flowing meadow. Then he saw her in white deer skin decorated with beads and painted signs of the Lakota. She reached out to him and he gladly accepted her slender, delicate hand. They smiled at each other, and then she spoke.

"My dearest Black Moon, let us now begin your journey. The Lakota people are suffering. Disease, starvation and relentless pursuit and killing by the white race—these things are our greatest test in time. We are of a great nation that will endure. But our strength must never be lost. You will show others that we are still of a warrior race. You must be great in the eyes and minds of our people. You have viewed spirits blocking the white masses, and like the buffalo you will be strong. You will show stealth and resolve like the wolves. You will move swiftly and silently like the golden eagle. Each strikes with power and strength. Let each creature's spirit join you in this quest. Then you will walk through this trail to my circle, and we will know the universe. Now return to the people under the eyes of Skar, the sky and Wi, the sun. I have sent holy men to show the start of your journey."

Black Moon tried to speak and could not. He knew it was time to open his eyes, but he did not want to. Maybe she would return.

No, it was over.

The vision of his spirit helper had passed. He stood up without a word and stepped outside to the chilly air of September in the mountains. He stretched out his arms to the east and greeted a sunrise. He had no idea how long the vision had taken.

The shaman and medicine man joined him outside, and they all rubbed sage and splashed cold water on their bodies, an ancient tradition. They did not speak or look at Black Moon; they simply dressed in silence. Then Black Moon began to speak the words from the vision and his spirit helper.

"The white man is here bringing his disease, death and suffering. He has pushed our people off their land in a quest for golden rocks. Many have died. Many more will die, though our biggest battles are over, and our numbers are fewer. It is time for some of us to remain strong and never let the Lakota warrior die. The strong must carry the fight to all whites. We will not win. But we will show them Lakota strength and resolve that will be praised in their songs and writings. We are Lakota. The land shall reclaim us."

The shaman and the medicine man sat nodding their heads in agreement. The vision was finished speaking through the mouth of Black Moon.

Now it was time for Black Moon to rejoin the living earth.

The shaman brought out a pipe filled with kinnikinic, a mixture of tobacco, dried leaves of sumac and dogwood bark. Black Moon held the pipe up to the four winds.

After the three took turns puffing on the ceremonial pipe, the medicine man created some cottonwood coals and tossed sweet grass on it. He soon followed this with a hand full of sage. Both created a musky smoke that would keep all evil spirits away.

Now it was time to dance. The shaman and medicine man sat cross-legged and made a rhythm with a drum and a rattle. Black Moon held out his hands and moved to the left, and suddenly he felt other hands touching his. Others had joined him to dance.

Black Moon chanted words that came to him from his spirit helper as many voices he could not identify joined him to sing these words:

Oh join me in my quest my brothers,
Let us be as one,
Let the Lakota stay together,
Form these earthly bonds.

The chant was repeated over and over during the dance until Black Moon fell in a trance, a vision of his spirit helper's face was before him. He danced some more, and then the dance stopped.

Those who had danced with him were gone.

Black Moon turned to the shaman and medicine man to thank them.

"Thank you my brothers for helping me find my vision. What tribe are you from?" Black Moon asked.

"We are not from a tribe," the shaman said.

And then they too disappeared.

Black Moon opened his eyes and found himself sitting cross-legged on the same cliff on Bear Butte where he had started. He stood up, staggered, and looked around to find there was no sweat lodge or sign of the fire he had built, and he realized that this had all been part of the vision.

Half starved, he decided to find some food. To his shock, a good-sized bowl of venison broth sat on a big, flat rock. He was surprised to find the thick broth warm and nourishing. He finished the gift and turned again to face the eastern horizon.

Once again the sun was rising, and he turned towards grandfather sun and raised his hands while watching one of the most beautiful sunrises of all time—truly a gift from the Great Spirit. He realized that now he was a leader of his people, and only now, he knew what it meant to be a leader.

I will continue the war against the whites, he thought. Many will die before I join my spirit helper. My actions will be the beginning of the Lakota returning to their birthplace, the symbol of our return.

LAKOTA CAMP
September 2, 1877

Bud and Benny were scared and homesick, but they were also curious about their new surroundings. The camp consisted of a dozen tepees that were positioned alongside a stream of cool water that slipped out of the hills. The boys had noticed symbols painted on each tepee, and small cook fires were positioned around the area.

Their journey from the Black Hills had been rough, and their dismount from the horses even rougher. They were dumped off the Indian ponies into the middle of several young boys their age or older who enjoyed delivering a few punches and pushes.

Red Hawk immediately proved to be a kind man who tended to the boy's needs and even their comforts.

Others were not as kind, especially a warrior named Mountain Rock.

The bitter warrior loved to give the boys a swift kick whenever possible, but he did not kill Bud and Benny because of his respect for Red Hawk, whom he had joined in many battles. The boys were lucky enough to be rescued by a well-respected warrior.

Their presence was not welcome by most at first, and the boys were quiet and unreceptive to Red Hawk's offer of pemmican, a mixture of sun-dried meat, fat, suet and dried paste from wild berries that actually tasted good to all but those who were scared and homesick.

A couple of days passed before the boys started realizing that they were safe while Red Hawk was around, and their empty stomachs made them accept his offering of food. They talked about escaping to find Birch, and then decided that he would eventually find them.

They could not understand a word spoken around them, but they started paying attention to the people, some of whom began warming up to the captive boys. They especially paid attention to Mountain Rock.

"Wish we had the rock sling," Bud whispered to Benny one day. "I'd love to send a creek rock flying at the injun who hurts us all the time."

"Yea, a smooth, black creek rock. Maybe we could hit him on the noggin or even in the rear," Benny answered.

"Yeah, maybe in the rear like that damned old goose, but we don't want to end up like that side of deer hanging over there with all of the flies crawling over it."

"Thought it was that color when we first was brought here," Benny said. "I thought it was black, but the meat is covered with flies. I've had bad dreams about them killing us and letting the flies cover our bodies and get in our mouths and everything."

"They can't. The guy who got us won't let that happen," Bud answered. "For some reason he likes us. We're safe when he is around."

"I don't like the way them injun women stare at us, and they never smile," Benny said.

"Yes, except for that young girl who smiles at me," Bud answered. "Did you notice how pretty her eyes are? Darkest eyes I ever saw. I think she is kind of pretty."

"Bud has a sweetheart, Bud has a sweetheart, and they smooch all over the place and Bud kisses her on the face."

"Just shut up Benny, or I'll give you a wallop on the side of your head."

"O.K., Bud the injun kisser, I won't say another thing."

Red Hawk let the boys roam around the Lakota camp that was located on the prairie just a mile from the Black Hills. Red Hawk figured that there were few places for them to go, and if they were foolish enough to run off, that would be two less mouths to feed.

At night they stayed in his safe tepee with Red Hawk's wife, Yellow Flower, who had faced too many bad times to retain her beauty. The boys noticed that she did not smile or talk much as she went about her chores. But Bud noticed a sparkle in her eyes whenever she looked at them; he had no way of knowing that her own two sons had died of small pox three years ago.

LESSONS LEARNED
September 2, 1877

The second search party had found a few more personal effects with the aid of a well-mounted Cavalry unit that happened to be on a scouting maneuver and moving in that direction. Patrols looked for the boys' bodies, but found no sign of them, only the bloody shirt. After so many days, no one believed the boys could have survived in the rugged Black Hills that was full of dangerous animals, and even more dangerous humans.

They had vanished and were presumed dead.

The Lakota had watched this strange procession slowly move 20 miles down the narrow path and back to town, but they had not interfered, waiting for a more opportune time to kill the whites, especially the soldiers. The older braves took this as an excellent chance to teach the younger tribesmen how clumsy and noisy the soldiers could be.

One experienced warrior, White Elk, explained to three young braves, "Listen to their approach. You can hear them for many miles. These men are not hunters like Lakota. They are loud and careless, and they are easy to sneak up on too. Just make sure the time is right."

It had been a very stressful trip, even for the veteran soldiers and seasoned mule skinners. No one saw any Lakota—that is, no one except for a young inexperienced private who stepped out of camp one night to relieve himself. The next morning they found him dead, naked, and scalped. He did not have time to relieve himself before a knife found his throat.

"You see," White Elk explained to the young braves while riding back to camp. "Just wait till the time is right. We patiently waited and easily killed one of the enemy without alerting the others."

The private's murder made even the experienced soldiers edgy. Several shots were fired, but always at shadows and once at the sound of a running flock of mountain quail. Nerves were raw by the time Deadwood was in sight.

The morning of September 2nd dawned bright. Two weeks had passed since Cookie brought Birch into Doc Crebbs' place for patching up. The wound had been serious, and he had lost a lot of blood, but Red Pony's knife could have done a lot more damage. Birch's fever was gone, and Doc allowed him to move around town, but told him to take it easy.

Birch Rose was not happy, and no one could blame him. Bud and Benny were dead. Somehow he could painfully accept that. But having his parents buried out in the woods really gnawed at him.

Mother and father should be dug up and buried in Whitewood Gulch, Birch thought. He could not see having his folks buried in a grave that would be unmarked and lost forever. Problem was, no one was willing to help him dig up the bodies, load them in a wagon, and then drive through the hills where Lakota warriors who would love to take fresh scalps could turn up at any moment.

So it came as little surprise that Birch could not find help moving his parents. Everyone considered him lucky that they had buried his mother and brought back the family's few personal effects, and as noted by many of the townspeople, after all, the effort had cost a young man his life.

Birch sat outside the general store on an old log bench stewing over how to bury his parents in Deadwood. He didn't notice Deputy Jim Mason leaning inside the store's door, rolling a cigarette and studying Birch while drawing the conclusion that he was looking at a real hayseed.

The tall deputy wore a black vest over his clean white shirt and black trousers, well fitted over black boots. His black Stetson was worn low over his eyes in a cocky manner that made his low-slung six guns look natural. Mason was a rugged looking man, not particularly handsome, but very appealing to the ladies who liked the type.

"Hey, Rose," Mason said. "What's your problem?"

"Just trying to figure a way to get my parents moved here."

"Well, let me ask you, do you believe in the hereafter?"

"Yeah, I guess so," Birch answered.

"Don't you think your folks are together there? How could it be heaven if they were not together?"

Birch thought about that.

"Guess that's right."

"So what does it matter where they're buried on earth? Now listen boy, I'm not sure about the hereafter, but you better toughen up or this country will kill you. Your family is dead, so you'd better get over it and get on with your life. And that's the truth of it."

Birch turned and took a long look at the hardened deputy who apparently did not know the meaning of sympathy.

What kind of man would say such a thing? Birch wondered. Had this place made him that hard or was he just a bastard?

"I don't know what else to do but sit here and try to figure things out," Birch said.

"Yeah, I know," Mason answered, "but nothing will bring them back. You're just eating yourself up."

Birch sat and starred down at the muddy street, wishing the abrasive deputy would go away and feeling thankful when he did.

"See you later kid," Mason said while walking across the street to the jailhouse.

No point pursuing this, Birch thought. Guess the folks being together in heaven will have to be enough. Got plenty to do though. All I've got is that mule that Cookie found me riding down the trail, still need grub and guns. Wonder if that trash found the secret compartment on dad's wagon.

Birch slowly approached the wagon, now kept at the blacksmith's shop, and immediately noticed that his mother's cooking stove had been taken apart. The thieves apparently thought she had stashed money or valuables in the stove's compartment. Then he saw the rock slinger that Bud used to shoot the goose.

It was covered in dried blood that Birch tried to wipe off without success.

He held the ancient weapon and cried like a baby.

You too, boys, he thought. My God, they're all gone, murdered like animals by trash and gone. I will never see them again. Damned bloody shirt. Maybe Cookie was right; animals or injuns, damn it, just not fair. They would have grown to be good men, but not now. I can't even bury them. They're just gone, damn it, gone! And I can't even visit my folks' graves without being scalped. I'm alone. My family is gone.

He thought about the goose and smiled before weeping again while sitting on the wagon's tongue.

Dazed, he decided to collect himself and get what he had come for.

Birch slid under the wagon and crawled to reach behind the spring to find the box undisturbed. He reached his hand in to grab the family Bible, his dad's medals from the war, about $300.00 of folded paper money, and his mother's broach brought over from Ireland by a family member many years before.

He choked back another sob while looking at the broach and saw his mother dressed for church in her Sunday dress with the broach pinned just below her high-lace collar. He grasped the plain-looking broach and cash tightly in his sweaty hand while opening the family Bible to his grandparents' written names and the date, 1824. He jammed the loot in his pants pocket and stepped outside carrying the Bible, knowing that he would never go near the wagons again.

Bullock watched Birch step out of the small wooden building where both wagons were stored and started guessing Birch's plan. This young fool is bound to get killed, he thought.

"Hey kid," Seth yelled across the street at Birch, "Come here. Let's talk."

Birch crossed the street with his eyes fixed on Bullock. Bullock noticed his red eyes and runny nose.

"Hello sheriff, sorry I ain't been by for that chat. I've been busy."

"So I heard, but let's talk about some facts you need to realize. First of all, you got lucky. You killed several able warriors and made quite a reputation for yourself. Now you'll have to live with it."

"What do you mean sheriff?"

"Places like this draw dangerous people. That's why I have a job. They'll know you killed six capable men, no matter what their color, and they'll come gunning for you to build up their reputation. Worse than that, you're planning to try and find that Lakota brave who killed your father, aren't you? How are you going to do that? Are you going to find a Lakota and ask him to help you? Don't work that way boy. That would just be another Indian you'd have to kill. If you'll remember, the last Indian almost killed you."

Birch knew Bullock was right about starting from scratch against a stacked deck. He had heard of this sheriff while his family still lived in Custer, but was too full of grief to care.

Damn, wish we still lived in Custer; everyone would still be alive, he mused. Then he quickly shook off those thoughts and returned to the business at hand.

"So what do you want?" he asked Bullock.

The sheriff hesitated before answering, "Let's just say you need all the help you can get and leave it at that."

The hardened sheriff did not want to show a soft spot, something he could not afford in those colorful days of Deadwood.

"Tomorrow you can move in with me for awhile," Seth said. "But first, do you have money for some new clothes?"

"No, I don't have a cent," Birch lied. "I'm skinned clean." The young man knew he might need the money when his time came to hunt down his family's killers.

"Well, I have a hardware store here with my partner, Sol Star. We have some of what you'll need. Poppa Sam's General Store will have clothing and boots. Can you read and figure numbers?"

"Yes sir, my mother taught my brothers and I so we could help with the business," Birch answered proudly.

"That will help some too," Bullock said softly.

59

BASIC TRAINING FOR BIRCH
September 3, 1877

The following day Birch walked into Poppa Sam's General Store. The door slammed behind him, and the door's sleigh bells made a bright jingling sound.

The store walls were covered with shelving filled with canned items and other necessities of life. A big, black pot bellied stove sat in the middle of the room, ready to be filled with wood and burnt throughout the long winter. Stacks of clothing and other material were neatly laid out on tables towards the back where Birch noticed a glass case full of handguns. He paused to look at each one before continuing on.

The young man walked back and forth, studying each item, pausing to look at the licorice whips and jawbreakers, both in tall glass jars. Then he remembered why he was there. Poppa Sam stepped out of the back room and took a long look at the young man.

"What can I do for you, son?" he asked. Birch took a step back and glared straight into the old man's eyes.

"Don't call me son," Birch growled. "Only one man has the right to call me son, and he's buried out on the trail."

"Whoa, I'm sorry, I didn't mean anything by it," the old man stammered.

Birch immediately felt bad about snapping at the innocent old man. He, in fact, was flashing a lot of temper around Deadwood. Most tried to understand, but some were losing patience. Birch nodded at the old storekeeper and stepped over to the clothing that was folded and neatly stacked. He quickly found two pairs of black denim jeans, two suits of flannel underwear and four blue and black shirts. A pair of brown rough leather boots, a wide leather belt with a big silver buckle and a black flat-brimmed hat was added to the merchandise stacked on the counter by the cash register.

Poppa Sam rang up each item, peered through his bifocals at the young customer in dirty clothes and moccasins and said, "That will be $29.50, young man."

60

"Put it on Bullock's bill. I'll even up with him later," Birch said.

"How do I know that Bullock will want all of this on his bill?" Poppa Sam asked.

"He told me to come here. Said something about telling the old goat that he would take care of it."

"Oh yes, he does like to call me an old goat, very well son, er, I mean friend, on Bullock's bill."

He thought about the candy jars. The young man stepped over and reached for a few jawbreakers and licorice whips. "Please add these to the bill, too," he said, carefully placing the candy into a bag and then in the side pocket of his new jeans. His boyish desires briefly had returned.

That evening over at Bullock's place Birch laid down to sleep, a time he dreaded because of the nightmares, but sleep finally came. He started dreaming of home and his family, and the nightmares returned. He could see his brothers smiling at him as he handed each a jaw breaker when suddenly, the face of that Lakota who killed his father appeared with an evil grin, moving closer and closer to his brothers with a spear. He sat up in bed, his face wet with sweat.

Birch smelled bacon and eggs, evidence that Seth Bullock knew his way around a kitchen. Birch needed to put on some lost pounds, but he could manage little appetite. At breakfast, Bullock handed Birch a present wrapped in old newspaper. It was a brand new .45 caliber 1873 Model Colt single action six shooter and a leather holster with leather strap tie downs.

Birch soon had the outfit strapped on. He stepped back into his bedroom and pulled the new revolver out, surprised at how heavy it felt in his hand. He turned the piece over and over, looking at it like a kid with a new toy. He had never seen such a beautiful weapon, let alone owned one. The barrel was covered in new bluing with walnut handle grips and the cylinders made a satisfying clicking noise as he changed chambers. He tried spinning the pistol and dropped it on the bed. Embarrassed, he looked up to make sure Bullock had not seen this stupid act.

Later he walked back into the kitchen with his pistol proudly strapped on his right side. He wore his new clothes and that curious turquoise necklace tied around his neck that he had taken off the Lakota brave. Bullock glanced at the blue stone and wondered if it was a trophy from the trail or just a reminder of what still had to be done. He deemed it a trophy; the kid did not need any reminder.

Bullock stepped beside him and said, "You know about killing. Now let's learn about living. That Colt will eliminate your chances for old age if you don't use your head. Many will come gunning for you if your reputation continues to build, so remember that gun is for self-defense and only for self-defense. In this country, a man has to know how to shoot. Shooting straight with a cool head will keep you alive, and trying to be a quick draw while spraying lead will likely get you killed by a gentleman who will calmly step back and fire once. Are you ready to practice?"

Bullock already knew the answer to that question.

They walked to the blacksmith's shop where a fine looking strawberry roan stood saddled. Bullock nodded toward the handsome mount and said, "You'll need a strong horse in this country, so I took the liberty of selecting this one for you. You can pay me back later. That suit you?"

Birch studied the beautiful mount over and did not answer. He only managed a slight smile, lately a rare expression for the young man.

His father had taught him how to judge horse flesh, and this was the most beautiful animal he had ever laid eyes on, with a head that was well proportioned to its body, a good, straight back, strong shoulders, a wide rump and a long, flowing mane. He walked around the horse, brushing against its butt to avoid being kicked and then carefully felt each leg for tender spots, bumps or swelling without finding any problems. Birch took several steps back and looked at the sturdy straight legs, thick chest and well-shod hooves before showing his satisfaction with a long whistle that picked up the horse's ears.

Bullock nodded his head and said, "Let's get mounted. We have some shooting to do."

Birch carefully slipped his foot in the left stirrup and swung his right leg over the roan's back, settled in the saddle, and instantly felt like part of the horse. Bullock twisted his rein over, and his horse moved out the stable door as Birch followed, still admiring his new mount.

During the ride, Birch suddenly felt a sense of guilt reassert itself over his elation about the new horse, gun and other equipment.

I have no right to feel happy when my folks are so recently buried, he thought. My brothers will never shoot a gun or ride across these prairies because they're dead. They will never ... he tried to stop thinking about his family. But it was no use. They haunted him and probably always would until, or even perhaps long after, the killers were dead. Bullock noticed this change of mood at a glance and understood that this young man was followed by a lot of ghosts.

Shooting was nothing new to Birch. He had shot his dad's old firearms many times, but this was different. Now he owned the nicest gun he had ever laid eyes on.

They finally arrived at an open green strip of grassland that bordered the Black Hills. Both men stepped down off their mounts and tied them in a shaded area.

"Alright Birch, now you're going to learn how to shoot that hog leg, but that is not enough," Seth began. "First you need to learn how to read men. You can almost always tell what a man is going to do by his actions. I say almost because the cowboy who is dumb enough not to be scared or show emotion is the one that will kill you. You'll meet some who talk a good fight, but freeze up when the action starts. Watch how a man carries himself and if he is wearing a tied-down hog leg. Now let's try shooting."

Birch had heard little of what the older lawman had to say. He was thinking about shooting his new six shooter that smelled of gun oil. He wondered if such a gun would have saved his father's life.

Bullock slipped him a handful of shinny .45 caliber jackets with lead bullets and watched him carefully insert one in each chamber, listening to that crisp-sound click each time the cylinder rotated.

Finally the moment came. Birch drew his gun, peered down the sights that protruded over the barrel, aimed the pistol, and took a deep breath like his dad had taught. His right index finger jerked the trigger, missing an old bucket about 20 yards away.

Seth laughed and drew his pistol in a lighting quick, smooth motion—the barking pistol planted three shots in the bucket. Birch walked over to find each shot was dead center and very close together, proving that the man could use a gun if necessary.

"Why would a man who can shoot like that never draw his pistol when making an arrest?" Birch asked.

63

Bullock reloaded his pistol and calmly answered, "If I don't draw my pistol, the other man will think twice before drawing his. They all know I can shoot like that. Some want to see if they can take me and that's why I have capable deputies. I don't give them the chance to try. We all get to grow older, and I no longer have any thing to prove."

During the next hour Bullock noticed that the young man had extremely quick hands and remarkable eye coordination. He spent a lot of time showing Birch how to point instead of aim, demonstrating the technique of pointing his Colt like pointing a finger before pulling the trigger. Birch drew fast and started shooting straight almost immediately with the best natural instincts Bullock had ever seen. More importantly, Birch had natural ability and coordination that could never be taught. Practice would make him an excellent shooter.

Soon the bucket was full of holes, most made by Birch. Seth declared it was time to go—words Birch was not ready to hear. This was the best he had felt since his family was murdered.

After the shooting lesson, Birch considered Bullock's words while riding home. Killing another man was possible; he had found this out the hard way. But what about finding ways to let them live? That is, except for those murdering bastards who killed his family.

How will I ever find the trash that killed my family? He wondered.

That night he thought about killing the murderers until sleep came and the nightmares returned. He woke up shouting night after night, and the horror was always the same. He could see a man pointing a pistol at his mother and then pulling the trigger, almost in slow motion. He would not stop shooting; he just kept pulling the trigger.

Bullock heard the shouts each night, and he just turned over and tried to sleep, hoping the boy would somehow conquer his demons. But he knew it would take time—lots of precious time.

BLACK MOON RETURNS
September 6, 1877

Black Moon observed a quiet camp where only two old women were visible, carrying baskets to find food in a nearby woodlot. Thin wisps of smoke ascended into the sky from cooking fires, and a good-sized doe hung from a lodge pole.

A dog lay in the sun, enjoying the last warmth before winter. The smell of wood burning filled Black Moon's nostrils, reminding him that he was hungry.

My people are still mourning, he thought, and so be it. I'm saddened by Red Pony's death, but more determined than ever to fight the white dogs. I know the Great Spirit and my spirit helper is with me now and no enemy bullets can hurt me. I will visit the elders and tell them of my vision and of my quest to defeat our enemies.

Black Moon held his hands towards the sky to pay tribute to his new allies. He had always felt the spirit world was with him, but now he had proof. The white invaders of his country would soon perish or be run out of Lakota territory.

The following evening he addressed the council of three small tribes that once had been large and strong.

"My brothers! Pay heed to my words, for they are the words of the spirit world that gave me a vision and a spirit helper," Black Moon shouted with his face turned upwards. "Many have claimed that the white man is falling on us like ashes, covering all and unstoppable. That is true, and we have fought this enemy bravely and with many deaths. The spirit world knows that we can not stop this scourge, but we can fight against it with our smaller numbers for we are strong and fearless."

Black Moon paused while several milled his thoughts over. He continued when their mumbling ceased.

"During my vision the spirits showed me how to do this and how to make them suffer and pay for taking our lives and the land we call mother. We will run in smaller bands and strike them when not expected. Then we will vanish back into mother earth where they will never find us. Their soldiers travel in big numbers; we will travel with few warriors in each attack."

The warriors' reactions of agreement to his last statement pleased Black Moon and made him feel powerful, like the leader he so desired to become.

"Their soldiers run through a village like a herd of buffalo; we will attack them like the trickster, by sneaking in and then back out," he continued. "My friends, we are Lakota, and we are too proud to let them take our land without a fight. Join me, and we will hurt the white man with every fiber of our being and for all of the spirit world to see."

More mumbling could be heard from the elders who nodded their heads in agreement.

"Black Moon has proven himself to be a good hunter," one elder stated. "Could he be the savior of our people?"

BIRCH'S NEW FRIENDS
October 2, 1877

The weeks passed slowly in Deadwood, and the ensuing practice sessions became the highlight of Birch's day. On several occasions, Bullock's deputies accompanied him to shoot, partly out of curiosity and partly to check his progress. Birch was not especially fond of Deputy Jim Mason. Mason had just turned 21, and he held the biggest ego of Bullock's deputies, partly because of his top-notch ability with a gun and partly because he was seeing the most beautiful woman in Deadwood.

Birch found the egotistical deputy to be on the strange side. Mason had the peculiar habit of reciting poetry at the strangest times, especially on the trail. He never recited an entire poem— just a couple of lines after riding in silence for a while, obviously deep in thought. The others would spend several minutes in silence after he quoted a verse, trying to figure out what in the dickens he was talking about.

Mason was a tough man with a sense of right and wrong that prompted Bullock to hire him. He sat tall in the saddle with a thin,

6'1, 160-pound frame that added well to Bullock's intimidating deputies. His unique hand slap on a .45 caliber Colt revolver produced a fast draw, close to Bullock's speed. Birch started practicing this move and was soon outdrawing Mason, a fact that was definitely unappreciated.

Buck Newton, the oldest deputy at 31, preferred to follow the crowd. The old cow herder was proud to be a member of Bullock's group, and he enjoyed the occasional fights—fist or gun. He sported a shaggy salt and pepper mustache, gray stubble, wore an old Stetson that needed to be thrown away and old buckskins that fit in with the shaggy-dressed crowd of miners, trappers, and drifters who enjoyed Deadwood's fringe benefits. Newton seldom talked; he mostly sat and listened to the others, until he disagreed. Then the argument started, and sometimes a few shoves followed. Birch liked this rough man who had spent more time on the trail than anyone and had more sand than most.

The man known only as Jed was different from the others. Birch noticed this unusual man sometimes silently watching him. Jed was about the same height as Birch, but carried more weight; his face was round and well structured. He kept a thick shock of raven-black hair pulled back and tied at the nape of his neck with a piece of rawhide, and he showed the confidence of a mountain lion. His hard, dark eyes and cold demeanor gave him a sinister look like the most hostile of his earlier captives and then tutors, the Cheyenne.

He wore a buckskin shirt and a Cheyenne necklace with a silver concho that highlighted a turquoise stone in the middle. A drunk had tried to buy the necklace some years back, but his offer had been ignored. As Jed turned to walk away, the unfortunate man grabbed Jed's shoulder and spun him around while drawing his pistol. His attempt to gun down Jed was rewarded with an underhand flip from a hunting knife. He took one surprised glance down at the knife in his chest—the last sight he would see in this life.

Jed's reputation grew quickly and no one tried to take the necklace again. He wore a black cowboy hat pulled low over his eyes, giving him an almost cocky look. Few doubted that his dangerous looks were only for show; the well-muscled man was no one to crowd. Only a few had tried, and they died for their efforts.

Birch learned the most from Jed's teachings of survival on the ever-dangerous plains and mountains, and he eventually became fond of this strange man who seldom spoke. Jed secretly admired Birch's warrior spirit, proven by his journey down the trail of death, but he never spoke of it.

Practice continued for several days, and the men were growing tired of shooting targets. One day, Birch was messing with his father's old knife, and Mason suddenly found another reason to be jealous of Birch.

Mason sarcastically asked, "Hey, can you throw that thing?"

His question was answered when a shinning streak slipped past his head. Astonished, he turned to look at the knife sticking out of a pine tree.

"Damn you! That just missed my ear! Where did you learn to do that?"

The other deputies laughed at Mason's astonishment.

"My dad taught me when we had a livery stable in Custer," Birch said. "He planted a plank, and we turned its center into toothpicks with his old knife. He taught me how to throw a knife overhanded and underhanded, tricks he learned from a Texan in his unit during the war. Yeah, dad could throw a knife."

Birch turned to look away, causing Mason to drop the subject. Birch occasionally would turn silent, thinking about the past. His new friends, including Mason, decided that it was better to leave him alone with his thoughts. Mason walked away, but looked back to see Birch sitting on the ground, starring at the horizon.

Days passed and soon Birch was giving knife-throwing lessons to all of the deputies except Jed, who was more than qualified at handling or throwing a knife. His adopted Cheyenne father had placed a knife in Jed's hands when most white kids were playing with a rattle. A competition started between the two, but neither man won consistently, or as Mason commented one bright summer's day: "I would hate to stake my life on any difference between the two."

Birch owned two knives—his father's and the Lakota warrior's more primitive version—until one day during practice when the deputies handed him a new knife to show their friendship. This knife was different than any he had ever seen before. The deputies had chipped in and bought him an Arkansas toothpick, sometimes called a Bowie Knife, named after the famous Texan, Jim Bowie.

Birch turned it over and over in his hands like he had with the single action Colt. He held the large knife at different angles in his hands and soon was satisfied with the balance. Then he slipped his right index finger up the blade, took a proper grip, and tossed it towards a wooden target made from a pine stump. The knife was larger than any he had ever held, but it turned twice in the air before sticking the stump, dead center to the deputies' approval. He made several more throws, sticking the well-balanced knife each time.

Two days later Bullock called Birch in for a talk.

"You're getting good with that hog leg and few in their right mind would challenge you with a knife. Now I think it's time for you to learn about men."

"Why?"

"I think it's time to add a new deputy. This entire territory will someday be enforced, and the law will make it possible for a man to raise his family without fear. But now we can only take care of our small part of the world. This town is growing by the day, and I can always use another good man. Want the job?"

"You bet, but understand that it is only until I'm ready to move on."

"I understand."

Both men knew exactly what Birch meant. Moving on meant finding those who had killed his family. Bullock knew that the young man was not ready; skill with a gun and knife is only a start, as many in Deadwood's cemetery discovered too late. Understanding men and their habits would be the last lesson.

Bullock knew that Birch could be the best with a six gun and still wind up dead. He was determined to teach Birch this last important lesson. The class would start tomorrow evening in the Number 10 Saloon, a bar filled with dangerous men who lived the hard life and felt little compassion for others. If anything, they enjoyed the adventure of a good fight.

-*>══◉ ◉══*-

BUD AND BENNY GET EVEN
October 6, 1877

Dogs at Native American camps tended to be vicious. Most were mutts that became useful as watch dogs, but pets were a luxury that most Lakota could not afford to feed, so the dogs had to fend for themselves. Only the meaner dogs managed to survive through a keen sense of smell and an aggressive nature.

So it was not surprising that Mountain Rock was chased and cornered by the camp's entire population of mangy dogs who faced him on both ends between two tepees. The man smelled like the bacon that had been taken by Red Hawk while attacking a miner.

Benny and Bud watched this drama unfold from a distance. They had hated this mean Lakota warrior ever since Red Hawk had found them wandering in the Black Hills after their mother's murder. Mountain Rock was a very cruel man, and the boys had endured several beatings by him when Red Hawk was not around.

Nevertheless, Bud and Benny still maintained their sense of defiance. They knew it was useless to escape; there was no where to go in the endless wilderness, only a maze of trees, rocks and mountains. Survival in the Black Hills was difficult at best, even for well-armed men who knew all of the tricks of survival. So instead of escaping, the boys tormented their captors when possible; this morning while he slept they had rubbed several pieces of bacon inside the Mountain Rock's buckskin pants, giving them a scent no dog could ignore.

"Serves the rat right," Benny said while watching Mountain Rock swing a stick at the stalking dogs. "Hope they chew his legs off."

"Naw, those dogs don't want rotten, stinking meat. It might make them sick." Bud added.

"I like this better than the time we propped that big, round, creek rock on the inside slit of the tepee at the end of a piece of stretched buckskin. Remember how old rat face yelped when the rock hit him on the forehead? That rock really knocked him flat

70

on the ground. Remember how he lay there with a stupid grin on his face and his eyes sort of squinted for a while? He had a big, red circle on his forehead for two weeks. That rock really clobbered him."

"Yeah, that was good," Bud said. "But do you remember when we stuffed our blankets with big rocks? He used to walk by and kick us with his bare feet 'til he kicked the big rock that would have been my butt."

"Yeah, he squealed like a girl and jumped around awhile— that was a good one. What about the time we put a dead June bug in his mouth while he was snoring? Remember his face when he woke up coughing and gagging?"

"I couldn't believe he swallowed it! What a sap!"

"Yeah, those were all good," Benny said. "But let's wait and see if the dogs tear his legs off."

"Yeah, that would serve the fat rat right."

Mountain Rock was panicking now as each snarling animal moved closer with the enticing scent of smoky bacon in its nostrils. He considered his situation and suddenly screamed, his voice high pitched and desperate.

Red Hawk arrived on the scene just in time with a rifle to see the panicking Lakota kicking at one dog, then the next. The panicked man did not notice that his friend had arrived to save him. Red Hawk pointed his gun in the air and touched off the trigger; the explosion frightened the dogs into a quick retreat.

Both brothers decided it was time to hide and avoid being seen by the irate Lakota who would eventually figure out their bacon trick.

Mountain Rock walked back to his tepee while a small dog continued nipping at his legs. The shaken Lakota kicked at the persistent dog who growled, took a few steps backwards and then charged forward again, this time getting a mouthful of pants and Mountain Rock's flesh.

Mountain Rock turned to Red Hawk, who had followed at a distance so the angry warrior could not hear him snickering.

"I know those two had something to do with this," Mountain Rock said in a frustrated voice, "I just don't know how they did it."

"I know why the dogs were after you. Meat. I smell meat," Red Hawk said. "Check your clothes; did you take meat out of your tepee?"

"No, I didn't even eat today," Mountain Rock answered while checking his clothing. His quest stopped when he noticed greasy spots down around his ankles.

"Please Red Hawk, let me kill them, please. They are constantly putting sand or small rocks in my moccasins, and yesterday the little brats caught a live otter and put it in my blankets. Do you want to see where it bit me?"

"No, I'll take your word for it," Red Hawk answered, almost laughing aloud. "Now look Mountain Rock, I will decide what will happen to them. You stay away."

Life became quieter a week after the bacon incident. Mountain Rock decided to act like nothing had happened, puzzling the boys.

"Think the stupid clod didn't realize we did it?" Benny asked.

"Don't know," Bud answered. "Maybe not. Thought he would have hit us or said something by now."

"Maybe we should lie low and see what happens."

About that time a shrill yell filled the entire valley, sort of an "eeeeahhhhhhhhhh," the sound of a man in great pain.

"Oh no Benny, what did you do with that weasel we caught in our box trap?" Bud asked.

"I sort of put it in Mountain Rock's buckskin bag. Do weasels bite?"

"I'd say so, judging from that horrible scream. I'm sure we'll soon find out."

Bud looked up to find a red-faced Mountain Rock with a weasel tightly clamped on his right index finger walking towards them. The boys almost felt sorry for the big Lakota. Tears streamed down his cheeks as the pain increased each time the weasel repositioned for a better grip.

Benny and Bud tried pulling the weasel's mouth open without success; the weasel's jaws were just too strong. Next they tried tickling the little animal's ribs, only to find that weasels are not ticklish. Finally, they slipped a piece of bacon under its nose. The little animal opened its mouth for a bite of the better tasting meat, and Mountain Rock was freed.

Benny quickly threw the animal on the ground before the grouchy Lakota could kill it. The weasel ran towards the creek and out of sight. The big man turned towards the boys, glanced at the glaring Red Hawk who had just walked into sight, exhaled a deep breath, and then walked away, defeated.

72

RICO AND HIS GANG IN DEADWOOD
October 10, 1877

ate in the afternoon, Rico rode down Deadwood's main street, trailed closely by his gang: Casey, Murray, Hawson and Taylor. Their torn, dirty clothes made them look like just another group of miners out of the several thousand who had invaded the area. They rode up to the Old Red Dog Saloon on the rough side of town, and Rico stepped through the door first. He eyed the place over, looking for a certain lady who had entertained him before. His gang sauntered in and roosted around a filthy table with old stains that looked suspiciously like blood. They were alone except for a small table of miners having a poker game towards the back.

The bartender, Matt Crawford, cautiously walked over while studying the group, a good habit he had picked up in other wild towns, a good habit for staying alive around the lower-class elements of 1877.

He recognized Rico and his band of cut throats and remembered that they became meaner than snakes after drinking too much rot gut whiskey.

That crap would make anyone mean, he thought. I wonder what it does to the stomachs of men like these who will eat or drink just about anything.

"Whiskey?" he asked in an uninterested voice.

"No señor, we came here to look at your beautiful face," Rico sarcastically answered. "Hell yes, whiskey. You pour."

Crawford, a stocky built man with a face that showed the scars of several bar fights and broken bottles, poured with a very stern look on his face. He was glad he had strapped on his six shooter under the old, dirty apron.

Rico watched the barkeep and waited until he was behind the bar before saying, "How about another drink of this fine whiskey?"

Crawford glared and walked back to the table, fully aware of what Rico had done and smart enough not to make a big thing about it.

73

"So señor," Rico asked. "What is new in this beautiful town?"

"Well, I guess you haven't heard, probably just coming off the trail, but a kid walked a long ways down the trail between Custer and here after his family was killed. Kid's name is Birch Rose. He killed 20 injuns or more and only with a knife," Crawford said.

"What a hombre this kid must be, 20 Indians and you say his family was killed on the trail?"

"Yep, his father was killed by injuns, but his mother was killed by men riding shoed horses. They never found his two brothers. The Army scouts found evidence, and now they are looking for his family's murderers. Bullock has made the kid a deputy because he's so good with a gun. I would hate to be the man who killed his mother and brothers if he ever finds out who did it."

Crawford turned and walked back to his bar, wishing for customers of a better class. Rico starred at Casey who looked kind of sick. Both knew that those kids might have seen their mother's murder and would talk if they were ever found alive. Worst, the Army scouts might somehow have evidence that connected Rico and his gang to the murder, meaning a fast stop at the end of a short rope. And if Birch Rose ever found out, revenge would turn him into a very bad enemy.

Truthfully, the Army had no idea who killed Susan Rose. Guilty consciences started working overtime, though, and their imaginations suddenly made Birch Rose a very dangerous man.

"Well my friends, I guess you know that we will only be safe when Rose is dead," Rico said in a low voice. "Who knows if he or someone else was hiding in the brush and watching us kill his dear madre? Even a miner or some damned Indian who was in the area might provide him with the information that could stretch our necks. So we must make a plan to kill this Rose, and his idiot brothers if they ever show up. But he is surrounded by Bullock's clowns, so what shall we do?"

"We only have two options," Murray said. "Either we shoot him in the back with a shotgun on a dark night or we hire someone to do it for us. I suggest we bring someone else in, because then the law will not be after us and we'll have a better chance to steal some gold. Especially when everyone is standing over his dead body."

"A fine idea. Casey, go find Reb Johnson and Shannon," Rico ordered. "They should be in town and they owe me a favor. And find that back shooter, Reggie Hillsham. He owes me too, and now it is time to collect my debt."

"Aw Rico, I don't like that Reb Johnson," Hawson complained. "He has eyes like a cougar and that Shannon don't talk—he just stares through folks. I don't like it. I just don't like it."

"You will like my boot in your ass even less, or perhaps even my knife in your ribs, now get moving," Rico snarled.

Several more shots of whiskey disappeared over two hours before four men appeared at the bar's swinging door. Rico slipped his knife across his whet stone while watching Reb Johnson survey the place before stepping in, followed by Hillsham, Casey, and Shannon.

Reb Johnson does have eyes like a cougar, Rico thought. But that damned Shannon is staring at me, and he never blinks or looks away.

"So my friends, how have you been?" Rico asked in his best Sunday voice, still slightly shaken by Shannon's gaze.

"What in the hell do you want, Rico?" Johnson growled while Hillsham, trying to seem dangerous, stood back with his usual dumb blank look.

"Oh, my friend, aren't you glad to see me, your old friend Rico who saved your life not long ago?"

"Alright, what can I do to repay you so I never have to endure the unpleasantness of your company again?"

"Have you heard about the kid who killed those Lakota with a knife?"

"Yeah, guys at the Lucky Lobo said he killed 30 injuns, but I don't believe it."

"Well, all debts are settled with all of you for a small favor. I want you to kill this young gringo, Birch Rose. Then we are even."

"What do you have against this kid?" Hillsham asked.

"That is none of your affair señor," Rico growled while glancing at Shannon and lifting his knife higher for all to see the razor-sharp edge. "Now will you do it or not?"

"That is already settled," Johnson said in a quiet voice that reminded Casey of a cat hissing. "Then we are even."

Suddenly Shannon stood up and walked across the room to look straight into Rico's eyes. The startled Rico could smell his foul breath and see teeth that were surprisingly white. Rico started to rise and was pushed back down in his seat by Shannon.

"Rico, if this is a double cross, I will look you up and kill you slowly," Shannon, the most dangerous of the three, said softly. "I will enjoy hunting you down, Rico. You might say that hunting a man and killing him is sort of an enjoyable thing for me. I almost hope you do trick us. I will kill you and take that knife you are always playing with, right after I stick it up your ass."

"I have no reason to trick you my friend," Rico said, trying not to show his nervousness. "Just make the kill, and then we are even," Rico said.

Johnson, Shannon and Hillsham slowly walked to the door, happy to leave. Shannon continued staring at Rico until he was out of sight. Rico focused his eyes on another shot of whiskey, then downed it to steady his nerves, and looked at his men.

"My friends," he whispered. "We must get out of town now."

"Why Rico?" Hawson asked in an innocent voice.

Rico looked at the floor and shook his head before standing up to leave. He knew that Hawson was not the smartest and decided there would be plenty of time to explain on the trail. They quickly mounted their horses and slipped out of town, unnoticed and happy to be back on the free, open range.

THE BOYS MEET BLACK MOON
October 12, 1877

Life around the Lakota camp became almost dull for Bud and Benny, who were treated with some respect because of their battle with Mountain Rock.

"Boy it's really cold outside, so put on your jacket," Bud told Benny. "Sure glad Yellow Flower made these buckskin jackets for us, or we would freeze."

"Yeah, I like her, but I miss ma, pa and Birch," Benny answered.

"Me too," Bud said in a soft voice. "Me too."

"Bud, look at that big guy riding in over there on that pretty horse," Benny said. "Is he is a big chief or something?"

"I don't know," Bud said. "But he looks kind of familiar. I've seen him before, just can't remember where."

The boys froze when Black Moon rode past before stopping to study them. They would have already been dead if he had realized who they were or if they had not been under the protection of Red Hawk. He would have killed them because they were white and unwelcome in his land.

Suddenly the big man stepped off his horse with a great deal of ease and walked toward the boys. Bud could see the fierce, intense eyes of this dangerous man who was studying them. Benny started to speak, and Bud slapped a dirty hand over his brother's mouth. Bud took a deep breath and prepared for the worse as the warrior walked closer.

"Hello my friend, welcome to my lodge," Red Hawk said from behind the boys. "Come and sit. Tell me about your life since I last saw you. Yellow Flower will prepare food while we talk."

The two men embraced and stepped through the tepee flap to a compact fire. Red Hawk explained the boys' story to Black Moon, and then told him of their exploits. Black Moon did not seem impressed, and Red Hawk realized that they would not be safe while Black Moon was around.

"My brother, we have ridden into many fights together," Red Hawk said. "You know my own two sons were killed by the white man's sickness. Now we have these two fine boys, and my wife has life in her eyes again. I only ask that you leave them to me."

"We'll see what happens, old friend," Black Moon answered in a voice that Red Hawk did not like. "Just remember that they are white, and you know what I say about that."

"Yes, but remember that I saved your life and you owe me this. I just want to keep the light in my wife's eyes a little longer. Besides, we could use two more hunters in camp, and they learn fast."

"I will speak no more of this, Red Hawk," Black Moon grumbled. "We'll see what happens."

THE FINAL LESSON
October 12, 1877

Over at the Number 10 saloon, Bullock met Birch the next evening in an advantageous table where the view was overall and safe. Bullock quickly explained, "enemies are made when you represent the law, and many will hold a grudge. Some will actually have the guts to face you. Most will try and shoot you in the back."

He paused to think about Hickok.

Bullock took a deep breath and glanced at the table before repeating, "Never sit with your back to the crowd. Now look around. I want you to just sit and watch. Look at the faces and how each man carries himself. Just watch. Tomorrow you can tell me what you saw."

Birch understood his role and the need to maintain a low profile, but he still proudly wore the Colt on his side, loaded, except for the chamber under the hammer, evidence of Bullock's teachings. Birch tugged at the collar of his new long, black coat Bullock had given him earlier that evening, and the coat easily covered up his Colt, a fact that Birch was not happy about.

He had spent very little time in any bar and was instantly fascinated as he glanced around at the drunken miners being sweet-talked by several girls who lived upstairs.

The music and the gambling looks like fun, he thought. I would like to try my hand at this kind of action sometime without this old fart dogging me.

"Remember earlier today when I told you to leave your Bowie knife at home? That knife is a sure invitation to a fight," Bullock told Birch. "The idea is not to start a fight. Your job is to make sure fights don't happen, or at least break up trouble before it goes beyond fists."

A loud female voice drew Birch's attention to a poker table in the bar's northwest corner. She was saying the foulest words he had ever heard a woman say. Birch stood up for a better look, only to see this awful woman shoot a stream of brown chewing tobacco to the floor.

Then, she wiped off her stained chin and squinted at her hand just dealt by a smallish man dressed in a white shirt, black pants, and a black and white checkered vest. She peered over her cards at the rather dapper gentleman and said, "You deal for shit mister."

The dealer looked down at the floor, partly out of fear of this foul smelling woman who was no one to mess with.

Bullock didn't have to look at who was making the commotion. He simply said, "That is Calamity Jane. See how she dresses like a man? That old gal can work a team of mules, peel the skin off a fly with a whip or shoot the ears off most men, but don't judge her too harshly boy. She has saved many men who came down with the pox and other diseases. That hard looking woman is an angel in disguise—although if I were you, I would never tell her that. She'll give you a poke but won't accept compliments. They make her suspicious."

Birch took a long look; he could see why compliments would make her suspicious. That woman was mud ugly.

Bullock watched Birch and wondered if he was too young and innocent to be a deputy. He most certainly had never tried a taste of real sin, so how would he react to some of the temptations that had destroyed men for centuries. Preachers write sermons about the temptations of sin, and much of Deadwood was built on sin, the kind that can pleasure a man or kill him.

Both men left the Number 10 with entirely different opinions about the place. Bullock understood the dangers, but Birch walked out intrigued. The young man was just getting his first real taste of sin and wanted to research it further.

They walked down the makeshift wooden boardwalk and came face to face with Mason and the woman he was courting, Amy Van Rijn. Dressed in a white, laced dress and a white sun hat, she smiled and looked over at the two men; her beautiful eyes accented brown hair and dark skin that showed she spent time outdoors during the warm months, quite a change from the pale prostitutes who spent their days sleeping. Both men tipped their hats to the lady, and Mason pulled Bullock aside to talk.

Birch stood looking at Amy like a farm boy looking at a red apple in the tree top—perfect but unreachable. He was taken back by her clear, blue eyes, well-shaped face with a slightly upturned nose and perfect facial lines that slipped down to a slight smile that occasionally opened up to reveal those perfectly white teeth. She tried not to look at the young man, but did and immediately blushed, instantly feeling attracted to the well-tanned and solidly built Birch.

Mason glanced over and noticed Birch and Amy looking at each other. His jealous nature flared. After all, a woman of Amy's beauty was noticed by all of the men in the dirty little mining town of Deadwood or anywhere.

Bullock noticed his new deputy looking at the lovely young woman and understood, but could only imagine the trouble this might cause. He knew that Birch was innocent as prairie grass, and once again, hoped he would survive his young, eager nature.

Amy had long been aware of Birch too. She had been courting the dashing Mason, but this new man, Birch, whom she had passed on the streets several times, quickly became unforgettable.

She lived in a two-story building that housed her dress shop on the bottom floor and her living quarters on the top. The place was purchased with money she had saved, combined with an inheritance from her parents. A dressmaker was needed for any growing city, the same as a church or bank. The two-story building suited her purposes perfectly.

A sign in Amy's front window read, "Dresses made to order with chain stitching, lock stitches, running stitches and blind stitches. I specialize in the latest French and English fashions."

The store was filled with scraps of fabric, a table where she designed patterns and an Empire Number One improved sewing machine made in New York around 1868. Women stopped by her shop to watch the incredible machine that was adorned by black with gold inlay designs work its modern magic.

Amy had hand-sewn dresses until her fingers bled to earn enough for this remarkable machine that could throw hundreds of stitches in minutes. She hand-sewed many of her detailed pieces and used a Finkle and Lyon pocket sewing machine for lockstitches. Two heavy-paper models held finished dresses made for customers who would eventually stop by.

Her home upstairs had two rooms. The living room and kitchen took up the big room with a small cook stove, two old chairs and a pot bellied stove. A bed, night table and wash basin were set up in the bedroom. Her bathroom was wooden, outside, and plenty cold in the winter.

Amy worked hard, but she had a somewhat boring life. She occasionally looked out her window in the evening to watch for the big, handsome deputy named Birch to walk past.

What kind of name is Birch, she wondered. Named after a tree. Big and strong like a tree, and those eyes, those blue eyes.

Amy had moved from a ranch outside of Deadwood where her father had been brutally murdered. She moved into town and sewed dresses and other apparel, mostly for the prostitutes before the so-called better class moved in. The "better" women in the area quickly discovered that the talented seamstress ordered the latest Paris patterns from New York and was skilled enough to reproduce almost anything when the correct fabric was available. Most women provided silks they brought from bigger cities or overseas, better than the plain cottons that could be purchased at the local mercantile, and were as overjoyed with Amy's finished products as the prostitutes who had ill-gotten money to spend.

Problem was, there were few decent places for women of standing to wear their finer attire. Amy's creations were often seen when the wearer's traveled back east. Naturally they claimed their dresses were made in Paris and not by a Deadwood dress maker.

Birch noticed her pretty smile one day in front of the dry goods store and never forgot it. Amy always had that effect on men, but she had yet to settle on one man. She was tired of being alone in this rough town and wanted to find the right fellow. She wondered if Birch Rose was the one and how Mason would react if he was.

Mason too would notice with time that his vision of eternal bliss with the beautiful Amy might slip away to his rival, Birch Rose. He became quiet around Birch and couldn't stand thinking about Amy in Rose's arms. The very thought made him crazy.

RICO LOSES A MEMBER OF HIS GANG
October 12, 1877

Rico and his cutthroats slipped into Lead City, searching for news under the noses of any posse that might be combing the hills for them.

"My friends, they don't know who we are or what we did," Rico said to his gang. "I think we are safe. The Army will never catch us. They are too stupid with their marching and foolishness. And Bullock doesn't know about us, so I think we should stay in the area a little longer and try to take a gold shipment."

"Aw Rico, I don't feel right about what we done, and I'm not so sure they're not after us," Hawson said. "They may have found the boys by now."

"They don't even know who we are, Hawson. Don't start acting like a big chicken."

"I ain't no chicken, but I'm moving on. I can't forget about killing that pretty woman in the hills. We shouldn't have done that."

Hawson pushed his chair back and stood up. Rico pulled his knife to kill this vermin who would dare walk out on him. He pointed his deadly blade at a very scared man.

Everyone in the room knew about Rico's hot temper and believed that Hawson was likely dead. The frightened man looked at the shinny blade's edge and thought about bleeding all over the floor, like a stuck hog. Then he thought about his family back in Iowa.

Sweat started dripping down his forehead to meet the tears on his cheeks, marks of a man who doesn't want to die.

Casey grabbed Rico's wrist and held it tight.

"No point in killing him," Casey whispered low enough so only Rico could hear. "That will just bring the law dogs down here to see what happened. Let him go. We don't need a coward anyway. We could never trust him in a tight spot when all guns should be shooting. He might be hiding in a corner and crying for his mama."

"No one walks out on me," Rico said in a deadly low voice. "I will kill this man."

"Sure, but later," Casey almost whispered. "We will kill him later where he can squeal like a frightened bitch without attracting as much attention. Now run away frightened bitch."

Casey's words made the others laugh and Rico lowered his knife. He wiped sweat off his brow and glared at Hawson.

"Ride away, you coward," Rico hissed. "Get out of my sight! I don't want to see you no more. And know when I run across you on the trail, the buzzards will eat good that day."

Hawson quickly grabbed his meager belongings, saddled his horse and rode out before dark. He did not want to spend a night in the same town or camp with Rico, who had slit the throats of sleeping men before. He knew staying would be fatal, especially after Rico had more time to think about him.

I wonder what's in Rapid City, Hawson thought while riding east into the evening light. He followed the trail throughout that night to get many miles away from Rico.

THE OLD NUMBER 10
October 12, 1877

Later that evening, Birch tried to sleep, but only tossed and turned while thinking about Mason's girl. Sleep became impossible, so he decided to revisit the Old Number 10 without an escort for a real look at this den of inequity.

When he arrived, he hung his long coat on a hanger so his Colt was in plain sight, and his well-polished badge reflected the flickering lantern light displayed throughout the bar.

A collection of barn lanterns and coal-oil lamps offered only dim light; unfortunately most of the seasoned dance-hall girls looked very different in the daylight. A young, attractive natural blond woman who easily filled out her red dress and actually did look good in daylight watched with much interest as Birch walked through the door. She glanced at the bar's mirror to make sure her makeup looked right, then walked up and rubbed well-skilled fingers across his left shoulder.

She found the man handsome, but very young. She wondered how old he was; she had just turned 20, but light wrinkles made her look older. She'd led a hard life in Dodge City, and her eyes held a sharp edge from seeing the worst. No one could deny her beauty, although some men did not trust the night-time girls who worked Deadwood's bars. She was no exception. Many men just sat back, drank and looked at her, trying to imagine what was under her dress.

"Hey deputy, want to arrest me?" She whispered in Birch's ear.

"Why no miss, I just wanted to see what was going on in here."

"Didn't you see enough with Seth earlier this evening? I saw the two of you sitting near the bar, gawking."

"Naw, we just stopped in for a drink. He was showing me around."

"My name is Debbie, and I know you're Birch Rose. In fact, everyone in town knows about you. Did you really kill all them Indians?"

"Yes'um, I did. They didn't leave me much choice."

"So tell me deputy, what is it like to kill a man?"

"Not much fun, but it's better than them killing you."

"Let me look in your eyes," the rather attractive Debbie demanded. "I want to see if you have the eyes of a killer."

She held his face in her hands and took a long look into his deep blue eyes. Birch felt a warmness throughout his body. Her green eyes made him uneasy.

He started thinking about things that he probably shouldn't have before she said, "You don't have a killer's eyes, but the gentle blue eyes of a gentleman who should never have killed anyone. I guess you didn't have much choice. I just hope you don't want to kill me. I can think of better ways for you to use my body."

He didn't answer, but sat pondering this amazing new circumstance as the warm feeling in his body increased. He had never met a woman who talked like her, and she looked mighty fine.

By now Birch had a shot of whiskey sitting in front of him. Everybody wanted to buy the hero a drink, and Birch liked the attention from a world he had only wondered about. He had never been a hero before, but could easily get used to the adulation. The trouble was, this kind of attention had been the death of many before him, and Birch Rose had a lot to learn.

Debbie hung on to him and helped share some of the drinks from miners, cowboys, and ranchers who wanted to shake his hand. Word spreads fast in a crowded bar, and everybody wanted to know the big, good-looking kid except for a stranger who was sitting exactly where he and Bullock had sat earlier that evening.

He sat with his chair tipped back against the wall and watched like a hawk watching a mouse as the young man enjoyed this steamy side of Deadwood. The killer's eyes seldom blinked, and he liked the fact that Birch was becoming extremely drunk. In fact, he sent over a shot of whiskey once to satisfy his sick sense of humor and allowed himself a slight smile as Birch downed the whiskey along with many others.

His dark brown eyes studied the young man with a sense of fascination and a twisted affection he saved for those he was about to kill, a select group whom he considered his only friends because he knew what to expect from them.

Birch started telling the crowd how he had killed each Indian for what seemed like the twentieth time. By now the whiskey had elevated his voice much louder than normal, and his story became more colorful as each thrilling detail brought cheers from the crowd. The young man had become that evening's entertainment for a bunch of drunks. His story took them away from their failures of looking for color in an unforgiving ground, and they were having a grand time listening to one hell of a story.

Suddenly the cheers stopped. The bar room became silent, a sure sign of trouble brewing. The stranger stood up and walked over to Birch, his gun strapped low on his right leg over old blue jeans. His dark red shirt was buttoned high, covered by a faded kerchief and his black hat sat low over squinting brown eyes that never blinked. He held up a shot glass of whiskey for a second, and then threw it in Birch's face.

"I jest wanted to buy you a drink, hero. Want another one on Reb Johnson?"

The whiskey burnt Birch's eyes, and he couldn't believe this was happening. He didn't want a fight with this stranger, but everybody was looking at him.

He was their champion.

"I don't want no trouble with you mister. I was just having a drink with my girl."

"That two-bit whore?" The stranger spit out. "Hell, I had her last night. She paid me."

Birch looked at Debbie who shook her head no.

"I've heard of Reb Johnson," she whispered. "He picks fights with men who've had too much to drink. He'd never face you sober. Birch, forget about him and let's go upstairs."

But the hero of the trail of death was challenged, and after all, the town knew he'd taken on the whole Lakota nation and won. What could this gunslinger do to him that a bunch of skilled warriors couldn't?

Everybody in the room felt a quiet, sick fascination while starring straight at Birch to see what he was going to do. Walking out now would label him a coward, something he definitely was not. Besides, this southern white trash had insulted his new girlfriend. He had to stand and fight.

Birch stood up, took a long look at the stranger's face, and felt a moment of terror. Something new had been added to the game; the gunman had a peculiar smile of arrogance on his lips.

His beady eyes peered straight through Birch, who suddenly felt good—the best he had felt since his family had died. Then, even drunk, that old feeling that carried him through the path returned. He was facing death and had to do something about it, but what, when?

That question was answered a second later when a slow-motion scene ran through the young man's eyes and brain.

Reb Johnson was going for his gun.

Birch's answer was not quite automatic, but his quickness saved him with a pistol slap and draw. He fanned the hammer of his Colt, sending two bullets through Johnson's chest who had barely cleared leather.

Johnson's eyes showed a great deal of surprise, and his mouth fell open as if he was trying to say something. Then his legs gave out. The older gun fighter died on the filthy floor of the Number 10 Saloon.

The crowd cheered as Birch looked down to study Johnson's face whose eyes and mouth were still wide open, as if he was surprised to be dead.

With Debbie following close behind, the young man ran to the cool air outside and immediately lost the evening's whiskey.

This continued for several minutes, until he finally stood up embarrassed and turned to face Seth Bullock with two of his deputies, Jed and Newton. They all had their pistols drawn and pointed at Birch, who turned to throw up one more time before passing out.

Bullock holstered his sidearm and the others did the same. This boy poses no threat right now, he thought. He's too sick.

Suddenly Hillsham, dressed in a long coat and buffalo skinner's hat, stepped out of the shadows with a double barrel shotgun pointed at Birch, who was still unconscious. Hillsham took careful aim and started to pull the trigger when Jed's knife slipped though the muscle in Hillsham's chest, cutting off a generous piece of heart.

Hillsham glanced down at the knife, looked up at the deputies and said, "Rico will kill all of you, just like you did me."

He shook his head, died, and fell forward on the knife, driving the thumb guards through his skin.

Birch's luck had held again.

86

A PAINFUL LESSON
October 13, 1877

The following morning, Birch awoke in his bed feeling mighty poorly.

His head ached and his guts felt on fire, while the room seemed to spin. He felt clammy from sweating, mixed with a classic case of the shakes—common traits of too much whiskey in an untested stomach. He wanted to throw up again, but could not.

I'll just lay here and hope the world quits spinning, he thought, but the world continued to spin. Birch Rose had learned about drinking too much whiskey, a hard lesson.

Bullock stepped in the room and handed him a cup of beef broth.

"Drink this," he said. "It might make you feel better, but time is the only thing that will make you feel right again. Just live with it. You deserve to be sick. I ought to kick your ass for last night, but I suppose it was bound to happen. Now I hope you learned something. I checked with the crowd and found it was self-defense, otherwise you would be suffering in a jail cell right now. I will talk to the judge and there should be no trial."

Truth be known, Bullock was happy that it happened and figured that a lot was gained by this one act of stupidity. The country was rid of some murdering trash, and Birch had learned his lesson about whiskey.

Most importantly, Birch had won his first gunfight drunk and killed a capable gun hand. The kid was good, no doubt about that. Maybe too good and too overconfident—he was not afraid. Bullock knew that a little fear had seen him through the roughest situations.

No fear was the mark of a fool; a fearless man will make careless mistakes.

Birch has much to learn if he is to survive, Bullock thought. This kid will take some molding, but he has all of the tools.

Only two things bothered Bullock.

Who was that damned blonde-haired girl from the bar who kept checking to see if Birch was alright? Bullock knew that she could ruin this promising young lawman. Many men had been ruined by what came in a red dress. And who in the hell was Rico? Why did this Rico want to kill Birch?

The talk between Bullock and Birch about what was observed in the bar came a day later than planned. Birch still didn't feel good, but he was starting to get his strength back. Bullock sat across the kitchen table from Birch and looked at his still ashen-colored face. Both men knew that this would be an entirely different talk since the gunfight.

Birch didn't know what to expect. Will he chew me out for shooting that gunfighter? He wondered.

The old sheriff finally got down to business.

"You looked at the faces of those men in the bar. What did you see?"

"A bunch of guys trying to get drunk I guess."

"Yes, but what else?"

"I don't know. What do you mean?"

"I mean, did you study their faces?"

"I suppose."

The old lawman just shook his head. This kid has trouble listening, he thought.

"I'll be surprised if you make another year," Bullock said with a hint of disgust in his voice. "You'll only survive by learning how to read men. Did you see the fat guy with a big booming voice across from us?"

"Yes."

"He's a coward. He's a big man who stands tall and talks loud and deep to intimidate. He's worthless in a fight. What about the little Irishman, did you notice him?"

"Yep."

"He's a tiger who would fight the biggest buzz-saw at a saw mill. He never carries a gun or knife, but he's fast and can throw a punch. Now then, did you notice the man you killed?"

"No, he blended into the crowd."

"That's the kind to really look out for. He was sure watching you, probably for several hours, just sitting, watching and waiting for the right time to kill you."

Birch thought this over and immediately shifted in his chair, feeling uncomfortable and no longer safe.

"The hardest part of killing a man is killing," Bullock continued. "Most are not willing to do it. Pulling the trigger on a man eliminates him from this earth. Even the most desperate are never ready to leave. Years ago a man told me, 'Everybody wants to go to Heaven, but nobody wants to die.' I have learned that is true for most men. But occasionally you'll find that one guy or gal who lives to pull the trigger. That is the person who will end your time here. And you know what is strange about that?"

Birch did not answer.

"You can never tell who's the killer, because most don't show it. Most killers quietly blend in until the time comes, then they kill and slink off somewhere else. Most don't stay around for fear of being shot in the back by one of their victim's friends. They don't brag about it or accept drinks for a fine shot. They simply leave. I guess you learned that the other night, shooting your mouth off about the Lakota might have gotten you killed. So, you killed a gunman, now learn from it. Did you like the experience?"

"No, I didn't," Birch answered. "I didn't like it a bit, but I liked it better than him shooting me."

Bullock smiled, stood up, and walked outside. He was satisfied with that answer.

The kid might make a lawman yet, he thought. He could be the best if he survives.

THE BOYS PLAY A DIRTY TRICK
October 15, 1877

Mountain Rock had left the boys alone since his horrible ordeal with the sharp-toothed weasel. Bud and Benny were happy that the mean man stopped giving them a solid punch or kick.

"You know, I'm kind of bored," Bud told Benny. "Mountain Rock at least gave us someone to hate and now I don't even hate him."

"Well I still hate the fat rat," Benny said. "He kicked me and I haven't forgotten it."

"Yeah, I know," Bud agreed. "I don't hate Black Moon, but I'm sure scared of him."

"Yeah, I dreamed about him," Benny said. "And he almost got me."

That afternoon the boys took a walk past Mountain Rock's tepee and noticed he had built a spit to roast some meat. Further investigation found a skinned raccoon tied up on a flap of his tepee to be roasted.

"Hey Benny, do you remember where we saw that dead raccoon yesterday?" Bud asked.

"Yeah, down by that little river bed, it was starting to stink," Benny answered.

"Let's go get it," Bud whispered.

"Why?" Benny asked.

"You'll see stupid," Bud said with a mischievous look on his face.

The boys found their dead coon and started skinning it. Benny and Bud both gagged from the pungent odor, but managed to pull off the skin that detached much easier from rotting meat. They returned to camp in time to see Mountain Rock slipping a spit through his coon carcass, then laying it just above the fire. He made the mistake of stepping into the nearby woods for a nature break at that moment.

"Alright, he's gone, now let's switch coons," Bud whispered.

"Yeah, and I hope it makes the fat rat sick," Benny answered with a big grin.

Soon Mountain Rock's new raccoon was roasting and creating quite an odor. People throughout the village stepped outside and sniffed the air. A couple walking past Mountain Rock's fire gagged at the stench created by his rotten meat.

A woman looked at her friend and shook her head, "He really needs a woman," she said. "Can you imagine eating anything that smells like that?"

Mountain Rock soon returned to check his roasting coon, took a deep breath, and started looking around to see what stunk so badly. He finally leaned over the rotten meat and gagged, then stood up to look around.

The boys hid in a nearby brush pile out of sight, giggling and punching each other on their shoulders. Finally the miserable Lakota picked the spit off his fire, hurried over the hill and tossed the rotten coon carcass into a nearby hollow where vultures, wolves or coyotes would find it.

An hour later Bud and Benny presented Yellow Flower with a fresh coon carcass. She had heard talk throughout the village and quickly figured out what had happened.

She started preparing the coon for roasting and turned to look at her adopted boys, who were learning to speak Lakota from her. She tried not to laugh at their young, innocent faces, knowing what they had done.

"Boys, this is a very large coon so I think it would be good for us to invite Mountain Rock to share our meal," She said without breaking a smile. "I understand that his evening meal was spoiled."

"I don't want to eat with that fat rat," Benny spouted out.

"Yes we do, and alright, we'll ask him," Bud said while holding his hand over Benny's mouth. "I don't like it, but we'll ask him."

Later that evening Mountain Rock, Red Hawk, Yellow Flower and the boys dined on roasted raccoon. The men laughed and talked through dinner while the boys glared at Mountain Rock. He occasionally glanced up at their dirty looks and then glanced back at his real hosts. Dinner ended and he stood to leave. Red Hawk followed him outside.

"My brother," Mountain Rock said. "I should never have made those two mad. They have a warrior's spirit and an even longer memory."

"Yes Mountain Rock, the boys are of a fighting spirit and you were mean to them."

"What can I do to make them leave me alone? I know they switched coons on my spit today. Now it is I who looks over his shoulder daily."

"I will ask them to leave you alone and they will obey. They are good boys."

"Yeah," Mountain sarcastically agreed. "Very good!"

CHRISTMAS IN THE DAKOTA TERRITORY
December 25, 1877

Fall ended much too soon. November passed cold and wet, then turned snowy, with the occasional blizzard coming down out of Canada that sent everyone in Deadwood inside to a hot stove. Now the fierce Dakota Territory winter pushed through the country like a runaway train. Everyone dreaded the long winters,

91

but they learned how to work and live in the worst conditions. Even Christmas became just another day of survival.

Snow blew up Deadwood's frozen Main Street. Miners and trappers wrapped in furs huddled in tents and prayed for an early spring.

Birch Rose sat in the jailhouse with his feet under the pot bellied stove, thinking about Amy's pretty smile and wishing he was not on duty. Jed sat a few feet away, staring at the stove, thinking about the plains in springtime. Mason flipped his knife at a plank in the corner, still trying to figure out exactly how Jed and Birch did it with such incredible accuracy.

Soon Bullock would arrive with Christmas dinner, a beef roast with potatoes. Birch could not help but think about his family, while Mason wished he was with Amy. Jed starred at the fire, feeling like he was with his new family.

"What do you think of Christmas?" Birch asked.

"Don't know," said Mason. "Seems they make a big deal about someone who lived and died a long time ago."

"You don't believe in Jesus?" Birch asked.

"I don't know, maybe, how would anyone know?"

"How can you not know?" Jed said. "My Cheyenne and Rancher fathers both knew and they showed me. I can see God or the Great Spirit when the sun rises or sets and when a baby is born. But mostly I just feel his presence."

"Well, I don't feel nothing," Mason said.

"Then maybe you're not listening," Jed answered in a soft voice just loud enough to be heard. "Maybe you should pay more attention."

"Reckon so," Mason replied, baffled by Jed as always. "I just don't know what to listen for."

"You will know when you hear it, amigo," Jed answered. "You will not have a doubt."

The door suddenly opened and Bullock stepped into the room with a cast iron Dutch oven full of roast beef and potatoes.

"What are you guys doing here?" Bullock asked. "I thought only Rose was on duty?"

"Just hanging around, boss," Mason answered. "Thought we'd brighten up Birch's Christmas with our charming presence."

"Well, luckily I brought a lot of food, so you clowns might as well grab a plate. Guess I have adopted the lot of you, what a burden!"

"We love you too," Mason sarcastically answered.

"Shut up boy," Bullock shot back. "Or I'll feed this delicious dinner to that pack of dogs outside."

No more words were spoken.

Christmas, 1877: Snow blew over the plains. The few remaining buffalo huddled together here and there, clumps of ice sticking to their heavy, matted fur, while their cold breath visibly puffed out of each nostril. Wolves howled in the distance. Spring might come in April or June, depending on when old man winter decided to turn loose, but right now both people and animals managed to survive focusing only on the moment. Living—for those strong enough—would be revived by warmth from the sun that would fully return life to the Dakota Territory.

DEPUTY IN A DANGEROUS TOWN
April 11, 1878

Spring returned early to Deadwood, much to everyone's delight, even with the muddy streets. The gunfight and ugly drunken affair in October had indeed inspired Birch to become a better deputy. He visited the Number 10 nightly to watch and listen like Bullock had taught him and to visit Debbie, a fact that Bullock was still not happy about.

She no longer entertained gentlemen upstairs, but only made sure that her customers were happy and that no glasses were empty. Her upstairs entertaining was saved for Birch, and she made sure his cup was always full too, but with coffee or water because the smell of whiskey made him gag. He occasionally drank a beer when the bar had it. They often ran out and the customers had to wait for the next freight wagon to bring in several kegs. "A sorry affair," a miner moaned one cool, rainy night.

Whiskey was another story.

Several enterprising miners from Arkansas discovered that they could make a lot of money by producing decent whiskey. They were artists of their trade, and the wagon masters made sure they received everything they needed, including plenty of copper tubing and bags of sugar and yeast.

93

Kentucky bourbon it was not, but it was better than no whiskey, and most importantly, no one ever died or went blind from drinking it. They couldn't produce this rot gut nectar fast enough; after all, mining is and always has been thirsty work.

Birch's reputation grew to mammoth proportions as word of his lightning-quick gun spread through the Black Hills and surrounding plains.

Birch started feeling comfortable in his surroundings and would have been shocked to realize that Shannon had positioned himself to watch Birch's daily habits. The capable gunfighter had stayed alive by being cautious. He was waiting to find the right time and place to ambush the unsuspecting Birch.

The deputies became a tight unit, and the four would occasionally have a few drinks together. Their favorite watering hole was called The Lucky Lady Bar. They stayed in a group by themselves, like an exclusive club that others tried to join but were generally snubbed. Shannon sat in a corner of the bar nightly and sipped coffee while watching Birch Rose. He made a point to study each deputy's face, faces of men who would want to kill him after he killed Birch.

Then one night Pete Hammond, a big miner from Ireland who owned a working mine outside of Deadwood drank too much and decided to challenge Jed.

"Hey, half breed," he said in a loud, rough voice. "Why don't you quit hiding with your white buddies and come have a drink with me."

Jed ignored him and dropped another shot of whiskey as five of Hammond's miners stood.

"Ain't they pretty," one of the miners said. "I wonder if their daddy, Bullock, taught them to fight without those guns? I'll bet they ain't nothing without those guns."

Jed looked at the others and grinned, one of the few times anyone had seen this expression from the normally stone-faced man who actually was half white and half Spanish. He wore buckskins after adapting Plains Indian ways from his Cheyenne father who had picked him up off the trail after his real parents were massacred.

He took off his pistol and belt, laid it on the bar, and then slanted a threatening glance at Jim Mitchell, the bartender, who picked it up and gently laid it in a safe place. The other deputies laid their pistols on the bar. The place grew quiet, except for the scuffle of bystanders trying to get out of the way. Shannon continued to sip his coffee in the corner and watched how Birch handled this affair.

94

In the meantime, Jed walked up to Hammond and glanced up at the big man's homely face.

"Now what can I do for you, boy," the big man said, barely finishing the sentence when a fist under his chin made him lean slightly backwards.

Jed had given this huge man his best Sunday punch with little effect, so he gave a blood-curdling war whoop and jumped on Hammond while driving a knee to his groin. The miner easily flipped Jed over his shoulder for a hard landing on the filthy floor. Hammond picked Jed up and hit him with a ham-sized fist that sent him over a table.

The others by this time were mixing it up with Hammond's crew. Jed continued trying to attack Hammond with about the same results; he got knocked down time and time again. Birch threw several convincing punches at a miner about his size with little success, and across the room Mason traded punches with a miner who had huge fists—or it seemed like it—every time one slammed his jaw. Jed persistently attacked the big man who could take a punch and give one back even better; in fact, all of the miners were giving better than they were taking.

Finally, the well-beaten Jed took another swing that was caught by the big miner.

"Well I declare, son, you just don't know when you're whipped."

The big miner turned Jed around with the ease of turning a baby and yelled, "you boys stop that. I'm tired of this fighting. Let's have a drink. I want to buy my new friend here a shot of whiskey."

By evening's end the deputies and miners had gotten formally drunk together, paid for by Hammond.

Their laughing and drinking took over the bar, but nobody from either group was laughing or moving very fast the following morning except for Hammond, who ordered his men to work with these kind words: "You can drink with me if you can work with me the next day. I only have solid men in my outfit."

The bruised and hung-over miners knew better than to skip a hard day's work because Hammond was a fair man who expected a lot from his men and gave a lot in return. From that day forward the deputies welcomed Hammond and company into their little group without fanfare or fighting.

The fight made the deputies a closer unit. Bullock realized this and decided not to reprimand his men who had actually been set up.

Hammond and Bullock had planned this fight to see how the deputies would react. Later the big miner told Bullock all the details of the fight over their weekly chess game with some decent Irish whiskey provided by the Hammond Mining Company. They both had a good laugh.

AMY VISITS THE JAIL
April 15, 1878

Mason was disgruntled as usual. Bullock left him to protect locked-up drunks. He was delighted to see Birch, who stopped by for a word with Bullock. The smell of drunks in the back cells was unpleasant, but the deputies had gotten use to it with time. Snoring in the back told Birch that at least someone was enjoying the confines of Deadwood's jail.

"Hey Birch," Mason said. "I need to leave for a few minutes. Can you watch the prisoners?"

"Sure thing," Birch innocently answered. "How long will you be gone?"

"Not long old buddy, not long at all," Mason replied.

Birch sat back and leaned his feet on the desk, knowing full well he'd been had.

He was grumbling something to himself when the door creaked open and Amy stepped into the lantern light. She was dressed in a lavender dress with white lace. Birch, as always, was taken back by her wholesome beauty and remarkable smile.

"Oh, hello Birch," She said in a soft voice. "I was looking for Mason."

"He'll be back soon," Birch said while hoping he was gone for the night. "How are you?"

"Fine, but I'm chilly."

"Here, let me move this chair over so you can sit by our stove. I have a good stand of coals burning," Birch said.

"So, how do you like being a deputy?" She asked as she sat near the fire.

"Well, I don't much like being shot at, but it's a good way to make money."

"Kind of smells in here, doesn't it," she said.

"Well, yes, most of our guests are drunks who are sleeping it off. They never smell very good, especially after a night of drinking rot gut. Their bodies don't take kindly to a belly full of that stuff."

"Well, I'm happy to see you anyway, even here."

Birch answered by moving a chair over by her. He sat closer to Amy, but was suddenly shocked to see a red-faced Mason step in the door.

"What in the hell are you doing Birch?" Mason growled.

"Just doing your job Mason, right Amy?"

Amy smiled and tried not to blush while Birch stood up and walked out the door, satisfied with his evening.

UP JUMPED THE DEVIL
April 16, 1878

"Good afternoon. Might you be Birch Rose?"

Birch had just stepped out of the jail's smelly old outhouse late on a sunny afternoon, just after a brief rain, to hear a startlingly calm voice.

"Yep, who's asking?"

"Folks call me Shannon, but you may want to call me something else."

"Why is that?"

"Cause I'm fixing to kill you in a fair fight, and by the way, Rico sent me."

Only then did Birch fully realize what was happening.

Damn, not again, he thought. The deputy's stomach suddenly tightened. He tried to take a closer look at the man and realized that the late afternoon sun was bright and full in his face.

Birch was in trouble. This experienced gun fighter had gained that most important advantage—the sun was at his back. Birch would not be able to see when Shannon went for his gun because the sunlight blinded him.

Birch decided to try and stop this or at least postpone the inevitable.

"I think we should talk about this over a drink," Birch said.

"So, the brave gun fighter and Indian killer is a coward and probably a liar. I knew Reb Johnson; you probably shot him in the back."

"One of us will be dead very soon if this happens," Birch pleaded. "I don't want to die and I don't want to kill you."

"Come on boy, I rode a long way to kill you. Go for your gun. I want to have a steak and some whiskey before bedtime."

"This don't make sense. I don't know you, do I?"

"Shut up and draw, or I'm going to drop you right here."

Birch realized that there was no way out. The intense glare made his eyes hurt, and he would never see Shannon go for his gun, so he slapped his hand on the holster, drew up his Colt and fired three quick shots at the darkened silhouette.

The first bullet entered Shannon's belly button, the second his chest, and the third tore through his left shoulder. He only had enough time to say, "Damn you, Rico" before his lifeless body slammed down on the ground, his six gun still holstered.

A cloud of dust filtered through the sunlight as Birch took a closer look at the man's face and saw the same shocked look that Reb Johnson had died with. Bullock and Jed came running from the jailhouse with pistols drawn after hearing the shots while playing a checkers game. They both exhaled a breath of relief to find Birch standing there, starring at the body.

"He didn't give me any choice," Birch said in a remarkably calm voice. "I opened the outhouse door, and he was standing there, waiting. He said he wanted to kill me so he could go on to his evening meal. Swear I never laid eyes on the man. He said Rico sent him, and he said Rico's name before dying."

Bullock examined the body. "You didn't have to recognize him boy," he said. "He apparently was one of many who Rico has hired to kill you, and he may still accomplish that very deed. You're now a trophy for reputation hunters after killing two known hired killers in fair fights—and don't feel sorry for him. Just remember that he is dead on the ground in the mud and you're walking away alive. You'll be the one enjoying dinner tonight, and the worms will soon be enjoying him. Jed, go find the undertaker. He has some work to do. I just wonder why this Rico character wants to kill you so badly. He may be rich; poor people do their own killing. A poor man could not afford three guns, but I don't know of any ranchers named Rico, at least in this area."

Jed nodded. "Glad you are still among the living, Birch."

Birch nodded, took a deep breath, and walked into the jailhouse. He did not enjoy dinner that night, as Shannon would have.

A BAD NIGHT
July 4, 1878

Deadwood knew how to put on a party, and July 4th was cause for celebration. The morning started with horse races and a shooting contest that Bullock decided the deputies should miss. Their reputations as gunmen had spread across the territory; no need to add fuel to a raging fire. The Chinese planned a fireworks display after dark after much urging from the city council and a great deal of money. Whiskey flowed and different tunes from the many bars spewed throughout town with plenty of whoops and yelling. The good folks who had hopes of making Deadwood a decent town with churches and schools even joined in. Everybody was having a good time—except for the deputies.

The deputies knew they would soon escort a gold shipment somewhere out of town. Bullock purposely never told anyone exactly where each shipment was going until they were ready to pull out, a precautionary measure meant to keep any big mouths from giving up information that could risk his deputies' lives.

"Damn that Bullock," Mason said. "We are going out on escort duty soon, and he's making us patrol the town tonight for drunks or whatever scum decides to act up. This is going to be a very boring night."

"For once I agree with you Mason," Birch said. "I would rather be somewhere else with someone warm instead of you."

"Is your horse that warm?" Mason jabbed back.

"You know who I am talking about, and she is no horse."

Jed followed closely behind the others. He never complained, but his look was not of contentment. His eyes were constantly moving, looking for danger, a tribute to a lifetime of hunting. The fireworks display was sensational, and even the drunkest stopped to watch. The deputies looked up at the different colored fires flashing through the sky. Birch thought about Amy, and from the other side of town she thought about him.

The sound of several revolvers down the street brought Birch to life an hour after the fireworks display ended. He ran past the others towards the harsh sounds of danger. The others quickly followed to find at least six rough-looking cowpunchers on horseback shooting up the town after trying to drink dry the Roundup Saloon.

"Hey, that's enough shooting in city limits," Birch yelled at the closest cowboy who gave him a long look. Birch could see his weather beaten face and a thick mustache that turned down to complete a heavy frown in the saloon's kerosene lamp light.

"Well, well, if it isn't Bullock's idiots, trying to take on men," The man spurted out in a hard voice. "Tell me junior, which one of you has the guts to draw down and start trading some lead with Bob Mathews."

"Now listen mister, we are the law and you are only asking for trouble," Mason said in a surprisingly calm voice. "Now we know you had a good time in the saloon. So far, no harm is done and we don't want to hurt you. So why don't you drop those hog legs and we'll talk."

"Damn boy, I killed better men than you in the war and they was only Yankees, and I ain't about to back down from some dumb-ass kid now. So draw down or shut up."

Suddenly the street became very quiet while onlookers watched to see what was about to happen. The cowboys started maneuvering their horses around to better areas for clean shots at the deputies. Jed realized this and yelled, "Look out," an instant before the first shot was fired. Then all hell broke loose in Deadwood.

Lead flew through the air, making horrible sounds like a runaway freight train. The entire city stopped and listened to the "BOOMS" created by pistol hammers dropping on caps. The deputies ducked behind any cover available as six capable cowboys sent an incredible barrage of hot lead at their positions. Mason, Jed and Birch wanted to shoot back, but could only manage a chance shot. They were pinned down by six experts who had fought in the war between the states and numerous Lakota encounters.

For quick cover, Birch chose a water trough that had already started leaking from bullet holes. He looked up and was startled to find the cowboys were still on their horses, firing wildly at the deputies and having a damned good time. Bob Mathews was firing his pistol and occasionally laughing like a mad man.

Birch took careful aim and tried to shoot, hopefully to stop Mathews from shooting holes in the trough that was making the ground muddy where Birch knelt. But the shooting was too intense for a clean shot.

Suddenly Mathews yelled, "hold your fire, boys," and the cowhands sat on their horses laughing at the befuddled deputies. "Come on out kids, and arrest us, we won't hurt you."

Slowly, with their pistols still ready, Birch, Jed and Mason stood and walked over to each man who handed down their pistols and rifles.

"Boys, we have had our fun, now arrest us so we can get some sleep," Mathews said to the befuddled deputies. "You boys need to polish up your fighting techniques. Hell, we might have killed you."

"Did I say this would be a boring night?" Mason asked while leading the rough group of cowboys to their hotel with bars on the window.

"Shut up," Jed said during one of the rare times when he spoke. "Just shut up."

Seth Bullock arrived in time to see the cowboys and deputies moving towards the jail. He quickly heard what had happened from two old miners who laughed while saying, "Yer boys sort of took a whipping, Bullock."

Soon the cowboys were sleeping soundly in their cells. Bullock knew that his group had been embarrassed. His men had never been this quiet.

"Well deputies," he said in a very low, dark voice. "I heard you got the chips knocked off your shoulders tonight. Maybe that is a good thing. You were just lucky they were playing instead of really trying to kill you. Otherwise I wouldn't be talking to all of you right now. I suggest that you keep practicing, and remember how Bob and his boys had you. You boys met face to face with a group of very capable men who could have easily killed you. Now get out of here and don't ever forget this."

The deputies walked out of the jailhouse with red, angry faces. Each knew that Bullock was right and that they were not close to being the rough bunch required for their jobs.

"Guess we might as well practice even harder boys," Mason said. "But the hardest part will be showing our face around town. This kind of news travels fast in Deadwood."

101

⊹⟩▬⟩⟨▬⟨⊹

THE UNDERSTANDING
July 6, 1878

Mason, Jed, Newton and Birch enjoyed their daily target practice sessions by seeing who could shoot first from the holster and hit the target, which was usually a horse dumpling or a piece of old China dinner plate. Birch always won, but Mason found his speed and accuracy improving while shooting against the young man. Daily practice made Mason the best he had ever been.

Then one day he decided to challenge Birch. Mason had slightly warmed up to Birch, but he was still jealous of Birch's reputation and attraction to Amy, which had become obvious to everyone. Even worse, she was paying a lot of attention to Birch as well.

"O.K. Birch, let's stand next to each other to see who's fastest. I'll count to three, and then let's slap leather."

Birch moved in beside him.

"Ready? One, two, three."

Birch drew before Mason's gun left his holster. He watched with a slight frown as the young shooter fanned his six gun, sending an accurate spray of lead that destroyed a horse dumpling.

For the first time in a long time, Birch Rose smiled.

Mason was not surprised, but slightly dumbfounded. This was the fastest he had ever seen Birch draw. For that matter, it was the fastest he had ever seen anyone draw, and Birch killed the horse turd. Mason rode home that day sure that he had just watched lightning death. He never wanted to go against that gun and would be glad to be on Birch's side when the shooting actually started.

The real friction started between the two of them when Mason was riding home from patrolling Deadwood one day. He passed by Amy's back porch and found Birch sitting there, eating a piece of cake. Amy was upstairs prettying up for the handsome deputy.

"Just what in the hell do you think you are doing here Birch?" Mason demanded in a loud voice.

"Having a piece of cake, Mason. What in the hell does it look like?"

"You know, before you came along, Amy was pretty much my girl and we was working on an understanding."

"She never told me that," Birch answered while trying to swallow a big mouthful of the white cake with white icing.

"Well, she is and you aren't welcome here, unless I invite you."

"You know, I'm starting to get tired of your big mouth," Birch said. "I'm here because Amy wants me here, so maybe you're the one who better get."

"Alright, that's it, step off that porch and let's settle this like men."

"Fine with me bud, and may the best man win."

"I plan to," Mason said.

Both men took off their jackets and stood face to face, then shook hands and started moving in a circle like two rutting bucks facing off.

"Come on, you take the first punch," Birch said.

"No, you take the first punch and I will deliver the last," Mason answered.

"Come on, you called me out so take a punch and let's get this going," Birch said, starting to get angrier.

"Well alright," Mason said while throwing the first punch that barely grazed Birch's cheek. Birch stepped back and delivered a solid right to the startled man's stomach, knocking the air out of his diaphragm.

Mason sat back on his butt and grabbed his stomach. Birch bent over to help him up and received a solid fist on the chin. Birch fell back on his rear and shook his head. Both men sat in front of Amy's shop, starring at each other in disbelief.

Then Mason started laughing, and Birch soon joined in. Amy stepped out on the porch to find her two suitors sitting on the ground, laughing like mad men. She looked disgusted and stepped back into the shop, hoping both men would someday grow up.

"I guess you know that Amy is still my girl," Mason said while brushing off the dirt from his trousers.

"I haven't heard her say that," Birch answered, feeling the back of his neck get warm as his anger returned.

"Well, she will and then you'll know, so just stay away from her. She's mine."

"Mason, don't go buying your wedding duds just yet."

103

BLACK MOON GOES TO WAR
September 19, 1878

Black Moon's hatred for the white race grew as time passed. He still traded with white trappers who could give him items that were not available on the plains or in the hills. He allowed them to live, finding a useful source of information from this group of loners who knew better than not to answer his questions. They were allowed to trap in the Lakota region— or for that matter, survive—for their cooperation by providing important information.

Black Moon had a particularly interesting conversation out on the plains one day in the Lakota language with a trapper known as Missouri Mac, a big burley mountain man who gave Black Moon information because he liked him. Black Moon knew that Missouri Mac was no one to fool with, and he was one of the few white men Black Moon respected.

"Good day old son," Mac said in perfect Lakota tongue. "We have been blessed with a fine day for travel."

"Yes my brother, the spirits have given us a good day in preparation for the hard days of winter that toughen us as men."

" I might head up to higher ground west of here, maybe find some elk or other meat. Come hunt with me."

"No my brother, I must stay and fight my fight against your white brothers."

"Black Moon, your people are more to me than the whites who keep hogging their way across this land. I am white and sometimes ashamed. The soldiers killed many of my friends from your tribes. The dirty bastards killed my woman, Little Dove, the most beautiful flower that was ever raised any damned place. No my brother, they are not my people."

"Then you are part of us. My heart is saddened by this torment across our land, so I will stay and fight."

"Guess it would do me little good to tell you the fight is over. No, it would do no good at all. Fight a good fight, and I will see you again on the other side."

"Yes, I feel the spirits are with you, but for now I need information."

"What can I tell you?" Mac asked.

"What do you know about the man who killed six Lakota on the trail by the village you call Deadwood?" Black Moon asked.

"That man is a famous deputy in Deadwood, a Birch Rose I hear," Mac answered. "They say he is the best with a knife or gun."

"Where can I find this Rose?" Black Moon countered.

"I guess in Deadwood. Guess you could find him there."

"The killer of my people on the trail will die soon, that is Black Moon's words and vision."

"Go with God, old son," Mac said, realizing that Black Moon meant business.

GOLD
September 19, 1878

The enviable big strike finally occurred when Cookie pick-axed a good-looking creek bed south of Deadwood. He was only just out of yelling distance of town when his pick ax struck something hard. A bit of scraping and digging turned out color like no one had ever seen.

He squinted his old brown eyes at the color, took off his old hat, and threw it in the air.

"Yeehaaa Ginger, we is rich."

The old prospector who had saved Rose received the Karma of good fortune. Cookie danced around the curious mule.

"You'll never have to eat stink weed again old girl. It's oats three times a day."

The old miner had struck the mother lode, and so had Ginger because the old mule was his only family who would have anything to do with him.

That night Deadwood witnessed one of the biggest parties of all time, paid for by Cookie. Miners yelped up and down the street, celebrating that their friend had hit it big, and even more importantly, he was paying for this shindig. They could drink until dawn and longer if anyone was still standing, but not everyone was celebrating.

Bullock knew that this big strike would bring on a new set of problems, and no one had moved in a safe big enough for a big strike or had hired armed guards. The gold would have to be protected 24 hours a day, a feat that would fall to him and the deputies.

His men were going to really earn their money.

"Now listen, this new surge of gold could get you all killed," he told a sober-faced Newton in front of the bank where Cookie had cashed in some of his gold. "You have to watch each other's backs and watch for strangers. I know that's hard in a town that could see 10,000 miners daily, but your very life could depend on seeing thieves before they see you. Remember, even an honest man might be tempted to step outside the law for that much gold. So watch out and stay alive. I'll count on you to tell the others."

Newton, the oldest deputy at 31, walked away grumbling and knowing that everybody would be having a good time while they worked. Their free time was over until a sound bank was built.

AMY'S JOURNAL
September 19, 1878

A my was glad to be home after a long day in the dress shop. Might have to hire permanent help, she thought while slipping out of her light blue dress and gratefully unbuttoning the tight black leather shoes that made her feet sore. Other shop owners warned her to stop doing business with prostitutes to avoid chasing her "better" clients off. She refused, saying, "I am sure God would not turn them away. How can I?"

Her clothing and shoes were soon traded for a flannel nightshirt. She ate a quick meal and gratefully moved to her bed. Amy laid down and started writing in her daily journal:

September 19, 1878

> I saw him again today. I can't believe he got in a fight with Mason over me. I feel bad for Mason. He is a gentle, capable man who would make a fine husband. But I can't stop thinking about Birch. The thought of his lips on mine makes butterflies dance in my stomach worse than a real kiss from Mason does. I wish my mother was still alive to tell me what to do. I guess that it is all up to me. I have to make my decision. That one prostitute I can't stand, Debbie, who claims Birch is courting her, stopped by to buy a dress today. She was short on cash and traded a derringer for the balance. She included several bullets. I think the gun is old, but it is solid and I can't wait to shoot it. I loved shooting with dad when I was a child.

She gently closed the journal, laid it on the table, then leaned over and blew out the flame of her kerosene lamp. She lay in bed comparing Mason and Birch and fell asleep with Birch's face in her mind. He would have been shocked to realize that she was thinking about him.

The following morning Amy unlocked the front door of her dress shop and stepped outside to sweep off the walkway. She was startled by Birch, who had been waiting there over an hour. She noticed that he was starting to dress more like Mason, with a dark brown vest, hat and trousers. Even his boots were dark brown to match his outfit.

"Hi Amy," he said with a hint of shyness in his voice.

"What are you doing here, Birch?" She asked, already knowing the answer.

"I guess you heard that Cookie is having a party tomorrow night to celebrate his strike."

"Yes, I heard that the foul smelling old goat was having a party."

"Well, would you consider going with me to the old goat's party?"

"Why Birch, what would Mason say?" Amy asked in mock surprise. "You already got in a big fight with him in my backyard. What would I do if the two of you got in a big knock down drag out fight in front of everyone? I'd be so embarrassed."

"Well then, let's just not go to the party, how about that," Birch asked. "Why don't we just go for a nice, quiet walk."

"Well, alright Birch, meet me here at sunset. But we may sit more than walk. My feet hurt at day's end."

"Great, then we have a date to sit and talk," Birch answered while trying to hide his absolute joy. "I'll see you then."

The next evening, Mason was enjoying the free booze at Cookie's party, oblivious that Birch and Amy were taking a walk just down the street. The couple had been seeing each other more and more, a fact that Mason had become painfully aware of.

"So, what do you think? How about a first kiss?" Birch teased Amy.

"Oh Birch, what would Mason say?" she answered.

"I really don't care. You are my girl and not his now."

"Oh, is that so? Since when do you make my choices for me?"

"I'm sorry Amy, but don't you see how perfect we are for each other?"

"Yes Birch, I do, but don't start telling me what to do. That is the main reason why I'm with you tonight instead of Mason. He always bosses me around. I will not live my life like that."

"Great," Birch said. "Then how about that kiss?"

Amy planted a sweet kiss on Birch's lips. He noticed how soft her lips felt and how sweet she smelled. He was feeling a great deal of arousal when a big hand grabbed his shoulder, jerked him around and planted a right cross on his jaw producing a blue flashing light in his brain.

Birch looked up to see a red-faced Mason starring down at him and shouting something he could not understand. The well-placed punch had dazed him, and the fight ended before it started.

"Mason, leave him alone," Amy shouted. "Don't you see how it is?"

"I do now," Mason said in a suddenly controlled voice as he turned to walk away. "Everything is clear now, and I won't be bothering you no more Amy."

She helped Birch up and tried to help him walk before he pushed away.

"I can walk on my own," he said in a grouchy voice. "Mason hasn't heard the last of this. I owe him one."

HAWSON'S BIG DRUNK
September 22, 1878

Hawson had made it big after leaving Rico and his cutthroats. He had made some money gambling, robbed a stage on the trail to Rapid City, and pulled a drunken dandy's billfold that was loaded with greenbacks. He was living the highlife and wishing the boys could see him now—everyone but Rico, that is.

He was having quite a time until the night when he entered the Derby Saloon with a snoot full of rot gut whiskey. The hall was darker than most, with only a few tables and low oil lamps for poker games. An old deer head was nailed above the wooden slat bar. Hawson studied its face and decided it had a very stupid look, the sign of poor taxidermy.

Guess I'd look stupid too if they nailed my head over the bar, he thought.

He ordered a drink for everyone at the bar and then proceeded to get even drunker. He befriended a cowpuncher, and they soon sat at a table, crying in their beer.

"You know, I did a bad thing, and I haven't told nobody, ever," he said in a loud voice.

"What did you do, chum?" the cowboy asked.

"I was with a gang when they shot and killed a woman on the trail from Custer to Deadwood, or maybe Deadwood to Custer," the drunk Hawson surmised. "Well, however it is, we did it."

"You killed a woman?"

"Naw, I held the horses while Rico and the others did it. Now I feel real bad."

"That's alright chum, we all do bad things sometimes," the drunken cowboy answered. "But killing a woman, that is real bad."

"Yeah, real bad," Hawson blubbered. "And I feel real bad, too. She had two little boys with her."

Later in the evening, Marshall Jim Cox stepped into the bar for a badly needed drink. His lined face showed he had seen too much while marshalling in several frontier towns, and a bullet hole in his right leg was about all he had to show for his efforts. The cowboy stepped up to the marshal, tripped, and almost fell on him.

"Hey marshal, I got to talk to you."

"What can I do for you?" Cox suspiciously asked the very drunk man.

"Do you see that man with his head on the table over there," he asked.

"Yes."

"He said he killed a woman in the hills close to Deadwood. Can I get a reward for turning him in?"

"I don't know what you are talking about," Cox said. "But I am sure going to find out."

Hawson went to jail without a whimper because he was passed out and carried by two rough-looking men. He awoke the following morning to a cold bucket of water thrown rudely in his face by the marshal. He looked straight up at bar cells over the window.

He stared at Marshal Jim Cox with a horrible look on his face and asked, "What did I do?"

"That is precisely what we are going to find out my friend," Cox softly answered. "You and I are going to know each other very well before you kill another woman."

HUNTING
September 22, 1878

Birch, Jed and Mason rode into the hills in search of elk or a mule deer. The cool fall weather was perfect, and yellow aspens shadowed by dark green pine trees were scattered across creeks and small rivers that drifted clear, clean water down endless shoots.

The deputies had decided to make up. Mason figured it was no use trying to change how Amy felt and decided that he was better served to be friends with the man who could save his life. Birch knew the same was true for him.

The deputies watched as an old female beaver slapped her powerful tail in a damned-up pool on a particularly large creek, sending a signal of danger that sent all beavers diving for the sanctuary of their well-constructed dens.

Birch turned to look at Jed who actually briefly smiled; this was his element.

Hunting had been good on the plains in those days, at least for deer that were plentiful. They had heard a bull elk, but never got close enough for the shot.

Mason and Birch had shot fine mule deer bucks while Jed shot a doe, claiming that she would be better eating. The others had shot deer with wide antlers. Mason left his antlers with the gut pile while Birch kept his and quickly discovered that the antlers were constantly catching limbs and brush like a hook. But they soon would be stored with the rest of his gear.

Upon arrival at camp, the young men quickly gathered up enough wood for Jed to cook the deer's back straps over an open fire.

Birch ate until he felt sick; few meals had ever tasted better. Birch lay on his blankets with a full belly and studied the stars— a habit that Mason found to be peculiar and a waste of time.

"Just what are you looking for up there Birch," Mason asked. "You lie down and stare at the stars every clear night."

"Maybe I'm looking for my family, I don't know."

"Well, there ain't nobody up there, just a bunch of old stars."

"I think you are wrong," Jed said. "There are many great spirits among the stars. My Cheyenne father is there, and all around me."

"You ain't making any sense," Mason said.

"That is why I seldom speak," Jed countered. "Most of you can't understand me."

"I understand you," Birch said. "I hope you're right."

Jed smiled and then fell asleep.

The following day Birch and Mason rode to the next hunting spot and argued while Jed silently followed behind, his eyes constantly moving in search of danger. The veteran prairie man constantly thought ahead, surveying gullies and hills for possible ambush sites. His time with the Cheyenne had taught the advantage of surprise; he quietly rode while the others argued.

"I still don't know why you kept those damned antlers," Mason gripped. "Hell, you can't eat them. The rodents could use them to gnaw on."

"You sure complain a lot," Birch answered while cutting off a piece of chewing tobacco with his sharp pocket knife.

Jed rode behind while allowing himself the luxury of another slight smile. He liked these two, but thought both were crazy sometimes.

Birch enjoyed taking verbal jabs at Mason, but liked him, even though he knew resentment would never go away. Birch had stopped visiting Debbie, because she was not a real lady like Amy.

Birch caught himself having the wrong kind of thoughts about her; he could not help himself. She was just too beautiful.

The hunt only lasted another day. Birch managed to shoot a doe on the last morning, providing enough fresh meat to hold them for a while.

DEPUTIES ON THE PLAINS
September 26, 1878

Most gold shipments were transported in strong boxes on stagecoaches through Wells Fargo, which was the transfer agent for many of the larger mines. But several smaller mine operations around Deadwood decided to let their deputies guard the larger gold shipments during the first 200 miles to a predetermined spot just outside of Fort Pierre where another group would take over. Bullock was not overjoyed by this arrangement, but he reluctantly agreed, and Birch, Mason, and Jed accompanied two wagons and drivers on the long trip across the prairie to Fort Pierre, east of Deadwood.

The teamsters driving the wagons were two brothers from Germany, Lester and Joseph Fizer, who were still trying to learn English. They had moved to a German settlement several years before, where Lutheran missionaries taught them English. Both men were short and stocky with wide shoulders and exceptionally thick arms built up from many years of hard work around mules. Their neatly trimmed mustaches and sideburns set off their closely shaved heads and gave them a fierce look. They didn't socialize much, but were known to be honest, steady men, and Bullock considered them perfect for this difficult job.

The group would be met by Wells Fargo agents, who would take the gold to Yankton, the farthest point west that the railroad had reached. The first wagon was loaded with four strong boxes of gold while a chuck wagon brought along extra supplies. Once there, a hot bath, dinner and drinks were planned to celebrate this first historic trip. Deputy Newton stayed in Deadwood to help Bullock maintain law and order, quite a feat for two men.

Jed started showing Mason and Birch how to track and survive on the trail. His Cheyenne past had taught him to listen instead of talk, a trait that he wanted to instill in both young deputies. He seldom showed emotions, but he liked both men more than any he had known, and they in turn admired him and hung on every word he spoke. He enjoyed teaching these two "greenhorns" how to read signs. Besides, moving a gold shipment across the prairie was slow and boring. Jed's teachings were never more welcome.

"Look," Jed said while pointing to a deer track. "See crumbling dirt from that track's edge—old track. But look here at the fresh track without crumbling dirt. Much fresher. See the dew claws behind its hoof print? There is probably a buck laying in that stand of mesquite, but we don't need meat now, maybe later."

Birch learned a lot from his friend on that trip. Jed showed them where to find water, and what plants could be eaten, and he showed them different kinds of snakes that could be eaten including a non-poisonous bull snake that resembles a rattlesnake without rattles.

On the second evening, Jed did something very strange. All three had settled in for the night as the campfire burned down, when suddenly a coyote started howling. Jed immediately sat up, obviously studying what the lonesome animal had to say. He listened for a while and turned to Mason and Birch.

"The coyote was called the trickster by my Cheyenne family. He is wise and warns me of a black danger ahead. Beware, something is going to happen very soon."

Birch was taken back by this strange speech. I've never heard Jed refer to the Cheyenne as his family before, he thought. For that matter, I've never heard Jed speak that much at one time. Danger ahead? What was he talking about? Was a pack of coyotes going to attack them?

He decided to forget it and get some sleep, a feat that was a challenge with the big German teamsters, Lester and Joseph, snoring and grumbling in their sleep.

Might not be so bad if they would mumble in English, Birch thought as sleep started to settle in.

Mason had shrugged off the coyote's warning as Jed's babbling, but Jed was certain. He knew that crooks were not their only concern.

The following morning Jed was proved right when bullets started whizzing through the deputies' camp.

Birch and Jed rolled under a wagon and started shooting back at Black Moon and several warriors who had been following the wagons. Birch took aim and grazed the side of a big warrior who seemed to be in charge. Jed shot at the same man, a complete miss, unusual for the sharp shooter. Both would have been shocked to realize that the big Lakota had killed Birch's father.

"That Lakota must have the devil on his shoulder," Jed mumbled. "I had him dead to rights. He must have moved when I shot."

"Maybe you're getting old and your eyes are too weak to hit anything," Birch teased as a bullet barely missed his head. "Just keep shooting—you're bound to hit something."

"Shut up Birch," Jed answered while rolling a brave off the nearby ridge. "I don't think that man will ever doubt my shooting."

Suddenly the shooting stopped as Black Moon and his bunch disappeared over the hill. Birch started to chase them, but was stopped when Jed grabbed his ankle on the way by.

"Why'd you do that?" Birch asked.

"To save your life," Jed answered. "That's an experienced group of warriors who will not just turn and run. They will likely stop this fight for now, but you will die the second you step over that ridge. Go ahead if you want to die."

The young man decided to listen and started tending to his equipment that had been scattered during the brief fight.

"This is how Lakota and Cheyenne fight, sort of hit and miss," Jed told Birch. "By the way, I got one. How many did you hit?" Birch just shook his head and walked away, knowing that his friend had won that contest.

Later that morning Birch surveyed the open country with understandable feelings of danger, but decided that it was all clear and the wagons could move out. A sea of prairie grass ran into draws and rolling hills each capable of hiding many men on horseback.

Black dots in the distance spoke volumes to the Lakota who were patiently watching. They would love to have a mule. The village would feast, and the warriors responsible would be heroic because mule cooked properly was really quite good. But preparation of this stringy meat meant little to the Lakota; they just wanted to fill empty bellies. They would wait until the time was right, perhaps at night when the deputies were asleep, but for now they watched and waited, a fact very well known by the deputies.

THE FIRST CLUE
September 29, 1878

On their return to Deadwood, Bullock called Birch over to his office. The young man immediately realized that something was wrong and that Bullock meant business.

"I really don't want to tell you this," Bullock said. "I have some news that you'll find interesting. In fact, it will probably get you killed."

"What could be that important?"

"A man dressed in a buffalo robe walked into a Rapid City bar and proceeded to get real drunk. After a bottle of rot gut, he started getting mouthy, bragging about the easy pickings him and his gang had been finding throughout the Black Hills. Then, another bottle later, he started saying how bad he felt about what his gang did to a woman with two little boys. The cowhand told the marshal. The man is now sitting in the Rapid City jailhouse. Would you care to go interview him?"

Birch didn't answer. His mind raced at this unexpected news. Bullock knew that the young man could never be free until this was resolved; otherwise, he might not have told him. Birch was almost out the door before a big hand on his shoulder stopped him.

"Now look, I haven't finished talking. This is not to be your personal vendetta. You will do this by the law. Talk to the prisoner, then track down the others. But bring them in to be hanged. Do this by the law, or I will personally come after you. The marshal is expecting you and has agreed to give you all cooperation. Do you want someone to go along?"

"No, I have to do this alone. I'll try to bring them in alive, but I'll have to defend myself. What if I have to kill them?"

"If possible, get witnesses to sign a paper saying what they seen. Make sure they sign it. Those who can't sign can make a mark. Just make sure you write down their names."

"Anything else?" Birch asked.

"Yes, make no mistake," the big sheriff answered. "I would rather see them dead than you. Come back home to us."

Birch turned and walked out the door. The hardened old sheriff watched Birch walk down the street as if he were his own son.

Later that afternoon Birch knocked on Amy's door.

"Amy, it's Birch. I have something to tell you."

She could tell by his voice that there was bad news. She opened the door and looked up into his eyes. Her blue eyes melted into his for a brief moment. Birch felt a moment of indecision, knowing she gave him a great deal to live for. But he had to see this through, and she would have to wait.

"I'm leaving for Rapid City," he said. "They found one of my family's killers. I'm going to talk with the man and hopefully persuade him to tell me where the others are."

She did not like how he said "persuade." That likely meant bad news for the prisoner, but she didn't care about him. She cared about Birch.

"I'm going with you," she said. " I will not stay here wondering everyday if you are alive or dead."

"No, you have to stay here. This will be dangerous."

"Then don't be gone too long," she said, as a tear dripped down her smooth cheek. "Patience is not one of my virtues."

"I'll be back as quickly as possible, count on it," he smiled and gently kissed her forehead.

She reached up and kissed him with all the passion she could find. Her embrace lasted even longer, squeezing the back of his neck. He looked into her eyes and stroked her beautiful hair one more time before turning to leave.

"I love you," she said softly.

Then he was gone.

She sat on her bed as tears dropped on the pillow that she was clutching to her heart. "Come back to me, Birch Rose," she whispered. "You will never be sorry."

She watched him ride away and prayed that he would make it back from dangers that lurked on the plains.

PART
THREE

A VISIT TO HELL
October 1, 1878

Birch took a deep breath of the open country afternoon air that was chilly, but refreshing. He was grateful for the survival tricks that Jed, Bullock, and Mason had taught him. Jed had been quite an expert at survival in the roughest conditions, and they had camped on several hunting trips. Birch watched in amazement at how Jed made their camp comfortable in winter or summer.

He followed an old road commonly used by the teamsters transporting supplies to Deadwood in their heavy wagons. He rode until dark, completely haunted by his family, who no doubt were riding with him. He had a promising future, but his main concern was finding the murderers who killed his mother and brothers. Later he would find that murdering Lakota who killed his father. Bullock had been right, only then would he be free.

The first evening's camp would have been pleasant on a hunting trip, but his memories made it uncomfortable. He wanted to ride through the night, but experience had taught him that most things would wait until morning. Besides, he would get farther much quicker on a fresh horse.

Need to stay sharp, he thought. Who knows what I might find in the middle of this wilderness? Maybe the booger man. He laughed at that suggestion, something he had not done lately.

The trip went smoothly, and he woke up on the third morning without nightmares and with a dusting of snow on his blanket, but the daytime temperatures stayed wonderfully mild. Soon Rapid City was in sight. Birch marveled at the long lines of wooden and stone buildings, quite a contrast to Deadwood's shacks and tents that pushed up against several well-constructed buildings, mostly bars and whorehouses.

He rode straight to the jailhouse that was easily visible on Main Street.

Birch walked up to the solid oak door with steel bars vertically nailed across its width about a foot apart. The windows were fitted with the jailhouse style black bars. Birch stepped inside.

He felt his stomach tighten up in knots to find a pot-bellied marshal with his feet up on an old beat up desk. The man had a big white mustache that spread across his round, wrinkled face. His big shoulders evidenced the type of man he once had been. The old man stood up and held out his hand.

"Marshal Jim Cox," he said with a toothy grin. "I'll bet you are Deputy Rose."

"Yes sir, I'm Birch Rose."

"I guess that you'll want to be seeing the prisoner immediately?"

"Yes sir, I want to see the man now if possible."

"Alright, but let's get one thing straight," the suddenly stern-faced marshal said. "That man is my prisoner. You will not lay a hand on him, understand me?"

"Yes sir, but I need information."

"Don't worry, boy. We will get the information. Seth Bullock is an old friend of mine. We spit some trail dust together, and I promised him that I would take care of you."

Both men turned and stepped to a narrow door. Marshal Cox took a big, black key from an old rusty nail on the wall and slipped it into the big lock. The basic jailhouse lock turned and the door slipped open.

Birch had to duck his head when stepping into the room with six cells; three had become home to men who looked the worse for wear and wore the look of defeat.

The smell in that room of body odor and human waste almost made Birch gag, but he quickly regained his composure and looked straight into the cell of a tall, raw boned man that was clinging to his buffalo coat. Room conditions were below freezing at night and small windows with black bars offered little light and less warmth even when the sun was shining.

The men all seemed sick, too sick to look up. They had come to think that death might be a welcome release from this hell hole and didn't care who was looking at them.

Marshal Cox unlocked the cell door and let Birch walk in to see the man clad in his buffalo robe. The door made a sinister sound as it clanked shut. Hawson glanced at Birch and then turned away, as if not wanting to look into the eyes of the young lawman.

Marshal Cox said, "Birch, meet Paul Hawson."

"What in the hell do you want?" Hawson asked in a hoarse voice. He still avoided Birch's cold eyes.

"I just want to ask some questions."

"I don't got nothing to say."

"No, I think you do have something to say, and you are going to say it. You and your gang murdered a woman and her two little boys on the trail between Custer and Deadwood. You are going to tell me the names of everybody in that gang and where I can find them."

"What's in it for me?"

Birch was going to answer, but Cox beat him to it.

"Right now, you're set to hang. That's what the judge decided at your trial. But if you give us the information we want, I'll bet the judge would be willing to change the sentence to life in territorial prison instead of hanging," the old lawman answered from outside the cell door. "I've already talked to the judge about it. Otherwise, we are going to drag you from this paradise next Monday and hang you on our new gallows. In fact, you will be the first to test its strength. I only hope the rope doesn't stretch too much. That would choke you instead of breaking your neck. Have you ever watched a man choke to death on the end of a rope?"

"You son-of-a-bitch."

"Well maybe, but if you don't cooperate, I'll be the son-of-a-bitch tying the noose. My hands aren't strong like they used to be, and the thing is, if I mess up that noose you might take 20 minutes to die, just kicking and choking at the end of that rope with your eyes bugging out and your tongue turning black. I'd feel plumb sorry about that."

Hawson dropped his head and starred at the stained floor. His lips whispered "son-of-a-bitch" before he finally turned towards Birch. Hawson spoke slowly and quietly, as if embarrassed that the other prisoners might hear that he was ratting on past comrades. But he knew the marshal meant what he said, so he talked.

"I didn't want to kill anyone. I was sneaking in from the back, trying to find the horses. Hell, there weren't any. Guess the damned injuns must have took 'em before we came. The other guys did the shooting and kilt the woman and the boys ran away. We couldn't find 'em. I swear in front of my maker that I didn't do it."

Birch tried to keep his composure, but his tempter began to rise.

"Yeah, you bastard, but where are the others now?" Birch asked in a deadly whisper while grabbing the front of his shirt under the buffalo coat. "Where are they?"

Hawson looked into Birch's glaring blue eyes and saw the devil starring back.

"I've heard they're holed up in a little mining town called Tinton, about 15 miles from Deadwood. The mine doesn't turn out much, but enough to keep them there. They're waiting to make a big score from the gold shipments out of Tinton or Deadwood. So you be careful, deputy, and remember that your friend, Hawson, helped you."

"What are their names?"

"Rico is the leader. He is a nasty half-breed who kills for fun. Taylor, Casey, and Murray ride with him. Taylor and Casey are ignorant, but watch out for that Murray. He loves to kill with a Bowie knife."

"Much obliged," Birch mumbled as he stepped out of Hawson's cell.

Birch was glad to leave that hell hole. He took a deep breath immediately after stepping out the front door. The air smelled clean, especially after visiting that cell. He took time to roll a cigarette while starring down the street. He felt the marshal step next to him.

"So what will happen to him?" Birch asked without looking at Cox.

"That has already been decided by the circuit judge. He will hang next Monday."

"After you told him he would get life in prison for talking to me?"

"Yep. Boy, the law decided his fate. I didn't talk to the judge about changing the sentence, but he don't know that. I have no power over it now. You should be grateful. He probably was one of the bastards who killed your family. Are you going to stay and watch him swing?"

"No, I have business elsewhere."

"Tinton?"

"Yep."

"Well, just don't forget that you swore an oath when you pinned on that star. You are sworn to bring in that trash alive so they can be judged in a court of law, and that badge don't give you the right to go killing for revenge."

"How would that make me different from you lying to that man and then hanging him. Isn't that a form of murder too? Don't you think that making him expect to live and then killing him is cruel?"

"No boy, he was fairly judged and now he will swing."

Birch turned and walked away without saying goodbye. He did not like Marshal Cox. The old lawman had become hardened in this hostile place, and Birch only hoped that he would never become that immoral.

He mounted his pony and slowly rode out of town, still thinking about the marshal's last words: "He was fairly judged and now he will swing."

Surprisingly, Birch wanted to stay and watch, but for a different reason. He wanted justice for his family, but he actually felt sorry for Hawson. He needed the information, but damned that was cruel, he thought. Wonder how long Cox will wait before telling Hawson he is going to hang? Wonder if the big man will break down and slobber all over himself?

Birch decided to think about the business at hand. What about Benny and Bud? Birch remembered Hawson's words: "We couldn't find 'em."

Might they still be alive? Probably not. Anyway, life was over for Hawson, even though he did not know it yet.

Besides, he might have been one of the killers.

IN PURSUIT
October 3, 1878

Birch decided to spend his second night out of town in a gully many miles outside of Rapid City. He stretched out on an Indian blanket and looked at the stars.

He started to think about his murdered family, then quickly changed his thoughts to Amy, his only pleasant thought these days. He closed his eyes and imagined how she looked and how her kitchen always smelled like cinnamon, kind of a sweet smell like when his ma made apple pies. He thought about her hair, her blue sparkling eyes and that body. She filled up her dress in the right places, and she always smelled so damned good.

He started to sleep when a twig cracked behind him. He looked up to see a man's silhouette in the moonlight as a chill ran through his body. He silently drew has pistol and waited, but nothing happened.

Was the man a cactus or just my imagination? He wondered.

Birch jumped up, but found no one in the immediate area. He laid down and thought about the man that he must have dreamed in his tormented mind. Yet, in the darkness any man could easily be hiding nearby.

That was the end of sleep. The young deputy pressed his back against a depression and waited for dawn to break while buttoning his jacket up and pulling his Stetson down lower to accommodate the early morning chill.

At first light he checked for tracks where the man had been, but only found smooth dirt.

He started back on the trail, rode through a small valley, and slipped out into an array of God's colors well displayed across the sky. The eastern horizon turned orange, providing enough light for Birch to travel without fear of his horse stepping into a hole.

His hand ached from a cactus sting he suffered while checking for signs of an intruder. A yarrow plant poultice had been applied to ease the pain and hopefully fight off infection.

He gently clicked his tongue to encourage a faster pace as the horse started across the rolling prairie. Birch was on a mission and nothing would stop him now. The killers would not stay in Tinton forever; he had to ride hard. He hoped that the killers were having a good time in the small mining town, or they might move on.

His hand throbbed as he rode across the rough prairie, and the sun seemed warmer than over the past several days. His bandaged hand started sweating, increasing the pain. Once he stopped and removed the yarrow plant to find the poultice seemed to be holding off the infection. He applied a second poultice to make the wound heal faster, another trick he learned from Jed.

That evening Birch decided to make camp earlier than usual. The horse had put in quite a day's work. He had led the horse about the same amount of time that he ridden it, and Birch was ready for some rest, too.

126

Early the next morning, Birch broke camp and spent a couple more hard days on the trail, dreaming at night about his parents and brothers. Finally, with the inflammation just about gone from his hand, Tinton came into view. From a high hill Birch could see the welcome sight of lights from the small town, shining like jewels.

RATS IN A TRAP
October 7, 1878

The small mining town had a saloon called The Gold Rush, with rooms for rent upstairs. Tinton also had a blacksmith, a small dry goods store, and a barbershop where the barber also served as the town's undertaker and numerous other tasks if a dollar was involved.

The saloon was the largest building in town, hosting a good supply of booze and a few Mexican women who served drinks and entertained upstairs after the bar closed. Nearby Deadwood had a better variety of this form of entertainment, but the Tinton girls from Mexico were better looking and less expensive.

Birch decided to check the saloon first. If he was lucky, he might find the gang there, and if they weren't there then he might find information on their whereabouts.

He felt a hunter's high, while looking at the saloon that was lit up and bristling with men drinking their fill or chasing whores. He didn't feel angry or scared, only numb knowing that the men who killed his family might be drinking in that bar. Best of all, they wouldn't know who he was or realize that the hunter was closing in.

Problem was, he had only learned their names from Hawson and had no idea what they looked like or how many gang members might be in the saloon.

Birch soon stood at the double doors, peering into the bar. A poker game to the left was illuminated by a coal-oil lamp that hung low enough for the cowpunchers to read their cards. Several cowboys leaned against the long, wooden bar, sipping on whiskey or beer.

A woman's laughter drifted through the bar from a back room where cowboys could enjoy different forms of female company for two bits, a dollar for upstairs delights. Smoke from cigars and hand-rolled cigarettes hung in the air like low clouds over a mountain, and the floor was littered with saw dust and wood shavings for dancing or spitting tobacco juice.

An old faro table sat vacant. The last faro dealer had been shot and no one wanted the job. But the crowd was content and plenty drunk as The Gold Rush did good business that night like most nights.

Birch's facial expression might have startled anyone who noticed him. His eyes were squinted, and a scraggly beard had formed under wrinkles from fatigue and pain, giving the image of a much older man. A hand-rolled cigarette dangled from the left corner of his mouth as he stepped into The Gold Rush where Casey and Murray were both enjoying a double shot of the bar's best.

Both studied the tall stranger and noted how he wore his well polished six gun. There was little doubt that he meant business, but just what business? Birch noticed the two scrubby characters who looked as bad as he felt.

"How about a whiskey mister?" the old bartender asked. "My name's Jonas, and who might you be?"

"None of your damn business," Birch answered in a threatening voice.

Birch stared through Jonas, who started to have second thoughts about conversation with this dangerous looking man.

Jonas had worked in many saloons throughout the Dakota Territory. Most were dusty holes that had included a healthy share of death, and he quickly learned to recognize a shooter by the look in his eyes. He also had seen crazy, scared, and stupid, but this stranger was none of these. Jones recognized the look of grim determination, making this stranger twice as dangerous. Jonas only hoped that it didn't have anything to do with his own checkered past.

"Where ye hail from stranger?" Jonas asked, trying once again to sound friendly.

Birch didn't answer, but quietly slid the shot glass towards the old man who automatically poured. Birch slipped down a second whiskey while trying not to gag.

"I told you once old man. It's none of your business, but I do want some information," Birch growled. "I was supposed to meet a friend here, a Paul Hawson. Heard of him?"

"No, can't say I have. What does he look like?"

"An old buffalo skinner, and he generally smells like one too."

"Naw, can't say I know him, but who should I say is looking for him?"

"Ask me that again, and I'll have to find a bar without a dead bartender," Birch bristled, trying to sound tough for Casey and Murray's benefit. "You just tell him a man was looking for him, follow?"

"Yes sir, I'll do that," Jonas meekly answered while returning to his bartending duties.

Casey and Murray had listened to the conversation with much interest. The ever-cautious Murray decided to watch this stranger for a while, but the less cautious Casey jumped in, hook, line and sinker.

"Hey mister, we're friends with Hawson, too. Ken I'ah buy ye a drink?" Casey asked, while Murray lit up a cigarette.

"Sure," Birch answered.

"You use that friend word might loosely," Murray grumbled.

"Ah, don't pay attention to him. Where ye hail from?" Casey asked.

"Here and there."

"Are ye prospecting?"

"Yep, I'm looking for the mother lode."

"Well then, you might find some color here, but most don't."

"I'll take my chances," Birch quietly answered without looking up from the bar.

"There's more than one way to find gold."

Birch looked up in time to see Murray hit Casey in the back.

"Shut up you idiot." Murray whispered. "You don't know this feller. He might be some kind of traveling lawman or something."

"Aw hell, he's alright. He's just another prospector looking fer color."

At that moment Birch knew he either had the right two men or at least a couple of thieves, and he decided to stay and drink with the two. He despised their kind of border trash and would have little trouble killing them on general principle, but he had to make sure that Hawson had told the truth. "Bartender, three whiskeys here and keep 'em coming," Birch demanded.

"Well, that sure is neighborly of ye mister," Casey said as he turned to Murray. "See, I told ye he was alright."

"Don't get the wrong impression mister," Birch answered. "Let's have a few drinks and see how the evening goes before we decide who is alright. But for now, let's have some fun!"

Birch drew his six gun and shot a neat, round hole in the ceiling. The bullet passed by an occupied bed, almost grazing one of the working girls. The bar drew silent and everybody looked to see what was happening.

"Damn boys, I am ready for a wild evening, especially if Hawson shows up. Let's do this right!"

"YEEHAAA," Casey yelled. "This will be a night to remember."

"Sure will," Birch whispered.

Birch had to make the two skuzzy cowboys think he was matching them whiskey shot for shot, a task that became easier as the night progressed. He poured a round and then carefully poured it into the spittoon on the floor next to the bar while the others swallowed their rotgut, an act noticed by Jonas who wisely kept his mouth shut. Rose was feeling his booze, but not like the others who acted slobbering drunk.

"I've been thinking about a plan to get rich," he quietly told Casey.

"What's that," the drunken man asked.

"Why don't we start prowling around the trails in them hills. People with money sometimes travel, and we could jump them and take their money and whatever else they have. What do you think?"

Casey held a finger to his lips and said, "Shuusssss, I have to tell ye something. We're already doing that and it sure is easy pickings. Hell, we once found a woman with two little kids all by themselves on the trail between Custer and Deadwood. She was a looker and I wanted to take her, but the others shot her full of holes. After all that trouble, we couldn't find much truck to steal. I think the damned Indians had already stolen her horses. Hell, I didn't even get a kiss from her, but she was a good-looking woman. I would have done fer her better than anyone ever had."

"So what happened to the little kids," Birch asked, dreading the answer.

"I'ah don't know. They got away. I expect a wild animal or two has et them by now."

"Were you the only two that killed the woman?" Birch asked while trying to hold back the anger that would soon overflow.

"Naw, there was your friend, Hawson. He rode away after we did that. There was me, Taylor and Murray and Rico. Rico is sort of the leader. He is smarter than all of us. Him and Taylor are looking for some gold to steal right now."

Birch found out exactly what he wanted to know and had these two dead to rights. But where were Rico and Taylor?

Should I wait and let these two lead me to them, he thought. Or should I take them in now?

A sickening "CLICK" behind his left ear made that decision for him as Birch felt a horribly cold feeling. This was not like a gunfight.

This was waiting to be murdered.

"You asked the wrong questions," Murray whispered in his ear, seeming a great deal less drunk than he had only minutes before. "Just what in the hell are you looking for—us by chance?"

Birch knew that the time had come as the .45 caliber bore slipped from his ear to the base of his skull. A finger twitch would quickly end this, and he waited for the explosion. He felt a flush of anger and dropped while pulling out his deadly Colt. He quickly emptied his six gun into Murray's belly and chest.

Startled, the very drunk Casey drew his pistol and missed Birch's head by inches.

The trapped deputy, still on his knees, tossed his Bowie knife underhanded, and the blade seemed to flash in the lantern light once as it sliced into Casey's chest. He laid back, staring at the ceiling.

Birch leaned down to ask about Rico.

"My God, look what you've done to me," Casey stammered. "I come from a good family back east. Please don't let them know that I died like this; you promise, mister."

"I promise," Birch said, realizing that Casey was not going to shut up long enough to answer any questions.

"I'ah wanted to do right, but I was not smart like my brothers. I was too tough and now I'ahhhhh," and he died on the dirty barroom floor.

Birch quickly pulled his knife out of the dead man and walked out the door backwards, his pistol in one hand and the bloody knife in the other, while watching the crowd who watched back in amazement. They didn't care about the dead trash; they wanted to know who was the guy that just killed two men?

Birch untied his horse, leaped into the saddle and paused to glance back at the saloon for any friends of the two dead men. The crowd watched him, but no one pulled a gun. They held their hands up to make sure he knew that no one planned to shoot. In fact, several waved.

They talked about the shooting and knife play throughout the night and for many nights afterwards. The bar sold a lot of booze that night—especially after the two bloody bodies were removed and the blood was mopped up by a very angry girl who was told to clean up the mess.

Damn it, Birch thought, where are the other two holed up? Let's see, their names were Rico and Taylor, and they are looking for gold to steal. I wonder if they headed for Deadwood? Where else could they be? They're both probably under Bullock's nose right now.

A FAST RIDE TO DEADWOOD
October 8, 1878

B irch rode through the cold night and straight to Bullock's office.

He stepped in the lantern-lit room to the smell of fresh coffee. Seth makes the best coffee, he thought while helping himself without a word before hearing a deep voice behind him.

"What happened?" Bullock asked before sitting behind his desk. "And why don't you help yourself to some of my coffee since you already have?"

Birch told Bullock the whole story and admitted he'd left the saloon without signed descriptions of what happened. Bullock was not happy about the absence of written witness descriptions, but he realized that Birch had escaped with his life. If anything, he seemed pleased by this keen job of detective work.

"We may just kill two birds with one stone," he quipped. "We might get the last two killers and the same two men who plan to rob a gold shipment. Damned good work. I only wish you could have kept one of the two alive to identify the others. After all, there are a few thousand miners, teamsters and other folks moving in and out of town these days. All we have to do is sift through this group to find the two."

"I have a plan," Birch quietly said. "Let's make it known that I killed those two in Tinton and plan to kill Rico and Taylor. Then we can set a trap and get both at once."

"I'm sure you realize the danger you'll be putting yourself in?"

"Doesn't matter. I have to finish this, even if it means my life."

"Well, alright. Guess I'll have to tell Amy that. She has been bothering me something fierce about news concerning you since you rode to Rapid City."

"Amy," he said. "I have to get her out of town. Those two might try to get her to get me."

"Let's get moving," Bullock said.

Deadwood was extremely busy as miners, soldiers and many other walks of life crowded the streets. Women of the night laid across the upper balconies of The Gem and other houses, shouting obscenities at men on the street who looked up in wonderment. Many walked in the bars and straight up the steps. Piano music drifted though the air from several different bars as a boy finished lighting his last oil street lamp. War hoops of excited men could be heard throughout town.

After all, it was Saturday night and women and booze were plentiful.

A group of wild men were ready to let the badger loose. Saturday was not Bullock's favorite night. Too many arrests would be made before morning.

I need a bigger jail just for the God forsaken night, Bullock thought.

RICO'S PLAN
October 10, 1878

Patrons in the Lead City bar sat quietly while drinking and watching a mad man throw chairs and dangerously swing his knife around. They wanted to leave, but the raving lunatic would not let them go.

Rico was out of his head with blind, heated rage.

First, he had learned about Hawson's hanging from a saddle bum who witnessed the whole thing. The bum said Hawson kept yelling, "this was not supposed to happen! I told them everything!"

Then Rico learned that a very fast man with a gun had killed Casey and Murray in Tinton. Witnesses said the man was a deputy, a man named Birch Rose.

"Damn him!" he yelled at Taylor. "This Birch Rose is soon going to be dead, dead, dead! I want that trash buried so the worms can feed on him!"

Some of the customers took their opportunity to slip out and have a safer place to spend their evening. Rico calmed down, paused and took out the fixings for a cigarette. He lit the hand-rolled smoke with a stick match and immediately blew out a long puff of smoke before turning towards Taylor.

"Most of our gang is dead," he continued, "and we will not be safe to steal gold shipments as long as Rose and his friends are still alive. We must do something quickly or leave this country. Our amigos are dead, and we may be next, just for killing one stupid woman who was abandoned on a meaningless trail."

"I think we should pull out," Taylor said. "You can't go against Bullock and his deputies, especially that Birch Rose. I heard he is greased lightning with a six shooter, and his buddies are pretty good too. What can two of us do against those guys?"

That was the wrong thing to say. Rico glared at Taylor with the look of a dangerous animal, and he pointed his knife at Taylor's chest.

The barroom's silence was deafening as Taylor starred at the big blade that would soon split him wide open and to hell. Others starred at the frightened man, fascinated at the chance to see a man's guts spilled across the barroom's floor.

Suddenly, Rico realized that Taylor was his only friend. He lowered his knife and kicked another chair that slammed into the spittoon, causing it to roll around and spill its sickening contents across the floor.

The big bartender gently pulled a scattergun from under the bar and looked at Rico, who quickly pointed his .44 at the very frightened bartender's forehead.

"Now mister barkeep," Rico said in a surprisingly soft voice. "What is it like to soon die? Are you wetting your pants? Do you know that my bullet will soon rip through your brain and you will be gone? So how does it feel?"

The scared bartender dropped the scattergun and felt a tear drip down his cheek while looking at the .44 caliber pistol's bore that look mighty big.

"Ah, look Taylor, the big man cries like a little bitch. Maybe I would do him a favor by killing this little bitch. What do you think amigo?"

"Don't shoot this idiot Rico," Taylor said. "The idea is to not attract attention, and we have done enough here. Put your gun away and let's get out of here. We need to plan how to take care of those who threaten us. What can we do?"

"Aw, you forget my friend, they don't know what we look like," Rico said. "I think we can slip in, kill them one at a time and slip out. But we may need some help."

"Who can we trust to help us?" Taylor asked.

Rico smiled. "Why, my friend, the devil himself."

AMY'S NEW RESIDENCE
October 11, 1878

Earlier that evening Birch knocked on Amy's door. She dove into his arms, and they hugged in the doorway for quite a spell before going upstairs and stepping into her kitchen where they sat down around a fine round oak table from Arkansas. She stiffened as he told her of his plan to get the last two killers. She was distressed at thinking about the man she loved as a sitting duck.

"We will have to move you out of here for a few days," he said. "Our love is no secret in this town. Those damned miners are worse than a bunch of old ladies where gossiping is concerned. Rico and Taylor would love to find you, and I don't plan to lose you now."

"I'll do as you say. We have a lot to live for. But where will I stay?"

"Seth says you can stay with us. I'll let you have the bedroom, and I'll fix a pallet on the floor in front of his fireplace for me.

That'll give you privacy, and someone will always be watching you until this thing is over. I plan to be visible around town while Jed, Mason, and Newton shadow me until I draw out the murderers. All of them are capable, especially Jed. They'll keep me safe."

"God, I hope so," she said while reaching over to give him another long hug. "Please say this will be over after those two are dead."

"One part will be over, but I still have to find that murdering Indian who killed my pa. I'll never be a whole man until they all pay for my family's lives. I'm sorry Amy. It just has to be that way. You can open your dress shop during the day, but only with a guard on the front porch."

"Alright," she agreed, "but I don't think an armed guard will help my business."

THE DEAL
October 11, 1878

The Gem Theatre was extremely busy as usual as Al Swearengen loosened the top button of his wool shirt. His stuffy office was downright hot. He gazed across his desk at two uncomfortable-looking men who knew all about this medium-sized evil man with a thick black mustache. People had died in this very office by his hands or by his orders. Killing a man was only business for him.

Rico had that in common with Big Al more than Taylor. Taylor could kill, but it always kind of bothered him, especially when it was murder instead of self-defense. Big Al looked at the two with disdain. He had heard of Rico, but decided not to stroke his ego by saying so.

He wondered, why does the trash always come to me?

"Alright gentlemen, what can this humble servant of Deadwood do for you?" Swearengen offered sarcastically. "What brings you to my modest dwellings and be quick. I'm a busy man."

"Well Mr. Swearengen," Rico offered. "We want to make a business proposition that could be worth thousands of dollars to you."

That got Big Al's attention. He reached into a desk drawer and pulled out a whiskey bottle and three shot glasses. Rico and Taylor watched each clear glass fill before reaching for one.

Big Al noticed their desire for whiskey and offered a sentimental toast: "Here is to new and prosperous business. Now gentlemen, state your plan and hope I like it; otherwise you might die tonight. I may feel like you have insulted my character."

"The Golden Streak Mine will soon be shipping out a half million dollar gold shipment and we need help taking it," Rico said. "We need wagons, six good gun hands and a spy in the Golden Streak. We only heard about this shipment in the Number 10 last night, but we have been waiting for such a chance, my friend. We will cut you in for half if you help us."

This did not get the effect they had expected.

Swearengen laughed.

"Get out of here," he said. "Do you really think I am going to furnish wagons, hired guns, and pay for a spy while you take 50 percent? Why don't you just have me drop my drawers and bend over so you can take that too? What would stop me from killing both of you to keep your mouths shut while I take the payroll myself? 50 percent! You both had better get out of my sight."

Rico was not used to being talked to like that. He didn't like it, but knew better than to challenge this over-bearing wealthy man, especially with the burley bearded brute standing by the door with a shotgun.

The pair stepped out of the Gem Theatre and into the street when a voice from above called, "Wait, let's talk some more."

They both looked up to find Swearengen on his balcony just over their heads. His office was through one of three doors. The other doors were used by Big Al's prostitutes to get a breath of fresh air. Rico and Taylor hurried up the wooden stairs and knocked on Swearengen's office door.

A pleasant voice said, "Come in boys," once again in a sarcastic way.

"I have had a change of heart, so pour yourself a drink and sit down. Let's talk business."

Rico felt his cockiness coming back.

"I though you would realize you need us."

"Shut up you two-bit punk!" Big Al spat out. "I don't need you. You need me. Now sit down and listen. You are going to need a plan that you're not smart enough to come up with. You were right to come to me boys. Maybe we can work something out after all, maybe even the 50 percent that you mentioned earlier."

Rico was a lot of things, but he was not dumb. He quickly realized that any dealing with Swearengen would be dangerous and in fact, foolhardy. It would also be very profitable.

He decided he would go along with the plan while keeping a close watch over his shoulder. After all, he was as expendable to Swearengen as Taylor was to him, and a bullet was cheaper than half of $500,000. He knew that Big Al would be thinking the same way—business is business.

Swearengen explained the plan and added, "Now both of you keep your mouths shut. Loose talk will ruin this entire plan. If I hear that either of you mentioned this to anyone, I will personally cut your throat and deposit your bodies in a cave somewhere. Don't let my nice-guy attitude fool you. Cutting your throats would be easy. Wouldn't even hurt my appetite for supper. Now get out of here."

Both men walked away believing the devil himself had just spoken to them, and they may have been right. His dark eyes had been the last sight of many who had departed life in a violent manner.

"That man is even more evil than me," Rico said. "But he will make us very rich if we play our cards right and watch each other's backs. Now let's go have a drink to celebrate."

The Number 10 Bar was packed. Rico and Taylor squeezed in to find a drink and a whore. Soon they would be out of this territory and living the high life in St. Louis or some other high-class town.

No one knew who they were; both men just looked like a pair of range drifters blowing off some trail dust. Soon they were talking to a pair of rough-looking women who had seen too much of the upstairs, but both girls started looking better after several drinks and soon they all went up the steps for their evening entertainment.

⋆⋗═◉◌═⋆⋖

SHOWDOWN
October 13, 1878

Birch spent the next couple of days indeed feeling like a sitting duck. Newton and Jed positioned themselves on nearby rooftops, and both riflemen were constantly in position to take out Rico and Taylor if they made a move. Birch made a point of being fully visible to draw out the murderers.

The deputies worked out different places where Birch would be at certain times of day. For example, he might spend an hour in the Number 10 Saloon, or he might get out of the sun under a certain hotel's porch. But there was a problem.

Nobody knew what Rico and Taylor looked like.

Then during the second morning, Birch stopped to talk with "Colorado" Charley Utter, a colorful plainsman who wore a flashy pair of .45 caliber pistols that were decorated in silver and gold. Birch admired his leggings and elk hide coat with strips that were handy for tying or other uses. He decided to own a coat like that someday.

"Hey Birch," Utter said. "I have some news for you."

"Charlie, what can I do for you?"

"I guess by now you know that the whole town is talking about how you plan to kill two men named Rico and Taylor. Did you know that they're in town?"

"Do you know them?"

"Well, I don't know Taylor, but Rico is a bad one who would cut his mother's throat for a penny, so be careful. He is dangerous and crazy, especially with that knife. I doubt seriously if he would face those guns of yours. He'd back shoot you instead. Do you want me to stay around town?"

Birch declined the generous offer.

Utter walked to his horse. He would soon fetch and then lead a wagon train from Independence, Missouri. His cargo was a group of farmers who wanted to try mining. He did not like bringing tinhorns to this country, but it was reasonably easy money and those farmers' wives were good cooks and sometimes real friendly.

139

"Wait a minute Charlie," Birch yelled after some thought. "You know what Rico looks like?"

"Sure, I spent some time south of the border. He used to show up in cantinas for a poker game or just to get drunk. He is good with those guns, but not as good as you, and he knows it."

"I know, but what does he look like. We don't know."

"Why, shoot boy, why didn't you say so? He's a skinny Mex who wears black pants with round Mexican silver conchos down each leg and a black vest that has several white marks on the left side. Some claim that each mark is for someone he killed. His black hat is more Tex than Mex with the sides folded up. He carries two pearl handled .44 caliber pistols that he no doubt took off a dead cattleman somewhere. And he carries a big knife. Well, I hope that helps boy. I've got to hit the trail. Good luck."

Birch signaled Mason, Jed, and Newton. They quickly met in the jail where Bullock and Amy were playing checkers. Birch told the others about Rico's description, and they decided to work in groups of two while looking for this sharply dressed Mexican.

This dangerous work was starting to take a toll on Birch, a man who was never short of nerve, but being a walking target is never for the weak of heart. Little did they know that Rico and Taylor were watching their every move from Swearengen's Gem Theatre out of a whore's window.

"We have got to kill those gringos," Rico said. "We could shoot from here with rifles, or maybe just walk up and shoot him in the back. He is too dangerous for a fair chance."

"I don't think that Big Al is going to like that," Taylor answered, dreading Swearengen's anger. "I don't think he will like that at all. We should stay undercover before robbing a gold shipment. Shooting deputies would put the whole territory on alert."

"I'll tell you what, just let me deal with Al."

Rico knew that the young deputy was good, but wondered just how good and decided to wait for his opportunity when Birch was not expecting trouble. Then he would be easy pickings.

Rico did not mind setting up an ambush now and then. Besides, murdering Birch Rose was much better than dying himself. A rifle bullet in the middle of his back would do the trick.

Rico and Taylor rode to the edge of Deadwood from the north and noticed a man walking past the Chinese settlement.

140

He turned just long enough for them to see a badge under his leather vest.

"Rose," Rico whispered just loud enough for Taylor to hear. "This is our chance to kill him. Let's keep riding, and we'll plant two bullets in his back. Then we can get back to the business of stealing that gold shipment."

Both men continued riding closer to Birch, who was unaware of the danger closing in. Rico noticed the pistol that had killed many was hanging harmlessly where it would do no damage. He started feeling skittish—like he was killing El Diablo himself.

They were quickly close enough to see the drawstring on the back of Birch's hat when a frightening realization set in. Rico looked up to see three men with rifles on a nearby rooftop looking straight at him. The rifles were leveled at his chest.

"Trap," Rico said in a low voice. "Let's get out of here or those Winchesters on the roof will end this pronto. Birch Rose isn't going anywhere. Let's get moving."

The two quickly turned their horses to the opposite side of the muddy main street. Birch turned in time to see several silver conchos on the lead man's black Mexican leather pants, and only then did he realize that his time on Earth had just about ended.

"Alright you two, hold it," Birch shouted while drawing that deadly six gun. "I want to talk with both of you right now. Get your hands up."

Taylor responded by making the dumb mistake of going for his gun, and Birch answered by sending two bullets through the man's chest and head. Rico rolled off his horse and ran behind an old shack that had become a Chinese laundry. The entire action happened too quickly for Jed or Newton to get off a clean shot.

Birch jumped over Taylor's dead body in pursuit. He gave fair chase, but immediately lost Rico, who was hiding behind a stack of old rags. Newton followed a few minutes later to see Rico rise from his hiding spot. The deputy made the mistake of yelling "Stop," instead of shooting.

Rico did not make that mistake.

His quick six gun sent a .45 caliber slug through Newton's forehead, killing him instantly. The deputy's body slammed down on the mud path. Newton, in fact, never knew what hit him.

Rico had run away by the time the others arrived to see the ghastly sight. Birch, Mason, and Jed stood by their friend's body, starring in disbelief at their companion who had been alive just moments before. He seemed to stare back at them in total astonishment. Birch looked at Jed, and they turned without a word, guns ready to stop Rico forever.

The deputies quickly ran back and forth through the Chinese settlement with their pistols drawn, scaring the Chinese.

Both deputies searched from hut to hut, ignoring the protests of many angry residents who were not particularly fond of the white race. Drunken white men had entered their sanctuary before with evil intent only to turn up days later with their throats slit. But these two were wearing badges and would be allowed to live this time.

The frustrated Birch, Mason, and Jed soon gave up and returned to Bullock's office. Their plan had succeeded in killing one of the murderers, but one of their own had paid the ultimate price in return.

SWEARENGEN SAYS GOODBYE TO RICO
October 13, 1878

Rico slipped in the Gem Theatre's back door to find Swearengen. He had lost all of his men and needed help. He took a great deal of time studying the bar before slipping over to the rounded stairwell and climbing up to Big Al's office. He knocked on the door and was shocked to hear a pleasant voice say, "Come in Rico."

"How did you know it was me, Al?" Rico asked, seemingly unaffected by his close scrape with death an hour before.

"Where else would you go?" Al answered gruffly. "You couldn't leave things alone. You had to try and kill Rose. Now you are hot property and no use to me. But wait a minute. I'll bet there is a reward on you already. You might be worth something to me after all. Why don't you lay that hog leg on my desk, and let's get down to business."

Al had reached into the top drawer of his desk and pulled out a shiny new Colt .45. He slipped his fingers around the pistol and started to raise it in Rico's direction. Shooting this piece of trash would make Al Swearengen a public hero. Who knows, he might even run for public office. He pulled the trigger and felt an empty "click."

He had forgot to reload after trying the new gun out on rats at the city dump.

Rico responded before the hammer had hit another chamber by diving through Al's office window, sending glass pieces everywhere. He jumped off the balcony and chose a good horse that by luck had a nice Winchester in the scabbard. The owner was in the Gem working on a good drunk.

Rico jumped on the dark bay horse that stood at least 14 hands high and headed west at a full gallop, throwing mud in all directions. He had chosen his new mount well; the gelding could run.

He imagined hearing faint gunshots, but in truth none were fired. In fact, Bullock and his deputies were planning their next move to find Rico. They never had a clue that the murderer was riding in a full gallop past the jail. Only a Chinese child who had stepped out in the street got a good look at the escaping Rico before being brushed aside by the galloping horse. The little girl was mostly unhurt, but understandably frightened.

Rico soon realized that he was not being followed and stepped off the gelding to rest. The horse was gulping for breath after sprinting up several steep hills. He led the horse farther up into the hills. He would shoot a rabbit or something for dinner when he was sure a posse was not in pursuit. For now, he would remain hungry. There was no use in advertising where he was holed up.

Only then did he notice a big drip of blood from his forehead, evidently cut while diving through Swearengen's window. He searched through the saddlebags and found an old sweat rag and some jerky. He wiped at the bloody spot while chewing on this welcome dried meat. A half-full canteen quickly washed down the morsel.

"Well, things could be worse," he muttered. "I guess that it is time to leave the territory." He turned his new pony westward and then later headed north.

Birch and Bullock learned about the Chinese girl's close call days later. The Chinese community was a close-mouthed group who took care of their own problems. The little girl had not been hurt and that was enough.

143

Yet a laundry man had mentioned the incident to Al Swearengen. The shady bar and prostitute owner immediately walked over to the jail and gave Bullock this important information. Big Al could be civic minded when it served his purpose.

Up until then, the lawmen only knew that Rico had disappeared. Swearengen's tidbit was proof that Rico had left the area.

They tried tracking, but heavy rains had washed away all evidence of Rico. Birch persisted longer than the others before returning to Deadwood, dejected.

Rico had made his escape.

BUSINESS AS USUAL
October 22, 1878

"I hope you clowns have finished playing around and are ready to work," Bullock said. "We have several gold shipments ready to go and one less deputy. I think it is time to hit the trail, gentlemen, don't you?"

"Uh, yes sir," Jed answered, "but can we leave tomorrow morning? I have some business tonight that I need to take care of."

"What?" Bullock shouted. "You have what?"

"I have to be ready to go this afternoon boss," Jed stuttered.

"Good, now get out of here and be careful."

The deputies stepped out of Bullock's office and looked at the sky.

"Clouds in the north," Jed said. "Plenty cold. Bring your warmest clothes. I think it is going to get bad."

That afternoon they started out, everyone thinking about someone they left behind. Mason couldn't help but think about Amy while harboring his resentment for Birch.

Jed was right as usual, and they soon were pelted with sleet and light blowing snow, a painful introduction to winter as it hit their faces. Jed's suggestion to bring hooded coats and wool clothing saved the day, and the gold shipment made it to the plains by mid-morning the second day.

Jed looked at the swirling clouds overhead and said, "Should be clear, but really cold in a couple of days."

"Now how do you know that?" Mason asked, certain that he was right.

"Just do," Jed said. "Survival out here means reading the weather. You don't want to get caught on these plains in a deep snow blizzard. That would be a rough trip."

"Rico will be snowed in too," Birch said. "Maybe we should postpone the gold shipments because of weather and try to find him."

"Where would we look?" Jed replied. "Those plains are no place to be riding during a blizzard. We need to hole up too, until the weather passes."

"I guess you're right," Birch said. "We might get word of Rico or Black Moon while we're in Fort Pierre."

BUD AND BENNY GO HUNTING
October 24, 1878

Red Hawk was communicating better with the boys, and they in turn were enjoying their stay at a camp where most white people would not have been welcome.

He fashioned bows and arrows for the boys, who learned quickly because of their rock thrower. The ancient weapon had taught them the hand and eye coordination required to shoot with a bow. Bud especially learned quickly and was soon killing rabbits and birds that helped the family survive.

The boys, who were now nine and ten, learned from Red Hawk by observing and imitating his actions. He was gentle with the boys and wondered what it would have been like if his own sons had survived.

The boys were still homesick, but adventures like rabbit and waterfowl hunting helped, and soon they were living normal lives by 1878 Lakota standards.

Red Hawk took the boys on their first goose hunt on a cold, October morning. He patiently guided the boys across an old marsh that was full by the grace of God and heavy rains.

"The Great Spirit has provided us with this pool of water to pull in geese and ducks. Now my sons, I want you to sit back and watch what I do. There will be plenty of time for you to hunt, but for now, sit quietly, watch and learn."

The boys watched as Red Hawk crawled under some weeds and cat tails and then lay still. Benny tried to rise up a couple of times to see if he was really still there. The big man had disappeared.

Soon a flock of Canada geese set their wings and slipped into the waterhole. The Lakota took careful aim and released an arrow that struck home. The last goose dropped his head in the water, quite dead. The second and third did the same before the lead goose signaled a warning with a desperate sounding "Honk" that alerted the remaining birds.

Benny and Bud watched the big geese fly out of sight before walking over to help carry the heavy birds.

"We will eat well tonight boys," Red Hawk said with a smile. "Yellow Flower's heart will sing when she sees our geese, especially if we pluck them before presenting her with the birds."

"Can't we shoot some more?" Benny asked.

"No my son, we have taken what the Great Spirit has provided, enough for today and it is getting late. We still have to peel the feathers off these great birds and that is not an easy task."

An hour later, the hunting party stepped in front of Yellow Flower's tepee, and both boys yelled. She peeked through the opening and flashed a big smile, something she did more often these days.

"Ah, my hunters have returned and look what they have brought me," she said while giving both boys a hug. "Now I will cook these fine birds for my men's evening meal. Hunters must eat so they will have the strength to hunt again."

The boys enjoyed their first roasted goose that night. Soon Red Hawk and Yellow Flower settled into their corner of the tepee to sleep while the boys curled up on the other side.

"Hey Bud," Benny whispered. "Have you heard the noises Red Hawk and Yellow Flower make sometimes late at night?"

"Yeah, I guess that is just the stuff married people do," Bud answered, slightly annoyed at the question.

"Sounds painful sometimes," Benny said. "I sure never want to do what they are doing."

"Shut up, Benny, and go to sleep," Bud said.

"Bud, think Birch is alive?" Benny asked.

"Maybe, but I'm not sure," he answered. "I heard the others talking about someone in Deadwood who was a quick draw like dad, but I have never heard a name. In the meantime, we are alive and Red Hawk and Yellow Flower are treating us good."

"I sure miss ma's cooking."

"Me too, but these people are giving us the best they can and I sure like them. Let's just see what happens, maybe Birch will come for us someday."

"Yeah, maybe someday," Benny answered wistfully. "But I sure hope we go goose hunting again tomorrow."

A VERY BAD IDEA
October 30, 1878

"You know who's the best looking woman in town?" Jess Phillips, bodyguard and bartender for Al Swearengen, asked an old miner while leaning against the bar

"Yep, it would have to be the dressmaker," the old miner answered. "She's pretty as a speckled pup, but don't she belong to that law dog, the hot shooter who works for Bullock?"

"I reckon she does, but he is out of town trying to guard a gold shipment," Phillips said in a low voice. "I've been thinking that maybe she needs someone to look in on her."

"I think that is mighty neighborly of you, pilgrim, but that kindness might get you killed. Hell boy, if you just want a poke, look at all these women Swearengen has working for him. Surely you can get some of that—and probably for free."

"Look old man, those whores might be good enough for you, but I want a piece of that beautiful young thing that hasn't been with every miner and drover in the territory. Now I guess you better move on old man. Your big mouth is starting to steam me."

The old miner had grown old in a hostile world by being smart. He left a full drink and walked through the door to unmerciful sunlight. Phillips watched with his hand on a very well used pistol. He surveyed the door a couple of minutes longer to make sure the man he had just pushed did not come back with a shotgun ready to fire.

I'll just pay that little diamond a visit, he thought while pouring another drink of whiskey. I think she needs protecting while her big, bad deputy is gone. Shoot, she might like it, and we can make it a regular thing. I can always unload a shotgun shell or two in the deputy's back if he finds out. These streets get mighty dark at night.

DEMONS IN HIS HEAD
October 30, 1878

Rico sat alone quietly sulking with both hands closed around a drink in an old saloon in Tinton that, like the Black Hills mining town, had seen better days. Swearengen had betrayed him, and a young deputy had wiped out his gang. He felt hatred and knew there was little to be done, except find a place to hole up for winter. Maybe he should forget about Deputy Rose and somehow come up with enough money to visit a big city where the women would love Rico.

"Hey bartender," he said in a rough voice. "Bring Rico another shot of that whiskey, or I will come and get it, and you don't want me to have to do that."

"Right away mister," the frightened old man answered. "I'm bringing the whiskey now."

Rico sat and stared at the bottle the old man had placed on the table before turning to quickly walk away. He glanced at the bartender who wore a black derby and black pants with a white shirt that had ruffles on the sleeves. Stains showed the shirt had been worn during many years of bartender work.

Rico's eyes narrowed and darkened at the thought of not returning to Deadwood because of a young punk and some half-assed deputies. He felt sleepy, but he dared not close his eyes and endure the dreams of being killed and going to Hell where demons would torment him.

The demons were always the same, slightly shorter than he was, with big yellow eyes and teeth like a mountain lion. The demons lowered him into the grave without a coffin, and he could see worms crawling out of the grave's side, companions for his long sleep. Soon an unknown man started shoveling dirt on his body; the first spade-full stung his face. He reached for the open air, knowing that soon it would be gone forever.

Then he screamed for help, help that never came as dirt continued flying in on top of his body. This dream always made him wake up in a cold sweat, and it had tormented him since he was grazed in the scalp by a bullet many years before.

He opened his eyes, drank several more shots, and then starred at the bottle again. The bartender noticed an evil look on his face and decided to step out the door and find help. Rico noticed him inching closer to the door and turned towards him, moving his head like a coiled rattlesnake.

"Old friend, where do you go?" Rico asked.

"Just a little stomach gas. Thought I'd step outside," The scared old man answered. "Too many frijoles last night I guess."

"I don't think so, my old friend. I think you look for someone to shoot poor Rico."

"No sir, why would I do that? You're just sitting there minding your own business."

"Yes my friend, and my business is taking what cash you have, so give it up, now."

The bartender turned and ran for the exit. He had barely opened the door when a knife slashed through space and caught him between the shoulder blades.

Rico stepped over, wiped the blade clean on the dead man's shirt, and stepped over to the bar. A cigar box held the cash the old man had died for—exactly $2.30.

Rico stuffed the money in his pocket and slipped out the back door. When he'd made sure all was clear, he stepped around the front and slipped a Mexican leather boot in his stirrup. He kicked the horse's ribs and turned east. He had to find another place to hole up, a place to do some thinking. No one had seen him kill the old man, but there was no use in taking chances for $2.30. That was just not enough money to risk having one's neck stretched by a rope of justice. Things had to improve, he thought. It was time for his luck to change. He was not some half-witted cowboy.

He was Rico.

AMY'S VISITOR
November 1, 1878

Amy, happy to be back home, leaned over and blew out her coal oil lamp that was well positioned on a table by her bed. She had moved back after the news was confirmed that Rico had left town.

The town seems quiet, she thought. Maybe I'll get a little sleep tonight. Sure wish Birch was back. I feel safer when he is around.

Towards midnight someone tried the front door by gently rattling it. Amy immediately awoke to the sound of bells she had tied on the inside doorknob.

Birch? She wondered.

Then she heard a sound everyone prays they'll never hear. A knee busted through the lock on her shop door, and heavy boots started walking up the stairs to her home quarters. She sat up to hear someone moving around and then saw a dim light filter under the door.

God, she thought as her breathing quickened and her heart pounded much too hard. Someone lit my lamp and is snooping around.

She could hear the boots moving closer to her bedroom on the wooden floor and suddenly she felt sick.

The steps stopped at her door. The knob slowly turned and then stopped.

Amy leaned over and lit her lamp. Guess he or she might as well have a good look at what they are going to get, she thought while trying hard not to panic or throw up. Suddenly the knob turned full bore and she strained her eyes, wanting to run but to where?

The single lamp threw sinister shadows around the room as her door slowly opened to reveal Jess Phillips standing in the doorway. His face showed more hatred than desire. The lamp made his face more hideous than it normally was when she saw him on the street. Phillips was a very cruel man, the exact reason Swearengen had hired him. He stepped in the room and flashed a horrible smile that showed he had arrived to get what he and many others desired.

"What do you want?" she asked while trying not to sound scared.

"I'm not after money. You know exactly what I am after little lady," he said in a low voice. "Now lift up your blankets and let's get it done."

"Just what do you think Birch Rose is going to make of this when he finds out? Don't you know that I'm his woman?" she said, hoping his common sense would end it there.

"He will never know bitch. Now peel off them clothes."

Phillips moved closer and started to reach out when a chill ran down his back. He was suddenly looking into the muzzle of a .41 caliber derringer and the hammer was locked back.

"Just what do you plan to do with that little thing," he stupidly asked.

Amy answered by touching off the top barrel. Flame could be seen coming from her derringer as the bullet entered his left shoulder, throwing him backwards on the floor.

He lifted up and realized that his desires for sexual exploits were over. He was losing a lot of blood on her floor, and he had to make it back across the street where Doc Crebbs was likely enjoying a nightcap. Amy followed him with the second barrel ready to make a more deadly shot as he trailed blood down the stairs and out her front door.

SWEARENGEN'S UNEXPECTED VISITOR
November 2, 1878

Al Swearengen hated mornings, crowing roosters, and sunrises. He woke up with a remarkable whiskey headache and new troubles. Someone had tried to rob his best bartender and now he had to find out exactly who was that stupid.

Someone will pay for shooting my employee, he thought. Now I have to find a replacement who can run my bar and not steal me blind.

Amy had stood outside the door of the Gem Theatre for a full minute before entering Swearengen's bar. She reasoned that the noted cruel man would not take kindly to bad publicity from an employee, and she wanted the most severe punishment possible for the man who'd tried to rape her. She decided that talking to the boss would get her farther than telling her story to the law. She didn't know what Swearengen would do, but it was worth the gamble of back-door justice that was not uncommon in 1878 Deadwood.

Swearengen hated surprises, especially the kind that walked through his door while he tried to swallow a mouth full of bacon to be followed by a sip of whiskey.

"Mr. Swearengen," Amy said in a calm, quiet voice.

"Why yes, my dear, how can I help you this fine morning?" Swearengen asked with more than a little sarcasm in his voice. "Did one of my girls not pay you for a dress?"

"I hardly think so," she said, feeling the back of her neck get warm. "No, I have other business with you. Last night a man broke into my home. I recognized him as one of your employees. Do you know anything about this?"

"Why no," he answered honestly. "I have not heard of this dastardly affair."

"Did any of your employees get shot last night, in the shoulder?" She asked.

"No, none of my men were shot last night," he said with a strange look in his eyes.

"Well please let me know if you hear anything," she said. "I have not gone to Sheriff Bullock yet."

"Wait, did this man who you claim works for me do any damage?"

"Yes, he ruined my door and bled all over my floor," she said, surprised that he smiled.

"Well, I don't know who did it, but I will be happy to pay for any damage if you are sure one of my people was responsible," Swearengen said with a very stern look in his eye.

"That won't be necessary Mr. Swearengen," Amy said while standing to leave. "I am sure everything will take care of itself. I trust you will talk to this horrible man when you find out who it is. Good day Mr. Swearengen."

"Good day, my dear," he said while walking her to the door.

A BAD MISTAKE
November 2, 1878

Jess Phillips was a very unhappy man. His wound from the gunshot was unbearably painful, and this was not how he expected to feel after walking into Amy's bedroom. Late-morning sunlight filtered through the window of his dirty room that was sometimes used on busy nights when the girls needed more rooms. Then he had to sleep in the same bed, a situation he hoped to soon change.

He figured the law would be by soon. The last thing he expected was an angry Swearengen to bust through the door.

"So Phillips," Swearengen growled. "You decided to pay the dressmaker a call last night."

"No Al, I was shot by a robber, just where I said," he lied.

"In what location did this robber shoot you?" Swearengen asked in a very angry voice.

"Down the street, in front of the bank, Al."

"Alright, I believe you Phillips, but I'm going to go look for blood in front of the bank and I'd better find some."

"Now wait Al, someone may have cleaned up by now."

Swearengen had expected this type of response, and he turned back and starred into the frightened man's eyes.

"Now then, why don't you tell me exactly what happened last night and I'll go easy on you."

Phillips knew he could not get away with lying to Al, so he told the whole story.

"You stupid bastard," Al yelled. "I have a business in this town and now you are going to bring the law in here. You are supposed to represent me, and now this dressmaker will squawk the next time she sees you on the street. Dumb bastard, do you see the position this puts me in?" Swearengen asked, while pulling a folded straight-edge razor from the pocket inside his jacket.

"Do you want me to leave town, Al," Phillips asked with a shaky voice.

"No, I want you to stay here," he said while swinging the razor and slitting Phillips' throat from ear to ear. "I want you to be buried around here somewhere so your body will never be found."

Al might have saved his words. Phillips could no longer hear him.

That evening two China men who did odd jobs for Swearengen carried a wrapped-up body out the back door. They unceremoniously threw his body on an old wagon and started out of town to the hills. The dead wagon stopped two miles out and both men started swinging picks and shovels under a kerosene lantern in a dip between two muddy banks. They completed Phillips' final resting spot a half hour before sunrise and drove back to town with a welcomed source of money to feed their families.

Amy had no way of knowing that her tormentor was dead and buried in the Black Hills where once again, the hunter had become the hunted. A new second derringer lay on the table by her lamp, loaded with the hammer cocked.

THE GERMANS MAKE A BET
November 4, 1878

Birch and Mason set up camp the evening before their arrival in Fort Pierre. Plans were made to change the guard every three hours, but for now the deputies and teamsters were sitting around the campfire and dipping into a pot of beans and ham that Mason had cooked. Jed, as usual, was on guard duty, never taking for granted that they were safe.

After dinner the Germans started talking among themselves in their native tongue. Birch listened to what he thought was a very strong argument. The older brother, Lester, seemed to be convincing his shorter, stouter brother of something. Joseph glanced at Birch and Mason several times and finally agreed to whatever it was. Lester turned to the deputies.

"You make bet with us?" he asked in thickly accented English. "We say Joseph can lift horse."

There was a long moment of stunned silence followed by Birch and Mason speaking at the same time.

"What?"

"Lift a horse?"

"Yes, Joseph lift horse," Lester replied.

"Now wait a minute. You're saying that Joseph can lift a horse clean off the ground." Mason said.

"No trick, no ropes or pulleys, or anything like that?"
"No trick, just Joseph and horse."

Birch noticed Jed at the edge of firelight taking in the strange exchange with a crooked grin on his face.

"Hey, Jed, you want some of this action?"

"Nope," Jed answered still with a small, half smile on his lips. He didn't care to bet, but was definitely intrigued by the wager and these two foreign men.

Lester gave Jed a long look, still unsure how to react to this unusual man of few words.

Mason and Birch exchanged a look, grinned at each other and shrugged a silent "why not?"

"Ok, Lester" Birch said, "We'll bet you a steak dinner in Fort Pierre that Joseph can't lift a horse, all four feet off the ground at once."

"It is bet." Lester walked to the horse line and brought the most docile mount into the firelight.

What the boys witnessed next became a tale that they would tell many times over, as the muscular Joseph patted the horse while speaking softly in German. Then he squatted underneath the gelding. He lowered his head, and when his broad shoulders were directly centered below the horse's middle, he put his hands on both rock-solid thighs and lifted with his legs. The horse was raised off the ground for a few seconds before the surprised gelding shifted and Joseph had to let him down.

"Holy cow! I wouldn't have believed it if I hadn't seen it with my own eyes." Mason yelped.

Birch was laughing out loud to see such an odd sight. "That was worth a steak dinner, Joseph."

The big sandy-haired man slapped his brother on the shoulder with a loud whack, and Lester returned the slap that brought on howls of loud laughter from both Germans. Birch watched the two bent over laughing, shook his head and laid down on his blanket, wondering if all Germans were that strange.

Jed shook his head, grinned, and resumed patrolling. The ever-alert deputy watched and listened to the surroundings after the German's finally stopped celebrating and went to sleep. But, the only unnatural sounds were the results of a camp full of men who had just eaten their share of beans.

Birch stretched out and starred at the stars as Mason glanced at him and shook his head, not understanding what Birch was looking for. Jed stood close by, but he did not speak; he only watched for any danger that might threaten this rare group of men whom he was starting to feel close to.

The night passed quickly, and they were soon finishing the last leg of their journey. The big Germans were first to rise and start cleaning up the camp. They had the first mule harnessed before Birch woke up.

Jed had finally settled in for a nap while Mason took over the guard duty. Joseph walked by and slapped the deputy on his right shoulder.

"Some joke last night, ya," he said. "We get you plenty good— you not believe, that I, Joseph, could pick up horse, ha, ha, ha."

Mason only rubbed his shoulder from the slap and smiled.

TRAGEDY IN FORT PIERRE
November 5, 1878

Birch and company arrived in Fort Pierre late the next morning, and many eyes in town watched their arrival while studying the wagon loaded with gold.

Birch, Mason and Jed felt relieved to deposit each strong box of gold in the bank's huge vault that morning. Now it was Wells Fargo's problem.

That evening Mason and Birch stepped into Fort Pierre's Cattlemen's Saloon to find decent sipping whiskey while Jed sat on the hotel's porch across the street. The teamsters quickly enjoyed their steak dinner, compliments of Birch and Mason.

Afterwards, Lester and Joseph found their own entertainment in the sleazy Blue Goose Saloon that was owned by a German immigrant, Gad Schuster, who happened to be from Bern, Germany where the brothers were raised. The owner knew their papa, and immediately the brothers considered him family, giving him a big bear hug that nearly broke his back.

The other Germans in the bar gave a loud cheer to find these stout lads were from their homeland, and the beer flowed. Soon the air was filled with Germanic songs sung by several very drunk patrons, including the brothers. That evening Joseph kept Lester and himself supplied in beer by beating all comers in arm wrestling. He tried to make another horse bet, but was stopped when Schuster warned the others that he had watched their papa do the same trick in the old country.

Jed stayed close to the Cattlemen's Saloon in case the others encountered trouble. He had learned long ago that he was not welcome in a white man's bar, even though he was not actually Cheyenne by blood, but by desire. Besides, he did not drink the spirits in the strange company of a different bar, only with friends.

Birch decided to live a little because he was healing inside. The nightmares were not occurring quite as often and besides, he was ready to howl.

Both Mason and Birch sat with their backs to the wall and watched the crowd, a lesson well learned from the cautious Seth Bullock. Most in the bar would occasionally cast a glance in their direction, a fact not lost on Mason who noticed the glances and worse, the bar was full of whispers.

Birch started feeling uncomfortable and decided to leave for the hotel. He stood up only to face three big cowpunchers that had obviously been drinking for a long spell.

Brandon Jones, Matt Sterman, and Jose Porperia's faces were red and their words slurred. Birch quickly took notice that their pistols were slung low and the leather strips that folded over the hammers were hung loose. He noted how they were standing with their left shoulders slightly cocked towards the deputies. This naturally let their right hand dangle close to those deadly pistols just waiting to be drawn, showing that clearly these guys meant business.

"Hey, ain't you those deputies from Deadwood?" Sterman blurted out. "You don't seem so tough to me. Hell boys, they look like a pair of scared coyotes. I heard you had a real live injun killer with you."

157

He turned to Mason. "Hey boy, are you the famous Deadwood injun killer? Are you the big, bad Black Hills booger man? I'll bet you'll protect us if the injuns attack tonight, what do you say boy?"

Mason had had enough. Many miles on the trail had given him little patience for a loud-mouthed drunk. He smelled Sterman's hard breath while the drunk haw-hawed at his own humor and tried to goad a fight.

Mason tried to walk past the tough range rover and was pushed back with a huge right hand. He grabbed for his gun in a flash, and Sterman was shocked by the deputy's speedy draw and even more shocked by Birch's gun that had appeared even faster. His eyes widened and showed surprise.

"Whoa, now hold on, boys," Sterman said. "We was just funning you."

Sterman and his men slowly turned towards the bar, and everyone in the room calmed down. The poker game in the corner resumed, as piano music once again filled the room. Mason noticed that Sterman was still mumbling to himself, so he continued to watch the bully.

Birch handed Mason a beer, and both men holstered their pistols. Both deputies continued watching the cowboys who were occasionally sneaking a glance at Mason, a fact that irritated him.

"Mister, I think you need to go home and sleep it off, " Mason said. "We don't want trouble."

"Hell deputy, we don't want trouble either. In fact, this ain't no trouble at all."

Like a flash Sterman drew his six shooter and pumped two quick shots into the shocked Mason's chest.

The deputy's mouth fell open as he dropped to the floor.

Patrons in the bar became deathly quiet. All ears rang from the deafening gun shots in the bar's enclosed area and all eyes looked down at Mason whose very lifeblood was seeping out. Some immediately turned their eyes away while a prostitute gagged and ran to a back room.

A frightening look crossed Birch's face. He was strangely calm, as if in a trance, while looking at his friend's lifeless body on the floor.

Smoke from Sterman's guns floated around him in the dim light to create a sinister scene. The killer looked into Birch's blue eyes and was shocked to see an intense stare that pierced through the three men like well thrown daggers.

Sterman stood there with his smoking pistol still drawn and slightly lowered. He started to speak, but Birch drew his pistols with the speed of a striking copperhead and sent two bullets through the startled gunfighter. Both pieces of lead opened his heart within a quarter inch.

Birch turned with amazing speed and sent two more bullets through Jones and Porperia, who only had time to touch their pistols. They had no time to fight back, only time enough to die.

Jed burst through the door with a shotgun. He moved the deadly scattergun back and forth with that same dangerous mountain lion stare that spoke of an intense, dangerous man who was trying to decide where to shoot.

No one dared to move a muscle, knowing he would not hesitate to kill.

Jed did not have many friends. Now one was dead and the other in danger. He was ready to kill or be killed for his remaining friend, and no one in the bar had any doubts about that.

Birch kneeled down beside Mason, lifted his head and closed his eyes. Mason had a death stare that would last in Birch's memory for quite a spell.

Didn't give Mason a chance to draw, Birch thought while looking down at the dead deputy. He bowed his head with eyes wide open, and a bar full of shocked patrons watched one of the fastest gunmen they would ever see pray over his dead comrade. Jed stood over him with a shotgun, ominously watching the crowd with the look of someone wanting an excuse to kill.

Birch's emotions were emptying out, partly because of Mason and partly because of what had happened over the past year. He had gone from a stable hand helping his family to what many considered to be a natural-born killer.

Jed took his eyes off the crowd for a second and looked at Birch, wondering how to get out of there without more bloodshed before looking back at the crowd. Two clicking sounds of hammers being drawn back somewhere in the crowd made Jed twist the shotgun back in a blurred motion. The would-be shooters lowered their pistols to avoid being torn in half by a shotgun blast.

Minutes later, Lester and Joseph busted through the door to take in the scene of carnage. They picked up Mason's limp body and gently carried him out to one of the empty gold wagons while saying a silent prayer. Joseph wiped tears from his eyes.

Jed grabbed Birch by the shoulder and edged him towards the door, his eyes and shotgun still glued to the crowd. Finally they stepped into the cool night air and followed the Germans back to their wagons.

The Germans wrapped Mason's body in a tarp, and then gently laid the dead deputy inside their lead wagon. Jed sat on the wagon and watched for danger while Birch quietly sat on the other wagon and starred towards the stars, remembering the ghastly scene over and over in his mind, amazed how quickly four men had died. He felt partly responsible for Mason's death; after all, the bullies were looking for the big bad Lakota killer from the trail of death.

They had meant to kill him.

The local sheriff talked with witnesses before making a judgment of self-defense. He knew the three cowboys were bullies and troublemakers from previous encounters. In fact, Sterman had been tried for the murder of Chess Atkins in Oklahoma and acquitted. Many claimed the jury was bribed, and no one ever believed that it had been a fair and just trial. Sterman had left the state and headed north before Atkin's family could unload their own justice.

The sheriff told Birch he could go, but first offered him a job as top deputy. Birch thanked him and refused.

When it was time to leave Fort Pierre, Mason was covered with a thick blanket and laid in one of the returning gold wagons beside a load of supplies. The silent Germans drove both wagons while townspeople standing along the wooden-slat sidewalks watched the strange procession leave town. Several had suggested burying the body at Fort Pierre, but Birch was determined to take Mason back to Deadwood.

Mason's horse was tied to the wagon that carried his body, while Jed silently rode behind with a scattergun, still constantly looking for danger. The three dead cowboys might have friends waiting in ambush, and he did not want to lose more friends to senseless violence.

Birch rode to the top of a small hill to look for danger. He glanced down to notice Mason's horse walking slowly behind the lead wagon and immediately felt guilty about Amy, whom Mason had found and loved first.

Birch softly spoke the words aloud that he planned to tell Amy as his big strawberry roan carefully stepped around yucca, cactus and huge stands of buffalo grass and little blue stem, but nothing sounded right.

Lester, who first drove Mason's wagon, turned over the reins to Birch several days into the trip. Even with November's nighttime freezing temperatures the smell of the partly frozen dead body was overwhelming.

Suggestions of burying the body there were quickly stifled by Birch. He took over the wagon, slapped the lead horse's rump with the reins, and continued on as both teamsters rode the other wagon well ahead of the ghastly vessel. Jed was determined to stay with Birch, no matter what.

The determined deputies wore kerchiefs over their mouths and noses to filter out some of the smell. Night was always a problem, as the smell of decomposing flesh drew in wolves and other predators in search of an easy meal.

Birch and Jed took turns at night watching the wagon. During the ride, Jed noticed several Lakota watching from a distance, but nothing came of it. Birch reached Deadwood days later, moving faster with the lighter cargo.

Birch drove the wagon straight to the Deadwood graveyard.

His next task was to tell Amy the news. He entered her dress shop an hour later and waited. He was glad to find her alone. She smiled when Birch walked in, but her smile quickly faded as she focused on his face while hearing about Mason. She started crying. He wrapped his arms around her and just held on tightly. There was nothing else he could do. He felt her take several deep breaths, then pull away.

"I'm closing the shop," she said softly. "I want to be alone tonight."

He started to walk away and heard her crying through the door.

Glad I shot those three bastards, he thought while walking down the street to Bullock's house. Nobody ever deserved to die more.

161

‹›═◯═‹›

BIRCH MAKES A DEAL
December 2, 1878

Rose realized that this life was not for him. He owed Bullock a great deal that could never be repaid, but he started thinking about moving on.

It had been a long, boring day in Deadwood. Too damned cold for anyone to cause trouble in town. Birch left the jailhouse and headed for Bullock's house where he still was staying. He opened the front door, found himself alone in the house, and slowly walked back to his room, rubbing his hands together to drive out the chill. He took off his hat and heavy coat, unbuckled his gun belt, pulled his boots off, stretched out on his bed and looked up at the ceiling. The room he had at Bullock's seemed to get smaller with each passing day.

Birch looked around the room—a bed, a dresser, a chair, a coal oil lamp, and his family's Bible. That was the extent of his personal world. Not much to talk about, but better than nothing.

Bullock hasn't said anything about moving on, but after all this time I'm sure he'd like to have his house to himself again, Birch thought.

Then he remembered Bullock asking about his family's wagons just the other day. They were still at the blacksmith's. What was he going to do about them? Been meaning to sell 'em, but it's hard to let go, he thought.

Maybe I could try gold mining? Aw, hell no, what a senseless idea. All the placer mining in the area is done, and what claims are being sold now are worthless. Maybe a piece of land and some cattle.

Birch looked over to the old Rose family Bible he kept on top of his dresser. Yea, dad would have liked that idea, he thought. A small spread of my own would be a good start. But I do need a grub stake. What about Cookie? He helped me once; I wonder if he would do it again?

The following morning Birch met Cookie at his old shack. Despite his fortune, the man had yet to change his lifestyle, not that he wanted to. The only differences were that he proudly wore new clothes and he always paid for the other miners evening's hooch. He had money to burn, and his friends lined up with their hand out.

"Glad to see ye young man," Cookie said. "Come in out of the cold and get warm by the stove. Whut brings ye up to see me an Ginger? You know thet damned old mule kicked me last night? I'm mighty sore this morning."

"Sorry to hear it," Birch mumbled before deciding to get straight to the point. "I wanted to ask you a favor."

"How much do ye want," Cookie quickly replied.

"How do you know that I'm here for money?"

"Well, whut else would ye be after?"

"I have a business proposition for you."

"Well, git on with it boy."

"Well, it's almost 1879, and things are changing around here. The Indians are getting to be less of a threat; there's only a few bands giving the settlers trouble anymore, and this town's booming. The Black Hills are getting civilized. I want to settle down, maybe start thinking about a family, Cookie."

"So you don't want ta end up like Ginger and me, an old bachelor? Cookie chuckled. "Cain't say I blame you with that pretty young dressmaker in town. That woman will either be yer salvation or real trouble—guess it depends on the cut of her sand."

Birch wasn't sure what he meant by that, but he continued.

"I need a silent partner in a ranch, someone with money 'cause I don't have any."

"How much?"

"Could you spare three thousand?"

"I think I could do thet, boy, hell Ginger and I air rich. I'll just make out a voucher you can use at the bank and we'll git started. Now tell me about this ranch I'm gonna be a part owner of."

The following morning was bitter cold, but dry; there was not much snow yet around Deadwood. Birch started looking over a few plots of land in the Black Hills that were now becoming available, and that had enough pasture for grazing a fair-sized herd. This project helped keep his mind off Mason's death as he surveyed a couple of good-looking spots.

Soon he had staked out a beautiful area that bordered the land that Amy had inherited when her parents died.

He decided he would still attend to his deputy duties until his unfinished business was over. He decided that killing the vermin that murdered his family was better with a badge than without. He did not want to end his time on the end of a rope—a horrible way to die.

CHRISTMAS
December 25, 1878

B irch knocked on Amy's back door in a suit and tie, an outfit he had bought at Bullock's suggestion. "Court her proper," the old sheriff had said. Amy opened the door and took a step back to take in the sight.

"Aw Birch, you look so nice," she said. "Where did you get that suit?"

"Bullock picked it out for me at Poppa Sam's General Store," he said. "I spent a month's wages on it."

"Well, it looks very nice and I am pleased that you wore it. By the way, do you like baked ham?"

"Yes 'um, I do."

"Then make yourself at home. Let's go upstairs and I will have dinner ready soon."

Birch looked around the room and noticed a small pine tree in the corner with shinny pretties hanging off the limbs.

"Why do you have a tree in your house," he asked.

"Why Birch, have you never seen a Christmas tree?"

"No," he said. "What's the purpose of this tree?"

"To celebrate the birth of Christ," she answered.

"Oh, a tree to celebrate Christ," he said. "Guess that's alright."

"The German's do it, and I think it is a good tradition," Amy replied, slighted irritated.

"Well, I guess that's alright for the Germans, but don't expect other folks to do it too. Kind of seems unnatural—a tree in the house."

Amy decided to let the subject pass and started stirring a cake batter. Birch sat down and watched how she gently stirred

164

the batter, just like his mother used to do at Christmas time. Suddenly he could see her stirring while Bud and Benny tugged at her skirt to see who would lick the bowl. The door opened and Jack stepped in, took the bowl, and held it above the boys' heads while they jumped up, trying to reach it. Suddenly he felt someone shaking his shoulder.

"Wake up Birch," Amy said. "Dinner's ready."

Birch sat up, realizing how much he missed his mother and father as a tear dripped down his cheek. Amy noticed the tear and decided to ignore it unless he mentioned his dream. She guessed where he had been.

"So, are you hungry?" she asked.

"I could eat," he said, still slightly shaken.

"Birch, I hope my cooking is almost as good as your mother's."

"You are a great cook. I will likely never get over thinking and dreaming about them."

Amy hugged him and said, "No my darling, you will never forget, but time will make it easier, a lot of time, and I have patience. Now let's eat."

THE GIFT
December 25, 1878

Bud and Benny lost track of time in the Lakota camp. They only knew when each season came and went. An old trapper passing through the camp wished the boys a merry Christmas, surprising both of them.

"Benny, where did we put that small box turtle shell we found last fall by the swamp?" Bud asked. "Remember the one we cut the belly out of and laid on an ant hill? The ants really did a good job cleaning the rest of the shell out. Let's make Yellow Flower a turtle bag for Christmas. What do you say?"

"Yeah, she would like that," Benny answered. "We can make it like that old man showed us. I wonder if he would loan us a stone drill?"

They took their box turtle shell to an old Lakota craftsman, who indeed loaned them a stone drill and helped them use it.

"Drill softly, young friends," the old man said. "The shell edge is brittle and will crack open if you drill too hard or too close to the edge. That's it, now drill another hole a finger's length apart."

Benny tried not to look at the old man's mouth. His teeth were almost gone and those that remained were discolored and nasty looking. Yet the old Lakota was a kind man, enjoying the company of two young bucks who would take time to pay attention to him and learn his craft. Bud examined his eyes and wondered what those eyes had seen during a very long life.

They made enough holes to tie a tanned buckskin bag in the turtle shell with sinew to make a present that all the other women would envy. Happy with their work, they took it to the surprised lady who was working outside her tepee.

"Merry Christmas," both boys said in English, not sure how to say it in Lakota tongue. "This is for you, Yellow Flower," Bud said.

"Yeah," Benny said. "I sure hope you like it."

Yellow Flower did not speak. She examined the surprisingly well made bag and then hugged the boys tightly against her chest. Bud felt a tear on the back of his neck as she squeezed them tighter, not letting go. While not forgetting their own mother, both boys had embraced Yellow Flower as their surrogate mom and had grown to love her.

Finally she released the boys and stepped into her tepee, crying. The old man watched from a distance and then turned to walk away, satisfied.

"Did we do something wrong?" Benny asked. "She was crying."

"No, you dope, those were happy tears, not sad ones."

"Oh," Benny said. "Girls sure are strange sometimes."

DANGER IN THE HILLS
April 2, 1879

Winter passed, and Mason's death drew Birch and Amy closer to each other than ever before. One day, they rented a buckboard from the livery stable and rode out to Birch's new ranch for a picnic. Spring was early for the second year in a row. The land was full of flowers, the songbirds had returned, and life was beginning again. The moment just seemed right. He asked her to marry him that day, and she accepted with a long, wet kiss.

Birch knew that the future looked bright, if he survived.

"We have a good-sized spread with both places, at least 6,000 acres," she said. "My dad's ranch plus the adjoining place you just acquired would make quite a cattle ranch."

"Yes, I think that we can work something out," Birch said. "But first I have some unfinished business. Rico and Black Moon."

"You can't be serious," she almost shouted. "You have a chance that Mason will never have now. Do you want to die, too?"

"Hell Amy, I don't have no choice. They killed my family! I have to track them down!"

"But you don't even know where they are! Don't you understand? I want you to live!"

Then, in a moment of blind passion, Amy kissed him with the abandon of a woman who had nothing to lose. He felt that same warmness spread through his body and started to hug her before she pushed him away.

Silently, they stepped back on the buckboard and drove away. Birch turned up a mountain trail just past his pasture when his instincts took over and he slammed Amy down across his lap and on the buggy floor.

An arrow made a zipping noise as it slipped past his neck. He tried to kick the team of horses into a run but found himself on the ground. A young brave shot another arrow before leaping off the hill.

The young brave rolled, then jumped up with his knife ready. He could not have been more than fourteen or fifteen, yet he had the vicious look of a wild animal. He made a leap at Birch, only to stop in his tracks while starring at that deadly pistol, the last thing that several men had seen on this earth.

He was shocked at how quickly Birch had pulled his iron. The .45-muzzle looked big and was pointed at his chest, so wisely he dropped his knife and stepped back, not wishing to join the spirit world just yet.

Birch was amused at the startled look on this young man's face and motioned him to run away. The brave turned and ran, stopping once to look back with a very surprised look like a fleeing deer.

"My gosh, are you alright dear?" Amy asked, still shaken.

"Oh sure," he said. "I'll bet that young buck is more scared than either of us."

"Why didn't you shoot him? Won't he come back later?"

"No, he was just a boy. The Lakota have lost enough people. Maybe he will manage to grow old."

"Not likely if he keeps on picking fights with guys like you," she said with a touch of admiration in her voice.

Birch turned his back on the young brave and stepped up on the buggy, gently clicked his tongue once again and rode on.

The young brave ran through the timber until he was out of wind. A half day later he reached the small hunting encampment that he had left the day before, breathlessly ran up to the leader, and tried to talk. He bent over to get his breath and stood up to face Black Moon.

"I saw the man I think you seek," Keowac said. "I tried to kill him, but he pulled out his pistol before I could move. He could have killed me."

"You did not see the killer of the path," the annoyed leader said. "He would have left you dead and gutted like a deer. His gun would have killed you. He would not have let you go. He is like a Lakota warrior who shows no mercy to his enemies."

The young man quickly retreated, not wishing to aggravate the tough warrior. Black Moon thought about what the young man might have seen for a couple of minutes and decided to investigate.

What if this was the man who had killed his friends on the trail, the man who they called Birch Rose, Black Moon thought. Maybe that young fool was right.

"Keowac, come and show me where you found this murdering white man who let you go," Black Moon sarcastically said.

"Right away Black Moon, but you go first. I don't want to see death again this day."

Black Moon shook his head and gave the young brave a dirty look as the two quietly moved through the timber without a word. Lakota braves seldom talked when traveling, a big difference between them and the noisy white men.

Late in the evening they reached the trail where Birch had escaped. He was long gone, so the Lakota moved to an opening where the pasture was visible.

"So this is where you saw the dreaded path killer?" Black Moon asked, almost sarcastically.

"Yes, Black Moon, they were here."

"I heard he had a ranch here somewhere," Black Moon answered in a quiet voice. "That is good news. I will be back here soon to meet our enemy."

JUST ANOTHER DAY IN DEADWOOD
April 6, 1879

Amy was happy to stay in town after the buckboard incident, but she would gratefully move to a ranch house after she and Birch were married and he was done chasing ghosts around the plains.

Spring made everyone anxious to start their plans again and everyone in Deadwood—everyone except Birch—had forgotten about Rico. Deadwood was brimming with business as gold was being pulled from mother earth. The miners had money to spend and every mother's son was ready to howl. A few saved most of their poke while others spent as if it was their last days on earth, and in some cases it was.

Evil eyes watched drunk miners open their gold dust poke to pay for a drink, then they followed the unsuspecting into the night where ambushes were generally swift and quiet. Many were laid to rest with a knife across the throat or a swift thump on the head. Gunplay might have brought the deputies, so common thieves of the night preferred a quiet robbery and killing without interference from the law.

Either way, many miners died and most were generally not discovered until the next morning. Many wound up in unmarked graves on a nearby hillside that overlooked the east side of town.

Bullock maintained law and order in Deadwood with what some might consider an iron fist. He prohibited guns, cussing, and other rude behavior in public. Failure to comply with his wishes often resulted in a night with free room and board—in a jail cell.

Night attacks made it necessary for the deputies to patrol late into the evening when they would have preferred to be home in bed.

Jed had excellent night vision and was rewarded with the first arrest in April. Standing in the darkness like a statue, he watched an old miner walk towards the livery stable after a long night of drinking in the Gem Theatre, and a shadow followed close behind. The shadow suddenly raised a knife. Jed yelled and the knife-wielding man turned to run until a bullet in his leg ended the chase.

Birch decided to sit tight and wait for news of Rico. He had feelers across the territory knowing that someone would eventually see the murderer and send word to him through the magic of telegraph.

Most evenings Bullock walked across the street to enjoy a drink at the Gem where he found the shady bar a good place to hear what was happening in Deadwood. Big Al tried to make conversation, but was generally cut short. The big sheriff could stare down the best, and the shady bar owner was generally given a dirty look for his efforts.

Truthfully, Bullock was enough of a politician to use Swearengen, if needed. Al accepted this treatment for his own reasons. He really wanted to be friends with this powerful man, a stature that would make him more accepted in the Deadwood society that was starting to develop and the fast approaching railroad would soon put this small mining town on the map. Big Al wanted to be a person of influence.

Bullock realized all of this and still considered Swearengen to be common white trash who found a seedy way to make money. He had seen too many of Al's prostitutes with bruised faces from severe beatings and knew the girls stayed on out of fear. Big Al had a reputation of bringing girls in against their will and chasing down those who ran. Girls who put Al to this trouble endured serious punishment; some disappeared, never to be heard from again. Many disruptive drunks had shared the same fate.

Life was occasionally still cheap in the Deadwood of 1879, partly because Bullock and his boys could not be everywhere at once.

The railroad was moving closer to Deadwood everyday, but it was still probably a year away. The harsh winters that slammed into the Dakota Territory slowed rail construction. Birch and Jed still spent a lot of time escorting gold shipments back east to Fort Pierre. More gold dug from mother earth meant more gold shipments loaded and shipped as many eyes watched each load leave town. Everybody knew what was packed on those wagons that left deep indentations in the trail.

NEW DEPUTIES
April 10, 1879

Most of the gold was transported by stagecoaches, but large, special gold shipments were packed in big wagons pulled by eight mules, a step up from the first gold shipments when oxen pulled a heavy wagon. A driver's duty was simply to move the team across open plains to each pre-planned destination. The Germans, Lester and Joseph, handled the teams and weather with ease, but both men and the deputies were starting to suffer from fatigue.

Birch and Jed planned to train ten young men to help escort this precious cargo. Bullock had been running newspaper ads that said:

"Wanted: Young men who love adventure and are excellent shots. Top wages will be paid for those accepted. No married men.

If interested, meet at the Deadwood Jail on Saturday, April 12, 1879 at 9:00 a.m. for more information."

Over 100 men showed up for the job. Each was interviewed and tested on the firing range. They started with rifles, shotguns and ended with pistols for accuracy and quickness. Bullock made telegraph inquiries throughout the territories about the character of each man, and finally the ten best were chosen. Most had worked on cattle ranches and some had mined, but all were tough men who were not afraid to fight.

Ernie Segal, Gary Defaro, Don Ammerson, Reynold Johnson, and Hank Fetterson had ridden in from the Decker Cattle Ranch that lay several miles northeast of Deadwood. They had punched cattle for two years and decided to find more adventure. William Harvey and Danny Mann were both from Ireland with red hair and hot tempers.

Harvey had stinky feet, a fact that would not be lost on the men each night in camp when he took off his boots. One evening on the trail, Harvey took off his cowboy boots only to be grabbed by three of the deputies. They carried the struggling Irishman to a nearby river where Joseph lifted him over his head and tossed the screaming man in the chilly water; a bar of soap soon followed.

"Now wash those stinking feet and your socks," Ernie yelled. "Maybe now we will be able to get some sleep."

Russ Jackson and Andy Karnes were college boys from back east, working their ways across the West. Both planned to co-author a book about their adventures. Karnes had boxed in college and was a handful for most men.

Greg Delgaldo did not say where he was from. Bullock, Birch, and Jed knew that he was a marshal from back east who was running away from something, but they considered him a good man. His troubles back east did not matter when trouble started.

Everybody had the job they were qualified to perform. Segal and Ammerson were selected because they were excellent camp cooks that the Decker Cattle Ranch would miss on their future cattle drives. Harvey and Mann had worked their way across the United States doing odd jobs and both men loved a fight.

Johnson found this out one night when he called Mann "a potato head." The short, red-headed Irishman walked over to the grinning cowboy and hit him square on the chin, laying him out flat. Johnson jumped up, but would have been well advised to stay

172

down as the Irishman gave him quite a whipping until Birch and Jed broke it up.

"You men will have plenty of fighting without fighting among yourselves," Birch told all of the deputies. "Now Johnson, you just got your back dusted by Mann in a fair fight. What do you have to say?"

Johnson looked down at his feet, then walked over and held out his hand. Mann took it while trying to hide his sheepish grin.

"Sorry I called you a potato head," Johnson said.

"Well, we did eat a lot of potatoes in Ireland. Just don't call me that again."

"That I can promise you," Johnson answered, rubbing his chin. "What did you hit me with? My jaw will be sore for a week."

"Just a good right cross," Mann answered. "Want me to show you how to throw the Devil's own punch?"

"I'd like to learn if you can show me that punch a bit easier. My jaw couldn't take another hit like that."

Bullock made sure each deputy was well equipped with the newest versions of Colt single action .45 pistols with shiny black bone handles. Other equipment was issued for survival and comfort. Deer skin moccasins were extremely popular on cold nights around the campfire. Each pair was a couple of sizes too big, allowing for the addition of straw for extra warmth. Being one of Bullock's deputies became a prestigious job that included on-the-job training.

Soon they had an efficient team, and they referred to themselves as Bullock's Bastards, but only baptism by fire would show how efficient they really were.

Remarkably, this group was the same age or slightly younger than Birch, who had just turned 20, yet he seemed like an old man to the team. Hard living since the incident on the Trail of Death had aged the once innocent young man and the love of a good woman had saved his sanity. Otherwise life might only have existed to exact revenge for his family's deaths.

Jed was barely 23, but he never remembered being young. He only remembered when he was still with the Cheyenne fighting like dogs in an alley for the last scrap of meat to satisfy an empty stomach. He ate regular meals after being adopted by the rancher Jim Henderson, and working as a ranch hand made him a thick-bodied tough man. The two men made quite a team to reckon with. Their combined survival instincts gave Bullock's Bastards tough and capable leadership.

Bullock made sure that they had plenty of ammunition for target practice. Plenty of shooting on the trail each evening served two purposes: the men were excellent shots and strangers or idiots tempted to try a robbery were made well aware of this. This group, and the German drivers who too were allotted ammunition and guns, seldom ran into trouble. Most robbers were not that stupid.

The deputies were honing their skills with both knife and gun, but all watched Birch closely when the shooting began. He could never escape without putting on a shooting exhibition for the young men, who like most had never seen such incredible, accurate speed.

Jed could not compete with Birch's pistol skills, but they had nightly competitions with their knives. Both were fast with pinpoint accuracy, and no one could determine who was best, but the point was constantly argued.

Entertainment was scarce on the trail in those days. On one occasion Jed and Birch had to laugh when they heard the German, Lester, ask one of the young deputies, "You make bet with me? My brother, Joseph, can lift horse."

Every deputy was leading a good life with top pay and all the perks. A flourish of gold in Deadwood had provided extra funds for anyone brave enough to guard this precious shipment. Every deputy realized that an attack might happen at any moment and all knew that instant death was a definite possibility, but by now they had become a team, each loyal to the other.

AMY'S FEARS
April 16, 1879

Special gold shipment runs began by the middle of April. Each round trip took just over two weeks, and Amy had open arms and a hot meal waiting for Birch when he returned. She always missed him, and she always watched until the wagon and riders were out of sight, praying that she would see him again—alive.

The two started talking about wedding plans, but Jed wisely suggested that Birch hold off on planning a future until the train track reached Deadwood. Both men realized they were open targets while riding beside a wagon filled with gold. A rifle could be pointed at them anytime during the trip and they would be the first killed.

Birch did not mention this to Amy and realized that Jed was right when he said, "There is no use in making future plans until there is definitely going to be a future."

He found out on a warm spring day on her shop's back porch that she was indeed well aware of the situation.

"I have started to feel responsible for Deadwood and the guys I ride with," Birch told Amy. "I feel like I am part of something here, and I have you—life is starting to seem worthwhile."

Surprise settled through him as tears started running down Amy's smooth face.

"Sometimes I can't love you. I don't dare love you," she sobbed while gathering up her skirts and running inside.

Birch stood up totally perplexed while watching the beautiful woman run.

What on earth did I say? He wondered.

"Amy, come back," he called, running up the stairs after her. "What is the matter?"

He found her on the bed in a crumpled heap, red eyed and breathless from weeping. Birch sat down near her for several minutes without a speaking a word and waited until she finally spoke.

"I have lost two men to the horrible violence of this country," she almost whispered. "I was 12 and helping my mother in the back of our cabin at the ranch I own now when three men galloped up into our yard. My pa came out the front door with a shotgun pointed at the ground, and the three strangers pulled their pistols and almost cut him in half—they just kept shooting, Birch. They ignored us as they unsaddled their horses and stole ours. They needed fresh mounts to stay ahead of the posse that was chasing them for robbing a bank. They were finally caught in the hills and hanged on the spot. My father was dead and the three men were dead—and now Mason is dead. I can't even bear the thought of losing you to violence, or any other way."

"I understand, Amy," Birch answered. "That's why I haven't tried to set a date to marry you and don't have a right to ask this, but please, stay with me until the train reaches Deadwood next year. Then the gold-shipment escorts will be finished and I'll turn to ranching."

"I don't know, Birch. I'm afraid."

"I know, dear, I am too. So let's be afraid together for just a little while longer."

"Alright Birch, just a little while longer."

Birch Rose started spending more time with Amy when he wasn't escorting gold shipments, yet they never talked about marriage again. The subject had been brought up, but both decided to wait.

THE MIGHTY LAKOTA WARRIOR, BLACK MOON
June 12, 1879

Black Moon became convinced that the spirit world was making Birch's medicine more powerful. He dreamed of killing the young man to take his strength. Killing this most terrible enemy would make him a respected war chief, and his powers might bring many of the warriors back from Canada. Some might even escape from the reservations where most Lakota resided in 1879. Sadly, few still roamed their sacred hills and plains.

Many dreamed of leading the few remaining free Lakota, Dakota and Nakota in driving the white man out of their territory. Black Moon, an Oglala from the Lakota, believed that killing Birch would help make the Sioux nations realize their vision of defeating the white hordes, and his powerful medicine would make it so.

Powder kegs still were sizzling in the Dakota Territory in 1879 after Congress had voted in favor of taking back the Fort Laramie Treaty only two years before. Remarkably, in 1875 the United States Senate had offered the Lakota six million dollars to buy the Black Hills region, but the Lakota nations refused. The smell of gold prompted the United States to take the Black Hills and an additional 40 million acres of Lakota land.

There was still much fire remaining in the Lakota who had avoided reservations and in some who had endured this "supervised" captivity. The Custer massacre in 1876 had been a powerful message to the American people.

In response, General Sheridan flooded the region with troops and many Lakota surrendered, but some did not. Sitting Bull and his band retreated to Canada while others, like Black Moon, stayed and dreamed of leading his people to victory against the white invaders. Some simply wanted to feed their people, even by taking the mules pulling wagons that made curiously deep tracks from the bulk weight of gold. Black Moon considered killing Rose even more important, and in fact, he became obsessed by this deed.

Lodges talked with reverence about how Birch Rose had survived the Trail of Death with only a knife. Some swore that he was from the spirit world and that evil spirits had sent the shooter to lead the white man against them. This same group believed that the mighty buffalo had disappeared from this land over the past decade as further punishment from the spirit world, although they did not know why or what they had done.

These thoughts served Black Moon well.

Black Moon's desires to save his people were focused on his becoming a great warrior. He wanted to leave this world as a great spirit that many would look to for guidance. Birch Rose's scalp, at least in his mind, was required to accomplish this ascent into power over his tribes.

Lakota scouts had watched the gold wagons for some time, and tribal existence was discussed over council fires that burned brightly throughout the night. Some planned to mount an attack on these strange white men who wasted precious bullets shooting at cactus and old buckets.

Black Moon was summoned to lead the attack because his battles with Birch Rose were legendary. He had fought this man of the evil spirit world and survived.

Black Moon's medicine was truly becoming greater, and he decided to play up the greatness of Birch with magnificent tales of conquest. Black Moon occasionally prolonged his stories of Rose's battles with the great grizzly bear and other horrible creatures.

He was not a liar, but a propagandist. Black Moon wanted to help his people and himself to power.

The young warriors listened with great interest while the older warriors and chiefs often looked at each other in wonderment. Many were sure that Rose had powers beyond a mortal man. Black Moon made sure that Rose would be legendary among the tribes by the time he took his scalp.

Some might call it obsession, while others might call it a vision. But, Black Moon read the smoke from his fire and it became a vision. He decreed that the spirit world gave him a plan to kill Birch, and the following evening he addressed his people:

"Our ancestors are angry. The man who took much Lakota blood on the Trail of Death is still among the living. I have learned in a vision that my destiny is to take his scalp and send him to his own warrior spirits. The white man known as Rose is a warrior who will give up his scalp to me. Then we will ponder on his medicine by the scalp that I will possess. I am to carry out this attack alone. I will sneak like the coyote and strike like the rattlesnake. We will add his medicine to our own in fighting the white soldiers for what is ours. I, Black Moon, have spoken."

The village was silent as many nodded to each other, but no one wanted to speak, and they walked away wondering if Black Moon's medicine was strong enough to kill Birch Rose.

BLACK MOON RIDES
June 13, 1879

Black Moon was given a hero's send off as he rode to his destiny the next afternoon.

He knew where the gold wagons traveled and rode to a spot where he could wait. The following evening he heard distant shooting from the east.

What makes men waste precious bullets like that, he wondered while riding towards the sounds of pistols killing buckets and trees. He waited for the silence that meant all had settled into camp for the night. He watched with interest as two men took guard positions while the others rolled up in their blankets around the fire.

Someone passing by might have thought that Black Moon was part of the boulders because he did not move a muscle for several hours. He sat stone-still, watching and waiting until about midnight when all was quiet before moving in.

Black Moon noted where Birch had rested earlier in the evening. He quietly observed when the lead deputy had laid on his back and studied the stars before turning over with his back against a wagon wheel, a trick Jed had taught him for partial protection from behind. Jed had not made this trip. He had become ill with a stomach virus. He wanted to go, but Bullock had insisted he stay in Deadwood.

Birch, six deputies, and the German teamsters enjoyed deep slumber while the fire burned lower each hour. The light was dim as Black Moon moved in. He crawled through an open space and stood up behind the two men on guard duty, Johnson and Fetterson.

Black Moon waited until Fetterson walked away before quickly and quietly slipping his hand over the startled man's mouth and easily sliding his razor-sharp knife across his throat. He held the man for a couple of seconds before removing his hand.

He laid the man down and crawled to Johnson who had stopped to roll a smoke. The Lakota quietly stood up, surprised to find that this man was much bigger than the first. He leaned up and slipped his hand across the second man's mouth, crushing the hand-rolled cigarette. He worked quicker this time with a deadly slice, and a slight gurgling sound came from the dying man's throat. A flush of excitement coursed through Black Moon's entire being.

Time to kill Rose.

Black Moon was a tough man. He had crawled across several sharp rocks, but was taught to ignore pain early in life. Pain and suffering were no strangers to the Lakota. He quietly crawled around the wagon wheel and squinted in the dim light to find a rolled-up body enjoying a deep sleep. Black Moon crawled closer to Birch and slowly pushed his hand under the blanket, then quickly drew his hand back in shock.

There was no body under the blanket.

Suddenly, a lantern flickered, and Black Moon turned to face Birch who was pointing a pistol at his head.

The shocked Lakota felt a grip on the back of his neck and at his buckskin pants as he was lifted off the ground. He barely turned his eyes to see the big German, Joseph, grinning and staring straight at him. Black Moon then looked away, wondering what kind of crazy man was picking him up, while praying to the spirits that he put him down. His pants were pulling up on his crotch. Joseph's massive fingers tightened to reach Black Moon's throat.

"Lester, look, real live Indian with paint on face," Joseph said excitedly. "He looks just like the books in our homeland described them. This one is very, very ugly."

Lester took a long look at Black Moon before saying, "put him down, Joseph, before you kill him. Can't you see his eyes are crossed and bugging out?"

Joseph obliged, and Black Moon slumped to the ground with a groan.

The only thing that had saved Birch was waking up to the horrible sound of his second deputy dying. The only thing that saved Black Moon at that moment was the dim light and his face paint—white with black streaks—that masked his identity from Birch.

Birch failed to recognize that he was pointing a pistol at the man who killed his father. He only knew that two of his deputies were dead, and this Indian was going to hang.

The other deputies had requested that Birch let them have the "murdering savage" without success. Birch wanted to let the law handle this, a decision he would regret for many years to come.

Black Moon had found some of Birch Rose's luck.

Birch sent Black Moon, escorted by Segal and Defaro before daylight, on to the Territorial Government in Yankton for trial and hanging. He really could not spare the two men, but he did not have provisions or desire to be burdened by a prisoner.

"Use extreme caution with this killer," Birch told Segal and Defaro, a fact they already understood. Many years of hard living were etched in Black Moon's face, and his eyes showed no compassion, only hatred.

Black Moon was securely tied to a horse and saddle that belonged to one of the dead deputies.

Defaro said, "I guess it's only fitting that this murdering injun is carried to the gallows on the horse of the man he killed."

Birch felt worried about Segal and Defaro while watching all three ride out of sight and only hoped they were trained well enough to complete their mission.

Birch's luck held, and the gold wagons reached their destination safely. Soon the gold was transferred to the next crew and headed back east while Rose and his remaining deputies turned their wagons back west towards Deadwood for the long ride home.

Miles away, the two men escorted Black Moon across the plains toward Yankton. Segal, the more experienced plainsman, had felt for sometime that they were being watched, but no one was visible.

He decided that it was his imagination or perhaps fear; besides, this cruel-eyed injun made him feel spooky. He was looking forward to reaching Yankton to unload their unwanted baggage.

Segal's intuition was correct. They had been watched and followed for several miles by a small band of fierce-looking Lakota warriors who had come to rescue Black Moon and kill his captors. They could have easily taken the group several miles back, but decided to wait for the perfect ambush spot.

Finally the deputies reached some low foothills, and their horses had barely started walking up the grade when the Lakota attacked.

Segal died first with a 45-70 round through the chest. Defaro briefly saw Segal's back literally split open by the large bullet. He drew his pistol in time to see a Lakota warrior charging him on an incredibly fast paint. He raised his Colt to shoot. The warrior leaned sideways to avoid the bullet and straightened up in time to wallop the deputy on the head with a war club. Defaro was mercifully knocked out before his throat was cut.

Their scalps were quickly taken and Black Moon was freed. He looked gratefully at the warriors as one asked if Birch Rose was one of the two they had just killed. Black Moon only shook his head and looked the other direction while two of the older warriors exchanged a worried glance.

Black Moon's action told them that the killer of many Lakota still walked among the living and now Black Moon had to go back and face his tribe. The medicine of Birch Rose continued to prevail.

Sadly, by now Black Moon's plight was the least of the tribe's worries. The remaining warriors were out hunting for precious food while most of the tribe had moved to the horrible conditions of a reservation. Stories of soldiers riding into camps and killing everyone including children prompted the abandonment of many traditional Lakota camps.

At Black Moon's camp, only about 30 old men, women and children still remained, unwilling to give up the old ways or their homeland even though less than ten able bodied men remained to support the entire camp.

AN APPROACHING STORM
July 8, 1879

Rose received word of the deputies' fate by the hands of the Lakota warriors because an Army patrol had found the scalped bodies and buried them. Sadly, coyotes and vultures had found the bodies first and devoured their fair share.

Birch, Jed, and Bullock sat on a bench in front of the jail and stared at Deadwood's activities. Few words were spoken.

Birch had questioned himself many times over for sending only two deputies out with the prisoner and had voiced his doubts to Jed and Bullock. Both assured him that they might have done the same thing.

"Might" stuck with Birch for many years and many sleepless nights. He only knew that his order had resulted in the killing of two good men while the murdering Lakota evidently escaped. He had learned a lesson of command the hard way.

Birch was not excited to learn that another gold shipment would be ready to go out the following Tuesday, but he had a job to do. Only six of the original ten deputies remained, not including Jed.

Bullock found four new men from the long list who wanted to join Bullock's Bastards. They were untrained, but good men who would learn quickly. Bob Erickson was an older mule skinner who would replace Segal. The eager new man had jumped at the chance to drive such a fine team of high-handed mules to occasionally spell the Germans. The others, Jim Anderson, Reynold Jackson and Randolph Newberry were cattlemen and range rovers who could shoot and survive in the worst conditions.

When Tuesday arrived, Rose studied each wagon and rider like a general surveying his troops before battle. The sense of adventure had passed, and now each trip was a matter of life or death.

The men seemed more solemn than ever before as the death of their friends had hit each man in a different way. Those who had been in camp when Black Moon struck were amazed that the murderer had killed the two men on guard duty. If not for Birch, none of them might have woken up, and each man realized that he could easily be dead.

Sleep would no longer be anticipated or enjoyed on the trial, at least for a while.

Jed rode up beside Birch and winked.

"We rode escort duty for several months without problems," he said. "We'll be fine now and besides, how can I be the best man at your wedding if we're dead? We will just be more careful."

Bullock watched from his window. His eyes showed the same type of worry a father might feel for his sons before they marched off to war. He stepped away from the window, walked over to the stove, and poured a cup of coffee while deciding not to watch them ride out of town.

Another pair of eyes did watch with much interest as the gold procession left town. Maxwell Braun was a dude from Chicago whose parents had brought him from Germany during his youth. The skinny man wore a gray wool suit, store-bought shoes with pointed toes and a derby that shadowed wire-rimmed glasses. He had been raised with education and more protection than a boy needed or should ever have. In fact, some might have called him a sissy, and they would have been right.

This out-of-place man had traveled to Deadwood with the smell of gold in his nostrils, but never planned to step foot in a mine. He would use his intelligence, not his back, to pan for gold.

Braun occasionally did clerical work for Al Swearengen, helping the saloon owner keep track of his rapidly accumulating assets. In fact, Swearengen was raking in hundreds of dollars daily in booze and prostitute sales, mostly from miners.

Braun was sworn to secrecy on his very life not to discuss Big Al's finances, meaning his very life in a blood oath. Well-educated men with college degrees were rare in 1870s Deadwood and Braun took very good care of Big Al's business dealings.

Braun was working for Big Al that day and making a tidy sum for delivering news that a big gold shipment was leaving town. He had plotted on a map the usual trail of each gold shipment from information gained by eavesdropping on Al's conversations. A day later he sat on his horse in silence and surveyed Swearengen's men, a nasty looking bunch who were operating under Big Al's nose. The lure of gold had made them turn on a very dangerous man.

Braun had never seen that many gunmen and saddle trash in one place. Even worse, they smelled mighty bad. Suddenly his trance was broken by a friendly voice.

"Good to see you, Braun," John Franklin, one of Swearengen's foremen, said. "What good news have you brought us?"

"Hello Mr. Franklin," the dude answered. "I do have news that I want to share with you alone, so can we talk somewhere away from these gentlemen?"

"Yes, we can talk over there by the wagon."

Braun was intimidated like most by Franklin, who had the eyes of a cold-blooded killer. His mouth was a constant sneer, and he constantly touched his holstered .45, as if wanting a reason to draw and shoot. He walked erect with his arms held slightly out to show he had muscles.

Braun was a meek man who did not want to irritate anyone, especially a man who clearly was constantly looking for trouble. He did not feel safe as he had with Swearengen, an unadvisable way to think. Franklin and the small man walked away from the crowd who stood back and watched with anticipation.

Franklin sat on the side of a grassy draw and lit a cigar while Braun closely watched him, occasionally glancing at the rabble that waited nearby.

"So, what news have you to tell me?" Franklin asked.

"Early yesterday a gold shipment on one wagon, followed by a chuckwagon, started out of Deadwood, and headed east for Fort Pierre," Braun said. "There were ten deputies, including Rose and Jed, and they all seemed pretty quiet after the four were killed. I only hope Mr. Swearengen doesn't find out about our double-cross. He might kill me."

"What four were killed?" Franklin asked, ignoring the little man's fears.

Braun proceeded to tell him about the dead deputies.

"Well, that means that they will be more on their guard than ever before," Franklin said. "But no matter. I have a small army here that will take them out easily."

"Will you remember my share of the gold?" Braun asked.

"Of course. You will get exactly what is coming to you, just be patient and wait."

Braun looked forward and walked over to his horse, mounted, and heard Franklin yell, "OK, boys, target practice."

The little man was literally cut to pieces as over 20 lead bullets hit his body followed by a brief silence. His remains fell on the grassy earth followed by laughter from the trigger-happy group.

Franklin looked at the little man scattered on the ground, shook his head, and walked away. Poor bastard, he thought. But that was bound to happen. He did not belong in this country.

Soon Franklin laid out the plan, and soon the gang was riding southeast toward the well-used wagon trail that moved from rolling hills to reasonably flat plains. Their course would come out far enough ahead of the gold wagon to set up a very effective ambush and crossfire where Bullock's Bastards would be cut to pieces without firing a shot in this open ground.

Very careless of Birch Rose and his idiots, Franklin thought. Constantly using the same trail without sending out forward scouts. I guess that makes them damned careless, very predictable and soon dead. But more importantly, that will make me a very rich man.

PRELUDE TO DISASTER
July 10, 1879

Several miles away, the gold wagon, chuckwagon, and deputies were moving slowly as usual, about four to five miles per hour, and this time there was a noticeable difference. The riders were not talking or joking; each man was quietly riding while looking around the plain for signs of danger. The death of their friends had been a timely wake-up call, and the entire group was all business as if by some premonition they knew what lay ahead.

That night three scouts—Newberry, Jackson, and Mann—patrolled the camp area, their eyes constantly moving with rifles ready. Each man occasionally knelt down to look under the wagons.

Birch figured that the first night would be the worst and he was right. The very idea of how that Lakota had crawled into their camp and killed two men without waking most of them meant almost no one slept well except Jed. He had learned how to sleep in a trail camp long before he was a deputy and besides, he knew the other men would be awake most of the night and he was right.

185

Birch slept very little and spent most of the night surveying the stars for signs of his family and perhaps the spirit of Mason. Every little noise was investigated by the jittery deputies, and the snoring German teamsters did not help. Harvey's stinky feet made sleeping even more difficult, and suddenly a coyote started howling. The deputies were mostly wide awake.

Birch looked up just as the eastern horizon started to look a bit lighter, and then he surveyed the land and watched shadows become recognizable objects. Everyone was grateful to see light orange shades—especially Birch.

Jed woke up annoyed by his lack of sleep. He'd been awakened several times by nervous deputies walking around the camp, stirring the fire and whatever else they did. A quick breakfast and hot coffee was cooked on a decent-sized wood fire. Birch figured that the deputies would be better off with a good meal after their lack of sleep, and finally they started heading east into a bright rising sun.

Franklin positioned his men behind rolling hills that looked squarely down on the trail. The wagons would not be there for several hours, and they had time to drag up old limbs and rocks to hide behind. Each man laughed and talked about what they would do with their share of the gold.

The position that Franklin had chosen was perfect; rifle fire from two directions with only short, grassy hills for protection would easily kill the deputies. All would hit the ground dead and the gold would be easy pickings. The grizzled foreman smiled and lit a cigar, took a deep drag and exhaled a pleasurable stream of smoke across the Dakota plains.

Franklin watched his men settle into their ambush spots through his binoculars. He was not obsessed with Rose, unlike many others; Rose was just another man who soon would be cut to pieces in a deadly crossfire.

Birch and Jed rode ahead of the gold shipment several miles to the East. Both men looked the countryside over with their binoculars, another perk from Bullock.

"I will be happy when this trip is over," Birch said.

"We just have to watch ahead for danger," Jed answered. "This will get easier with time."

Birch knew he was right and swung his horse to circle the strange procession, giving each man a reassuring nod. Most returned a weak smile.

186

The four lost deputies had taken away the remaining deputies' cockiness, and their very moods made each man extremely dangerous. They were still self-confident, just less indestructible. They would now fight back like wild caged animals—a state of mind that would serve each man well over the next several hours.

Every ambusher lay motionless. Most had slipped blankets around their still bodies, except Franklin. He did not move and barely seemed to breathe.

The outlaws were becoming impatient after enduring a cold camp all night; many would have liked a hot cup of coffee and hot food. But smoke from campfires could be seen for miles, and the gold wagon escorts might notice their fires and turn back towards Deadwood. This would mean chasing them down in open country without the element of surprise.

Franklin considered this attack an easy way to cut down the number of men who would receive gold shares. Their ambush was fool proof—or so they thought—so each man would have to suffer and wait.

This problem was solved when a scout who had been posted on one of the higher hills ran back with news that the gold wagon was in sight. He could see the wagons about three miles away. They had deputies on both sides, a man with a shotgun beside the driver, and the chuckwagon followed close behind.

Franklin signaled to his men across the trail to get down and ready. Soon his fortune would ride into sight, and he did not want any mistakes.

A COLLISION OF FORCES
July 11, 1879

The gold wagon moved into harm's way, and Jed felt that old sensation of being watched while Birch allowed himself a quick vision of Amy.

Birch's instincts took over when one of Franklin's men jumped up for a clear shot. He yelled at Jed as both men wheeled their horses and galloped quickly back to the west while bullets filled the air.

Jed felt a bullet tear skin on his right shoulder, but he managed to stay in the saddle. Two deputies, Harvey and Jackson, on each side of the wagon died immediately from a concentration of heavy rifle fire when most of Franklin's men shot at the same targets.

Lester took a slug in the shoulder, and the older German slumped down in his wagon seat. When Joseph saw his brother slip over, he jumped off the chuckwagon with surprising agility for such a big man and grabbed him off the gold wagon with remarkable ease. Both brothers took cover behind the wagon's front wheel where Joseph doctored Lester's wound.

"How bad are you hit, Jed?" Birch asked after they had ridden out of the range of gunfire.

"Just grazed me," he answered with an angry look in his eyes. "What do you want to do?"

"Several shots came from the hill behind the wagon, but I don't think there are as many guns on that side, so let's clean out that area. Otherwise, we're surrounded and no one will survive."

They knew that the gold was going to be delivered to the railhead, or they would die trying. No other option existed. But for now, they wanted to save as many deputies as possible from the murderous crossfire.

Birch and Jed tied off their horses, pulled repeating rifles out of worn scabbards, and slipped around a big grassy hill, where a quick crawl up the knob allowed a view of what had happened.

Jed surveyed Franklin's men on their bellies, laughing and shooting at the remaining deputies; the ambushers were simply enjoying a day of target practice on the plains. Many more gunshots were coming from the other hill, but Birch and Jed were not concerned about that now. Birch only hoped that the trapped deputies could survive the hailstorm of lead until they could think of something to end this.

Jed motioned to Birch and pointed at the shooters just right of the group. They each took careful aim with the rifle sight centered just below the shoulder blades, and squeezed their triggers.

Both robbers slumped on the ground, and their rifles slid on the grass; their faces would never look up again. The others did not notice that two of their friends were gone, and the deputies repeated their deadly barrage on the next four.

The final four men suddenly noticed something was wrong and stood up to look straight at the deputies. Birch whipped out his six gun and dropped the first three men before they could take aim, while Jed dropped the fourth man with his rifle.

Suddenly the shooting seemed to increase over the hill. Jed and Birch crawled to the hilltop for a look at the situation and decided to slip around behind the ambushers and ambush them.

They rode a wide swath around the hill's perimeter and slipped up behind Franklin, who was shooting at the wagons. He did not hear the first slug from Jed that ripped through his skull.

Several others tried to shoot back and were cut down when they rose for a shot. The remainder of Franklin's gang made for their horses and rode away.

Jed and Birch took stock of their situation—two dead deputies, one German wagon driver injured, and one mule killed. Both men looked at the dead deputies.

"Sorry to see those men killed, but it could have been worse," Jed said.

"Yep, most of us survived, and now we can go on."

"What do you want to do with their bodies?"

"Bullock said to bury them on the trail in canvas if this happened and he would send a detail out to dig them up for burial in Deadwood if anyone showed up for their bodies."

"And you call what we do a tough way to make a living?" Jed asked.

Joseph started plying Lester with whiskey for what was to come. He had been lucky—the bullet entered and exited the muscle portion of his shoulder, but the problem of infection still existed.

Soon the older German was singing German songs in a loud voice that showed the whiskey had done its work. Joseph insisted on taking care of the wound and touched the bullet's entrance hole with a red-hot piece of steel horseshoe that had been placed in the fire for several minutes.

Lester yelled, "Mein Gott, you swine!" and took a swipe at Joseph with his good hand, just missing the determined brother who had repositioned to place burning steel on the exit hole.

Another scream from the ailing German said the job was done, and soon a yarrow plant poultice was secured on both holes by clean rags to further impede the possibility of infection. Lester took another long swig of the whiskey, and then handed the bottle to Joseph who was ready for a drink.

Several hours later the deputies all stood in a circle around Harvey and Jackson's graves. Neither had next of kin, and each man figured this was a good spot to be buried.

Jed suggested that Birch say a few words.

The young deputy stood by the boards with each man's name and said, "Lord, I don't know the right words to say over these men, but they are yours now. I hope you can tolerate Harvey's stinky feet. Other than that, both men were good fighters and the best of company. Amen!"

Jed walked around the area, studying the ground and surroundings. The expert tracker soon found fresh tracks moving to the Northwest and marked several spots before returning to the wagons.

The gold was delivered two days later, and the long trip back to Deadwood started. Birch wondered what he was going to say to Bullock, not to mention Amy.

Birch Rose had a lot to think about on the long ride to Deadwood.

RICO'S JACKPOT
July 18, 1879

Things had not gone well for Rico. After knifing the old bartender in the back in Tinton, he had ridden around some of the mining towns that had sprung up seemingly overnight throughout the Black Hills. Things had been bad enough, but opportunity for wealth did not appear. A miner or two had lost their gold-filled pouches in the dead of night to pay for Rico's needs. Some of them had even given up their lives trying to fight back.

Rico trusted no one, rode alone and kept to himself. He moved in the shadows and kept his unshaven face down while visiting saloons and whorehouses. Depression fed his hunger for revenge.

Now it was summer. His wanderings had taken him over to Fort Pierre where he was able to rob from a few victims, then head south and away from his Deadwood experiences with the deputies and "that pig Swearengen." He found himself steadily moving across the Dakota Territory border and into Nebraska, southwest toward Fort Robinson. Rico was about to give up when he stumbled across his oasis—the Perry Ranch, a spread that visually spoke of a great deal of money.

His first sight of the ranch was from a long hill where some cattle were grazing nearby and others were in adjoining pastures. Don Perry hoped that the snows would hold off longer than usual so he would not have to start feeding his animals hay. He was one of the first to use the Midwestern method of storing grasses throughout the warm season. His tactic had resulted in providing some of the best stock by the following spring.

Perry's wife, Mae, raised a large garden in the short growing time allotted along the Dakota Territory border. Most of her canning was done on the ranch with her lovely 17-year-old daughter, Libby. They sometimes worked with Mae's family to put up jars of green beans, cabbage, carrots and other vegetables, and a stock of potatoes that were stored in a deep cellar under the ranch house.

The best cattlemen wanted to work for Perry, because no where else could they be that well fed throughout the brutal winter.

Rico looked the spread over and stood up in his stirrups.

Old son, he thought, you finally hit the jackpot.

I will ride in, a humble man from Mexico, he planned. I'll ask for a job, and they'll immediately know that I am too proud for handouts. They will get to know me very well, indeed.

He neck reined his big black stallion and proudly rode down the hill, sitting high in his saddle.

Libby had spotted this visitor first. Bundled up in an Indian blanket jacket, she stepped out on the porch and took a long look at what she perceived to be Mexican royalty. Rico needed a bath, but his dusty clothing showed Mexican leather with silver on each pant leg. He needed a shave, but had a good thick black mustache that made him look like a gallant English knight on a big steed, like she had read about in some of her mother's books. The young girl, who only saw her family, cow punchers, and an occasional group of Lakota looking for food, was in awe.

"Good day señorita. Might you be the lady of this ranch?" Rico asked in his best voice. "I am a weary traveler from Mexico just passing through. Would there be a chance of some work on this magnificent ranch?"

191

"My father owns this entire spread. You will have to talk to him."

A deep voice from behind her mildly startled Rico, perhaps because of what he was thinking about the beautiful young girl standing in front of him.

"What can I do for you, mister?" Don Perry asked, not looking particularly friendly. His hand was not far from the hog leg that had helped him create the remarkable ranch that had made him a wealthy man.

"Ah señor, I, Rico Peredes, only want food and shelter," Rico lied. "I am a traveler who is seeing this beautiful country for the first time."

Perry looked him over and noticed the Mexican silver on each pant leg.

Not a saddle bum, but better keep an eye on this guy all the same, Perry thought. Don't care for strangers, especially the way this one was looking at Libby.

"You can set up in the bunkhouse. Some of the others have moved south after our spring round up," Perry said. "Meals are at sunrise and sunset. Those who are late don't eat. Do you have any experience with cattle?"

"Ah, yes, señor, I drove longhorns through my home country of Mexico. I can tend to stock as well as the next man."

"Fine. I'll offer you some work if you're interested. But I'll say up front that you will work hard. I don't tolerate sliders."

"Thank you, señor, I will do my best."

"Then that is good enough," Perry said while turning to walk back into the house. "Get settled in and we'll talk later."

Perry walked into the kitchen where his wife, Mae, was just finishing a batch of sugar cookies from her custom-made cooking stove imported all of the way from Chicago. He walked over to pick up one of the still warm cookies, and she slapped his hand.

"Don," she said. "You are the one who wanted to lose a few pounds. I remember you saying last week that the saddle was starting to feel tighter around your rump. Do you think that cookie will help make the saddle comfortable again?"

"Do you think that I'm not going to grab one of these warm cookies?" he answered while stuffing it in his mouth. "Do you think I am not going to grab you?"

Libby rolled her eyes. She could hear them laughing and acting like children again from her chair on the front porch where she was watching Rico unsaddle his horse. She thought about his dark eyes and beautiful thick mustache.

She admired everything about this stranger who might just be her prince charming. She understood these matters of the heart from the countless books she read.

Reading—that's all there is to do in this God forsaken country, she thought. Bet he could find something more to do than read books or act childish like mom and dad. Bet he could show me plenty.

A HOT TRAIL
July 24, 1879

Seth Bullock sipped his coffee while taking a long look at the returning wagons from his jail house window. The chuckwagon had holes in its canvas, and horses were tied to both wagons—a bad sign.

He took another look at the telegram.

Should I show this to Birch, he wondered?

The telegram read: "Seth Bullock, stop. Man fitting Rico's description sighted here first and then riding south, stop. May be heading towards Nebraska border, stop. Suggest you send posse to investigate, stop. Signed, Edwin Starman, Justice of the Peace, Fort Pierre."

Almost wish I hadn't sent that damn description of the murdering trash, Bullock thought. Now I'll lose Birch and maybe Jed too.

Into his office stepped Birch and Jed, showing signs of too many patrols and worse, too many dead deputies. Bullock sat behind his desk and glanced up as they came in, no differently than any other day. Jed leaned against the wall and Birch sat down in front of the desk without a word. Bullock straightened up some papers and peered at both tired, dusty men.

"What happened?" he asked.

Birch told the story while Bullock listened with a deep frown. When finished, Bullock handed him the telegram, while saying, "I'm letting you know up front that this will be handled by a territorial marshal in Nebraska. You're not going. I still don't like the way you returned from Tinton without papers signed by witnesses. Otherwise, everyone in the territory will think I let you do whatever you want to do, especially above the law."

Birch read the telegram and laid his badge on the desk.

Bullock starred at the tin star for several quiet moments before asking, "Do you think quitting is the answer? Why don't you take a few days off, spend some time with Amy and then we'll see how you feel."

"I'm not leaving forever, just for awhile," Birch answered. "I have to go after Rico. You do what you have to do."

"But you don't even know if it is the same Rico," Bullock countered. "There are a lot of Rico's in this part of the country. Maybe he's the wrong guy."

"Naw, I think he's the right one. Starman says he fits the description right down to those fancy Mexican pants. No, it's the same man that killed my mother and caused the loss of my brothers, and I'm going after him."

"Me too, boss," Jed quietly said while laying his badge on the desk. "I am going with Birch."

Bullock took a long look at Jed's badge, inhaled deeply, and stared out the window.

"Alright, both of you go on this wild goose chase, and keep your badges, but remember this. That man is to be brought back here to be fairly tried. Don't forget he killed Newton. He will be hanged when he's found guilty. I will personally trip the gallows. Now pick up your badges while I write out a warrant for this murdering trash. You'll need supplies so use my voucher at Marne's store. You two idiots be careful and come back quickly as possible. I need you here."

Later that evening Jed disappeared like he always did after a patrol while Birch took a long-needed bath and got a hair cut. He paid an extra nickel for some good-smelling tonic on the back of his neck and head. This evening would be the last with Amy for a while. He only hoped that she would want him back.

A FAREWELL TO AMY
August 7, 1879

By now, business in Amy's dress shop was booming, and she was making quite a living. More so-called respectable women had moved into the area and her dresses were considered to be "quite the thing." She had a poke of money set aside with Birch Rose in mind. Soon the railroad would reach Deadwood and his horrible gold transporting duty would be over. She had yet to hear about the recent attack. She jumped, startled, when someone knocked on her front door.

She opened the door to find a cleaned up, good smelling Birch Rose with his hair slicked down. No words were spoken; she jumped straight into his arms and their lips met in a firm kiss and a spine-breaking hug.

Amy had become Birch's sanity during the long hours of gold wagon escort duty. They rarely saw each other except in their minds, and both found it hard to sleep during their many lonely nights apart. Amy and Birch lived for the day when a future would be possible.

Birch took note that Amy's décor had improved. Her successful dress shop had provided enough money for a parlor table from back east, a Persian rug and wallpaper. He shook his head and wondered what his mother would have thought about such luxuries. Probably would have wanted the same, he thought. Wish she could have lived to have this fancy stuff.

Amy prepared an excellent dinner of roast beef, carrots and potatoes, along with blackberry cobbler for desert, washed down with fresh brewed black coffee. Both sat quietly, eating dinner while exchanging glances. After dinner, she slipped over and sat on his lap for another long kiss, then leaned back and looked into his eyes.

"What's the matter," she whispered. "I know you're tired, but is something else bothering you?"

He told her about the killings and the telegram while she solemnly listened. The part about Rico brought a pained look in her eyes. She knew that Birch would go after the murderer of his family. She just didn't want to let him go.

"Damn it, Birch, do you know what it is like sitting here every night and wondering if you're still alive? Do you have any idea how it feels to wonder if I will ever see you again? I lay in bed every night wondering if you will ever be here with me again. And don't think that other men have not asked me out. Yet I lie in bed every night, alone, waiting for you. Do you think that is easy? Get it straight Birch. I am not going to wait forever. Now get out of here and go find your murderer. I don't want you to see me cry."

Birch grabbed Amy and pulled her tight to his chest. He squeezed her and felt the tears of fear and frustration let go. She reached up and gave him a long, hot kiss. He could taste the tears that had streamed down her face and stopped at her upper lip. Her mouth parted and they stood up. He swooped her up in his arms and carried her shapely body to the bed. This night would stay in both of their minds for a long time to come, an example of what was to be.

PART FOUR

BACK ON THE TRAIL
August 8, 1879

Birch met Jed and Bullock at the livery stable where the clinking of steel on steel filled the air as the blacksmith shaped a shoe. The smell of fire burning from his forge smelled good in the otherwise musty-smelling stable where several horses, mules, and donkeys quietly chewed on hay that had been loosely tossed out. Some of the lucky animals, owned by miners who had found color, dined on oats.

A noisy freight wagon rumbled past, pulled by four stout mules that were at least sixteen hands high. The wagon's metal parts made a jingling sound, and the mules' heavy hooves sounded hollow as they touched Deadwood's muddy main street. Birch and Jed were quietly talking when Bullock walked up.

"So boys, how do you plan to find this guy?" Bullock asked.

"We are trusting to luck in finding out how far south he might have gone," Birch answered. "We plotted out the direction he might have traveled in heading south from Fort Pierre. We will angle that direction and try to cut him off somewhere. Maybe we'll get lucky and find someone who ran across him on the trail. We are going to try and bring Rico back alive. I want to see him hang and even better yet, wait to hang like his friend in Rapid City. I think waiting for execution might be the worst punishment."

"I am glad to hear you talk like that, Birch," Bullock said, although he did not believe it.

I would have killed the murderers of my family if it had happened to me, he thought. But maybe the boy is different; maybe he will go by the law.

"Jed thinks finding this scum will be easy," Birch said. "He won't dream anyone is coming after him. We'll just have to ride a long way. No, I don't think that he'll be expecting us. This might be too easy."

"You know that I could organize a posse to help you catch Rico," Bullock said. "That would allow more of you to spread out."

"Thanks for the offer, boss," Birch answered. "But Jed and I will be more than enough. Make no mistake, we'll find him. His days are numbered."

"Now look Birch," Bullock said. "I know that we have talked about this, but I am going to say it again. Only heaven knows what you are going to do if this turns out to be the Rico you're after. You might charge in like an old buffalo bull protecting his cows or you might do the right thing and arrest him for trial. Again, bring him in alive if possible. Remember, if he's gone into Nebraska you won't have jurisdiction. You'll need to find help from a local sheriff. "

Bullock looked concerned. "Did you pack your warm stuff and extra blankets? You won't likely return until late Fall, and I don't have to tell you how cold it gets on the plains during that time of year. You guys watch your backs and come back alive."

Jed and Birch exchanged amused looks at the motherly advice coming from this legendary tough guy. They mounted their horses and rode out of the stable, leading an extra gelding that was loaded down with supplies that could mean the difference between life and death on the open plains during winter.

Riding out of Deadwood was tougher than either man expected. Jed looked over his shoulder several times while they passed through the Chinese section of town, starring back towards Main Street. Birch's horse raised its tail and deposited some horse apples in the muddy street.

"Just what are you looking for," Birch asked.

"Oh, nothing," Jed quietly answered. "Just looking."

"Oh no, don't hand me that. I know you're looking for somebody, now who?"

"Nobody."

"Alright, if you say you are looking for nobody, then I believe you."

"Damn it Birch, I'm looking for someone who should be looking for me."

"Who?"

"Just a girl."

"So that's where you've been disappearing to. To see a girl."

"Well, yeah, who do you think I'd be going to see?" Jed answered slightly annoyed. "And where were you last night? Who did you go to see? Miss Amy? So why can't I go and see a girl too?"

"Why sure you can, pard. I just wanted to make sure that you was behaving yourself."

"Shut up, just shut up," Jed growled before riding ahead of Birch and the extra horse.

Birch had to laugh. That was the most Jed had ever said to him. But even better, the normally in-control Jed was totally flustered and possibly in love.

Will wonders never cease, Birch mused as the two quietly rode on.

Deadwood lies in a little valley, and Birch and Jed rode a full day and a half through the hills before reaching the plains. Ponderosa pines and aspen made their late summer ride spectacular.

Birch took a deep breath of clean mountain air and exhaled, wishing this dirty business was finished so he could come back to Amy and life.

He glanced at Jed again and had to grin. The normally tough man who seldom showed emotion was looking at the lighter-green aspen against dark green pine and smiling.

Yep, my buddy is in love, Birch thought, but he knew better than to say it out loud.

UNEXPECTED COMPANY
August 9, 1879

Jed and Birch's first camp was south of Deadwood. Neither man was in a hurry. They would find Rico, even if he had moved on, especially with Jed tracking. They made fair distance into a stiff, east wind the next day. Both slipped their blanket coats over their shirts to stop some of the wind, and their hats were tied down for warmth and to avoid being blown off.

Later that evening a thunderstorm dropped torrential rains, and heavy bolts of lightning went crashing into the ground. The storm had approached fast, but Jed saw it coming. They rode to a distant shelter belt that had always been a source of water for the gold wagon trips.

An old Lakota lodge that was dug partly in the ground by an enterprising brave would shelter them from the intense thunderstorm, common during changing weather patterns on the plains.

Jed quickly tied off the horses, and both men crawled into the dugout. The top leaked, but it was better than being in the downpour and at least they were staying mostly dry.

The storm rapidly passed, and the sun shone down on the wet buffalo and little blue stem grasses. The air smelled sweeter than before the rain that washed down the plains.

Both men were preparing to move on when the first arrows flew over their heads. They turned to see five young Lakota riding in full gallop towards them with only bow and arrows; each skinny young man knew this was his day to become a warrior. Taking an enemy in combat meant gaining a feather and higher standing in their tribe, including with the women. They would return to camp with scalps from two white men on their belts.

Birch and Jed realized that these were only boys, although Lakota boys became men very early in those days. They drew their pistols and sent several bullets over the charging boys' heads. The sound of a bullet screaming through the air makes a distinctive sound, like a runaway locomotive, gaining in pitch as it passes by—a frightening sound.

The boys slid their horses to a rough stop, dropped to the ground, and raised out of the grasses with their bows to be greeted by several more shots just over their heads that spooked their horses. One of the boys lunged for the animals that were now bolting across the plains while Jed and Birch took this opportunity to mount and ride east, both men laughing and yelling at the boys as they rode.

The boys would have to find someone else's scalps.

That evening, the stars shone brightly. The open plains allowed an incredible vision of the sky, and the evening chill made a moderate fire pure luxury. They gathered a few pieces of wood. Starting a fire was much easier when the buffalo herds were roaming the plains in huge numbers, but sadly, the buffalo herds were diminishing. In the past, two to three bushels of buffalo chips could easily be gathered for a camp fire to cook dinner, but now most of these magnificent animals were gone and wood would have to do.

Jed and Birch relaxed in camp that night. Their jerked beef and muffins from Amy's kitchen filled their empty stomachs with a swig of water to wash it down. Both men rolled up in their Indian blankets and looked at the sky.

"We'll get an early start in the morning," Jed said. "We have to keep watch for Lakota warriors; those kids nearly took us yesterday. They were in bow and arrow range before either of us knew it. Now let's get some shut eye."

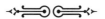

GHOSTS
August 10, 1879

The following morning both men turned south. The late summer air was crisp and refreshing. They chewed on a piece of jerked beef and a swig of water while they traveled.

Little brown shapes on a distant hill stretched higher to see the two travelers and three horses as the prairie dogs rose from their early morning dens, straining their eyes to decide if this was approaching danger.

Jed noticed that Birch had become quieter as they ventured farther into the plains. He knew that his friend was deciding what to do when they found the murderer, Rico. Jed could only imagine the tortured thoughts going through Birch's head, and he was quite correct.

Birch was filled with a mixture of hatred and revenge and the desire to uphold the law. He wanted to kill the animal responsible for killing his mother and his brothers. He wanted to torture this animal into a horrible death for ruining his life.

He fought off feelings of anguish for his family and blind hatred for a piece of trash who had taken the life of a very good woman—and for what reason?

Birch spent a good part of the ride slipping away from sanity while planning how to torture this vermin.

I will stake him out over an anthill and slowly peel his skin with my bowie knife, he thought. Jed once told me he watched a man take three horrible days to die like that, yes, that is what I'll do and Jed will help me, but what will I tell Bullock?

Bullock always came to mind, and Amy with her decent ways. During these thoughts his unsettled mind reasoned that bringing Rico back for trial would be the way of a civilized man—the man he had become.

Just have to keep reminding myself of that, he thought.

Then he started thinking about what his brothers might have become, perhaps college back east for one or both, and then he started thinking very unhealthy thoughts about Rico again.

He only knew for sure that one of the best trackers on the plains was on the final trail for the trash that took the best years from his family and left a painful memory instead—and for what purpose?

RICO MAKES HIS MOVE
August 13, 1879

Rico had been on his best behavior; new calluses and muscle aches vouched for his attempt at honest work. Rico had been busy in other ways, too. He learned that Perry had contracts with the Army to supply beef to Fort Robinson and to Indian reservations established near the fort. The contracts were lucrative. Perry's spread included a large, two-story ranch house, a bunkhouse for his cattle hands, a network of corals, and several out-buildings, including a small blacksmith shop.

Rico's charm had made the Perrys feel more at ease, and they accepted him into the ranch life. His ability to smile, to ask questions without seeming to be nosey, and to keep his mouth shut encouraged others to talk freely. He soon found that a cattle drive was going on and the remaining trail hands would be riding out to the north camp in search of strays. Perry had a big contract to fill, and also he did not want his stock trapped on the plains through winter; few cattle would have a chance to survive in the incredibly cold temperatures while being exposed to heavy winds and blizzards.

The following afternoon Rico watched the men saddle, gear up, and ride out. Rico was one of the few remaining hands to stay around the ranch in case they were needed. He waved as they crested the nearby hill, and then he did a quick clean up job. The

Perrys had invited him to dinner—mostly at Libby's insistence and her parents finally agreed. After all, it was not often that she had the opportunity to converse with a guest from a foreign land.

She took a bath before slipping into her best dress brought from Chicago. The long white skirt with purple embroidered flowers was a present from Don and Mae when the stove was ordered. She even sprayed a little of mama's perfume behind her right ear.

The evening meal was a great deal more than Rico was used to, as tall candles illuminated the beautiful setting of white china and red glasses. The amazed bandit picked up a glass and held it towards one of the flickering candles, marveling at the beautiful red light it created.

Don sat at the head of the table, and Mae sat to Rico's left with Libby across the table. The cook set a plate of steak, potatoes, and carrots in front of the extremely hungry Rico. He started to reach for a fork when Don suggested that everyone hold hands for the prayer.

Rico closed his eyes and felt the soft hands of both women. His thoughts at that moment were not about God.

"Our kind and most gracious heavenly Father," Don prayed aloud. "Thank you for our abundance of food. Thank you for this beautiful weather, and please bless the guest of our house. Please allow us to live in peace in this land of uncertainty. In Christ's name I pray, amen."

"Amen," Rico echoed with a sadistic smirk.

MURDER OF A GOOD FAMILY
August 14, 1879

"So Rico, where do you hail from?" Don asked the next morning while the two men were out by the coral.

"Mexico City, señor," he answered. "My family owns much property near there. I am the youngest of three brothers; one could someday be the president of our fine country. My father owns a lot of land and two huge herds of cattle."

"What type of cattle?" Don inquired.

"Texas longhorns, and we have some sheep, chickens and pigs, too."

"I wonder if your father might be interested in some prime Angus beef."

"Maybe so, señor Perry. Of course, he would have to inspect the beef himself. He is a very cautious man."

Rico was lying of course, and doing a pretty convincing job. Don Perry was being taken in by this thief and liar, and even worse, Libby was being pulled in like a big fish. She had met Mexican royalty; now she had to act before he moved on. That evening after dinner she made her move.

Rico had settled into the now abandoned bunkhouse when a knock came on the door.

"Señorita, what are you doing out here on this chilly night?"

"Mr. Peredes, I wanted to talk with you." Libby paused a moment before saying what she really wanted to know. "Do you find me attractive?"

"Oh yes, my dear, you are beautiful like a desert cactus flower."

"Would you like to kiss me? Am I that attractive?"

Rico did not answer with words; he wrapped his arms around her and planted a long, passionate kiss that made her a little dizzy.

"I don't want you to leave," she said softly. "I want you to stay here with me forever."

"No, my dear, I have to move on."

"Then take me with you," she pleaded.

"I am sorry little dove. I don't have enough money with me for both of us."

"I can get money," she said. "We have lots in a metal strong box in the house."

"How much money?" Rico asked.

"How much do we need?"

"A lot my dear, a lot."

"Alright, I'll slip back into the house, and I'll return after mom and dad are asleep. I'll get the money and my clothes, and I'll meet you over that hill by the old creek after everyone is asleep, about 10:00 tonight. They'll never miss me. Maybe you can take me somewhere like St. Louis where I can buy a new red dress and then we can go places—like the theatre or on a trolley and we can eat at nice places. I will buy you a new suit, and we will be the most beautiful couple there. Everyone will look at us when we walk in the door. Oh Rico, I love you!"

"And I love you, too, my little prairie flower," Rico lied. "But wait, before you go, take this, it belonged to my mother."

Libby held out her hand, and he gently placed a golden locket on her palm. He had stolen it from a whore in Kansas City years ago, but Libby believed a gift that belonged to his mother made her special. He moved behind her and slipped the necklace around her pretty neck.

She flashed him a big, bright smile and reached up to kiss him once more before turning to leave. Libby slipped back out the splintery door and disappeared into the night, still feeling the stretched out locket against her skin.

Rico lay on his bunk and waited, thinking. She is pretty. I can use her a while and all that beautiful money. But the parents will come after us; they will know where she has gone. The old man is not stupid.

Rico lit a match and looked at his pocket watch—9:30. He walked to the door and glanced at the house.

Good, all the lights are out. They are asleep, he thought, and she rode out a few minutes ago—she will be waiting.

Rico slipped across the yard and tried the front door to find it unlocked. Until that night there had never been a need for any type of locked door on the plains. The knob turned easily in his cold hand, and he stepped inside. He stood there, fingering the smooth blade of his knife and breathing hard.

"Time to kill again, amigo," he mumbled to his knife. He started to take a step and then stopped to calm down.

Finally he started moving towards the staircase again. Moonlight made it possible for him to see the stairs that led up to the bedrooms. He softly put his weight on the first step and second step without a problem. The third step made a high-pitched creaking sound that echoed through the quiet house. Rico touched his pistol and waited, but nothing happened. The next seven steps creaked a great deal less when he stepped on the edge of each slat just over the nails.

Rico finally reached the top and slipped into the Perry's bedroom. Their door was wide open. He could hear Don Perry's deep breathing as he slept soundly, covering up Rico's breaths of excitement.

The bandit started breathing even harder, lifted his knife, and briefly stopped to notice how the moonlight coming through a window reflected across the shinny blade's edge. The floor squeaked once more as he reached the man, and in one quick motion Rico covered Perry's mouth and slit his throat.

Mae stirred, saw Rico's dark shape over her, and started to scream before meeting the same fate as her husband. Rico had done his evil work with deadly stealth and silence, taking the lives of two respected and well-liked people in less than a minute. He sat on the deathbed for a few minutes, trying to calm his intense excitement from killing two innocent people. He stood, looked at the lifeless bodies that were barely visible in the dark room, wiped the bloody knife blade on a quilt that had kept the Perrys warm for many years and quietly retreated.

Later that evening Libby stood by the old creek and saw a horseman riding towards her. "Rico?"

"Yes, I'm here señorita. Did you bring enough money for us to travel?"

"Yes, I counted it. Over $3,000. We can do a lot with that much money, maybe buy a home."

"Alright little one, let's go before your parents awaken. We have much to do and the world to see."

"Yes, my darling, let's go before they wake up."

TROUBLE
August 16, 1879

Birch and Jed met their contact on the trail and had found out details about Rico's movements. He had been spotted heading south toward the Nebraska border, and a couple of dead bodies with their throats slit had testified to his progress.

The two Deadwood lawmen learned from a saddle bum who traveled around, working just enough to have his fill of whiskey and grub, that the most likely place to find more information about Rico's progress was at the Perry Ranch, a large spread just across the border into Nebraska.

All had gone smoothly with a clear trail and little interference from the few remaining roving bands of Lakota. Birch had caught Jed smiling a couple of times during the trip, a welcome interruption from his dark thoughts.

"What are you smiling about, Jed?"

"Nothing."

"No, I saw you smiling about something—is it about that girl?"

"Maybe," Jed answered, hoping the subject would end.

"What's her name, you old dog?" Birch asked while cutting off a piece of long green chewing tobacco.

"Maybe I'll tell you later—now that's all I'm gonna say."

Birch laughed. "Alright, I promise not to say another word about it. What's her name?"

"Carlotta," Jed said while starring straight ahead.

Birch gave him a long look, spit out a stream of chew, and then thoughtfully gazed ahead across the prairie.

"Carlotta," Birch said with a grin. "Good name for no doubt a beautiful woman."

"Shut up, Birch," Jed warned.

Birch chuckled and rode on without another word about Carlotta.

Then he became quiet again like many times before, and Jed knew to leave him in the silence.

Finally the ranch house was in sight, and the deputies were quickly intercepted by a group of riders. The lead rider was a tough looking man who was clearly in charge.

"This is Perry land and visitors are not welcome. Now just who the hell are you?"

"We're deputies from Deadwood," Birch said in a low, unfriendly voice. "I'm Birch Rose, and this is Jed. We're trailing a Mexican by the name of..."

"Rico," the ranch foreman interrupted. "Mister, you're standing in a long line. We're after that murdering bastard, too. He killed Don and Mae Perry, cut their throats, and kidnapped their daughter, Libby. We wouldn't have discovered them for several days if I hadn't sent a rider back with a message for Mr. Perry. So lawman, you might as well move to the back of the line. My name's Henderson, and I'm the ramrod for this ranch. I have my best trackers following him right now. They'll find him, and we'll hang him."

209

Birch shot a glance at Jed, then back at Henderson.

"Now look mister, we're the law and..."

"No you're not, deputy," Henderson said. "Maybe in Deadwood, but you're not the law here. This is Nebraska. I am the law on this ranch that spreads several thousand acres. I know about you and your reputation, but it don't mean much here."

"Mister, Rico will kill the girl if you go charging up with that big mob," Jed quietly said. "Let us get him."

"Hell injun, we don't know you. You might be going to join that murdering scum. I suggest you stay the hell out of our way."

Birch realized that talking to the mob was useless.

"You can join us, fight us, or ride on," Henderson said in a low, gruff voice. "My trackers will find them, and we'll end it for good."

Birch decided that there was nothing to do but get away from the angry mob. He knew that Jed would easily find Rico and the girl while the mob chased their own tracks. He glared into Henderson's eyes, neck reined his horse to the left, and both men rode over a nearby ridge and out of sight. Henderson scowled at the deputies as they rode away.

Jed started swinging to the east while watching tracks.

"Pard," he said softly to Birch, "These idiots will have all of Rico's tracks covered up soon. We passed several fresh tracks that probably were the trackers, but they're going the wrong way. Rico's tracks are over here and the horse riding beside him is carrying a smaller person, like maybe a young woman. Let's follow those tracks."

Birch followed, totally amazed that Jed could figure all of that out on the grassy slope. He could see the indentations from a horse and rider's weight, but nothing more.

By now Rico had figured that it would be several days before Henderson and company discovered the Perry family. The railhead was a day's journey, and the train would not pass though for two more days, so no reason to hurry now. He had snared a rabbit, cooked it over a spit, and tore off a piece for Libby.

"We will live like a king and queen, instead of peasants eating rabbit on the prairie," he said to Libby who chewed on the tough piece of rabbit thigh and listened, her eyes shinning. "We'll soon make the railhead, then to Kansas City where we'll catch a train to St. Louis. Then we will live like royalty."

210

ONE HELL OF A FIGHT
August, 17, 1879

Birch and Jed quickly moved across the plain's rolling hills. The expert tracker leaned down to study tracks as they pushed towards the unsuspecting Rico, who thought he was safe and on his way to paradise.

Jed continued to study the ground by torchlight, moving through the night with jackets tightened down against the cool prairie air. Studying tracks by torchlight slowed their progress, but they managed to keep going. Several hours later Jed saw a sliver of smoke on the morning horizon rising up from the bottom of a rolling hill.

"There," he said to Birch. "We can sneak up on the camp in that small valley and take him without firing a shot. But let's be cautious. He could see us and kill the girl, or that camp could be a small band of Lakota. They normally don't build visible fires, but maybe they have a good reason."

Unfortunately, Rico stood up at that moment and saw the two approaching riders in the distance.

He turned to Libby and said, "Bandits are coming to take our money!"

He slipped a pistol out of his saddlebag and handed it to Libby.

"Now little one, I will slip to the east side of this hill and try to draw their fire. You go the other way. They are bandits, so be careful. Shoot, and ask questions later."

"Rico, I'm scared," she whispered while hugging him.

"Just trust me little one. We will kill these two and then move on towards the train stop."

Birch and Jed decided to split up. Jed worked his way to the west side of camp while Birch went east. Jed slowly moved to the small grass-covered ridge, looked over the edge, and was rewarded with the bore of a pistol against the top of his forehead.

Then he heard a female voice say, "Give me your gun."

211

He laid the Colt beside his stretched out body and asked, "Are you Libby?"

"I am," she answered in a surprised voice. "How did you know that?"

"Henderson told me. They, like us, are looking for the one who killed your mother and father, the one they call Rico."

Libby shook her head in disbelief and felt hot tears slipping down her cheeks. Her mother and father were dead?

"No, Rico could not have done that," she whispered. "He is too good."

Jed dropped his head in the grass and moaned, "Oh no, just my luck!"

Rico had discovered some good fortune while crawling in the opposite direction from Libby's position. A three-foot prairie rattlesnake sensed that uninvited company was close and coiled up. The snake's delicate senses were not startled enough to rattle, but it was certainly on the alert.

Suddenly a heavy pressure pushed the snake's head down into the prairie grass, the toe of Rico's boot. He carefully grabbed the befuddled serpent with one hand while squeezing its rattle for silence with the other.

"Now, my deadly friend," he whispered. "Be patient, and I will let you do a favor for Rico."

Birch was crawling now with his pistol in hand and nearing the ridge top where Rico waited with his surprise. Rico heard a stick crack from Birch's weight and tossed the rattler toward the sound.

Birch suddenly tensed up as the unmistakable sound of dangerous rattling passed over his head.

The snake landed a foot from Birch's leg.

The startled deputy dared not react. Reaching for his pistol would require too much movement, but his hand was by chance touching his belt knife. He quickly threw his knife at the disoriented snake, which struck at the shinny object.

The knife barely missed while Birch took the opportunity to roll down the ridge, out of striking distance.

The snake slipped off in the grass as Rico peeked over the top for a look, and he almost lost his head from the shot that placed a neat hole in his hat. The bandit took off his hat and looked at the neat little hole.

"Who are you?" Rico yelled.

212

"Deputy Rose from Deadwood," Birch answered. "I am here to take you in for the murder of my family and the Perry family. I plan to see you hang and look forward to the prospect."

"Oh yes, you again, who survived la via de muerte and whose mother squealed like a pig before she died. Pity, she was a good-looking woman. What a waste. But she is dead my friend. What kind of a future is the gallows for me? I have a much better idea. Why don't I just kill you? Then me and the young lady will ride away to a much better life. Now doesn't that sound better than having my very pretty neck broken by a scratchy hemp rope?"

"Time to die, you murdering bastard."

"Si, amigo, but it is time for you to die first," Rico said while cranking off two rounds at the deputy who buried his face in the prairie grass while listening to bullets tear over his head.

Birch stood and fired three quick shots at Rico's barely visible head. Rico rolled to the right and shot several more times, then continued rolling before stopping at the low ridge's bottom where he slowly and carefully slipped his head forward for a look at his enemy.

He crawled over the hump only to find that Birch had done the same thing. A fist caught the startled Rico on the chin, and he quickly responded with two quick jabs that caught Birch off guard; Birch's pistol bounced over the prairie grass.

Birch was not an exceptional fighter, a skill that the quick Rico had acquired in many rough towns. He threw two more punches at Birch, and Birch stepped back to reach for his knife that still lay where the snake had been. Rico quickly drew his pistol as Birch desperately kicked it out of his hand before he could manage a firm grip.

Both men starred at the pistol—as time seemed to stop for a second—before they dove for it.

The two men struggled for control of the pistol, but Rico was quicker; he grabbed the grip and trigger. Birch knew that both the fight and his life were over.

Then his hand felt a sharp object in the prairie grass. He grasped a long, sharp piece of flint, and drove it into Rico's right eye and into his brain while pushing aside his gun hand just before Rico could pull the trigger.

The dying bandit screamed, the pain searing in his head, thrust his hands up to his face, rolled over and over in terrible agony, then—his body jerking in spasms—took his last breath and died.

Birch lay over on his back, took a deep sigh and thought about his family. Rico fought his last fight without drawing the knife that had taken many lives.

AN ANGRY MOB
August 17, 1879

O n the other ridge, Jed heard the gunfire and was desperately trying to convince the foolish girl that Rico had killed her mother and father. At the sound of the gunshots, she briefly looked away, and he grabbed the gun, knowing she really had not wanted to pull the trigger.

Jed ran to see if his friend was still alive. He stopped where Birch was lying on the grass and glanced at Rico, who was a ghastly sight. Libby ran up beside Jed, took a look at Rico, screamed and passed out.

Suddenly a gun shot from the next ridge signaled that Henderson and his men had finally arrived. Henderson rode his buckskin horse around the area, took a long look at Rico and then rode back where Birch and Jed knelt by Libby.

"Thought I told you we wanted this man alive."

"He didn't give us much choice," Birch quietly answered in an aggravated voice. "I gave him every chance to give up. Guess he didn't want to be hanged."

"Alright deputy, I am the law here and this is not over. We came to string someone up and it might as well be you."

Birch's patience was finished, and he drew his pistol with the speed of the rattlesnake that by now was burrowed up several feet away. Jed pointed his pistol back at the seven men who all pointed their guns at them. Birch had his pistol pointed at Henderson's forehead, and Henderson was pointing his pistol at Birch.

The ranch foreman could see Birch's clear, blue killer eyes calmly staring at him over the pistol's sights and his finger twitching on the trigger. He knew about Birch's reputation and decided that nothing was worth dying over that day. Suddenly nothing in the world mattered at that moment, only life or death. Henderson starred into those cold eyes and lowered his pistol.

"Alright men," Henderson said. "Lower your pistols. Rico is dead and we're finished here." The mob slowly lowered their pistols while keeping a close eye on Jed and Birch.

"This is over Rose," Henderson continued. "Let's end it now."

"Alright Henderson, but make a point never to visit Deadwood. I don't ever want to see any of you again. Now take Libby home to bury her parents. She's had a mighty rough day."

Libby climbed on her horse, gave a long, last look at the deputies, and rode away with the shaken foremen and his men. Jed and Birch walked back over for another look at Rico. The stone dagger sticking out of his eye socket was sickening to look at.

"Want to bury him?" Jed asked.

"I don't owe him a thing, not even a burial. Let him lie there for the animals and worms," Birch said while giving the corpse a disgusted look. The Mexican silver conchos that ran down Rico's pant legs reflected sunlight like a shinny decoration—a grotesque decoration in the prairie grass.

"So how do you feel now that all of the gang who killed your mother is dead?"

"Not like I thought," Birch said. "Not good. I feel like justice has been served for my mother and brothers, but I don't feel much better. I just miss them—everyday."

Birch felt a little sick. "He deserved what he got. Let's ride."

Jed looked at Birch, nodded his head in approval, and spit out some tobacco juice on Rico's chest. Both men neck reined their horses west.

Birch figured he had a four-day ride to Amy. His reins felt slick, and he glanced down to realize that his hand was cut from the fight. Blood dripped on his pant leg, but he didn't care. The cut was not deep and it would eventually heal. Killing his mother's murderer had in fact left him empty inside, almost without purpose.

He remembered Amy and the ranch and decided to think about good things. Part of the evil in his life had already started decaying on the plains. He should have felt freed from a burden, but he had a feeling there was something more. Jed rode on with his partner in silence.

215

─◆➤══◗ ◖══➤◆─

HOME AGAIN
August 21, 1879

When Birch and Jed quietly rode into Deadwood, Jed had that peculiar smile on his face that Birch had noticed before. No doubt, he was thinking about someone he considered to be special.

"Carlotta," he told Birch. "She works for Al Swearengen."

"What does she do?" Birch asked.

"She cleans, and she helps take care of the whores."

"Are you serious about her?"

Jed just smiled and rode on. The conversation was finished as far as he was concerned, and nothing more needed to be said. Birch just felt gratified that Jed had said anything at all.

Deadwood was busy as usual. Birch and Jed dodged ox-drawn wagons, a stagecoach and miners headed for some destination. Finally they reached the blacksmith shop and livery stable.

"Hello Hank," Birch said. "Can you take care of our horses? Give them both the royal treatment. They earned it."

"Sure thing, boss," the young livery man answered. "Hey Mr. Rose, when are you going to sell me this big strawberry roan?"

"When I have two more just like him." Birch answered, chuckling. He winked at Jed and they both stepped into the sunlight, dreading the moment when they would have to explain to Bullock why Rico was a dead man instead of a prisoner.

Bullock looked out his window and watched the fatigued men step out of the blacksmith shop where their horses were receiving a good rub down and brushing, soon to be followed by a double helping of oats.

The sheriff quickly sat behind his desk and re-lit his half-smoked cigar, business as usual. He was greatly relieved to see both men return—although he did not want them to know that.

The jailhouse door soon opened, and Jed stepped in first, closely followed by Birch. Bullock listened to their story, shaking his head in disbelief. He stepped over to his pot-bellied stove and tossed his cigar into the glowing coals. He briefly watched the butt flame up and then disappear.

"I should put out warrants on that mob," Bullock grumbled. "Guess I don't have enough to arrest them. What do you think?"

"I think that it is done," Birch answered. "Let's forget it and get on with our lives. I killed that man. That was a sickening sight, and I want to be finished with it."

"Agree, Jed?" Bullock asked.

"Yep," Jed answered.

"Alright, let's not waste any more time on this," Bullock said. "He got what was coming to him, and Birch warned those men to stay away from here. That should be enough. So Birch, what are you going to do now?"

"I'm going to clean up and go see Amy," Birch said, smiling for the first time in several days.

BUD AND BENNY, LAKOTA HUNTERS
September 1, 1879

Bud and Benny lay under cut weeds that bordered the Missouri River. They had found a small oxbow just off the river where huge flocks of snow geese occasionally landed. Both boys wore the buckskins that Red Hawk's wife, Yellow Flower, had sewn with some of the last buffalo sinew. Their faces were blackened with soot from a fire, and their hands were hidden. Soon a flock of about 60 sharp-eyed geese soared overhead, honking and flying a big circle while looking for danger.

"Keep your mouth shut, stupid. Geese crap when they circle, and some might get in your mouth," Bud told Benny. "And quit looking up. They might see your face. I'll let you know when to shoot."

Both boys had fine bows and arrows crafted by Red Hawk. Bud, in fact, loaded an arrow he had crafted under Red Hawk's instruction.

"Remember to shoot the geese nearest us after they land, and maybe we can shoot more than two," Benny whispered. "Just rise up high enough for a shot and make sure the weeds don't fall off your back."

"O.K.," Benny whispered.

Soon the noisy geese settled in, honking and splashing. Bud could barely see a goose eye swim past, not over five yards away from shore.

The boys raised up with arrows drawn back, and then released their arrows that struck home with resounding "THUMPS."

Some geese swam away from the dying birds without realizing the danger. Two more arrows quickly flew through the air, piercing two more geese.

The first goose screamed a warning "HONK" before dying. The flock rose as one into the endless sky, leaving two grinning boys who waded in the shallow water to claim their birds, quite a tribute to Red Hawk's teachings.

"Do you think Yellow Flower will like the geese we shot?" Benny asked in Lakota tongue.

"I hope so," Bud said. "Have you noticed how tired she looks all of the time?"

"I'm going to get her a rabbit or two," Benny answered. "She will smile tonight; I'll make sure of that."

"She seems to be getting fond of us now that we're bigger," Bud said. "But we need to get away; I guess we are going to walk out of here one of these days. We should have done it sooner. I only wish that Birch was still alive; he could go hunting with us and then take us home."

"Yeah," Benny said. "He would come and get us, but in a way, I like it here with Red Hawk and Yellow Flower."

"Yeah. Me too," Bud agreed. "Let's go try to shoot more geese. I love it when we make Yellow Flower smile."

Later that afternoon, both boys had several geese strung over their shoulders while trying to wade through a shallow marsh. Bud stepped around a high stand of cattails and came face to face with a grizzled old miner who looked older than the hills. The young man noticed the deep lines on his weather-beaten face that spoke of many years in the high lonesome trapping fur-bearing critters.

"Well," the old man said. "Those are fine geese, but what are two white boys doing in these parts?"

"None of your business you old goat," Benny said while being pushed by Bud.

"My brother don't mean anything by that, mister. He is just kind of sharp sometimes."

The old man laughed and said, "That's alright son, I admire a boy with sand, even if he could get killed by letting his mouth overload his ass. Now again, boy, what are you doing out here?"

Bud told the story and the old man finally left, satisfied that they were in safekeeping.

Just the same, he thought. Guess I'd better tell someone about those boys. They might have some kinfolk around who might be worried. Hell, might even be a reward out for information about their whereabouts, and I could sure use a poke. The trapping just ain't what it used to be.

NEWS OF TWO WHITE BOYS IN A LAKOTA CAMP
September 9, 1879

Bud and Benny had no way of knowing that Birch was indeed still alive and that he had made a reputation as a Deadwood deputy and as a well-known gun fighter. They would have been interested to know that Birch was preparing to go looking for them.

Birch had always thought his brothers were dead. His only family had been Amy, until he heard the boys might be alive, or so an old trapper had told Bullock.

"Yep," the old sourdough said. "I saw two white boys on the upper Missouri who had become Lakota. They dressed like injuns and carried bows, but you could tell they were white. I spoke to the oldest in white man's tongue, and he answered me back before herding the younger boy away. Both had taken a fine brace of geese, injun style. Now that's worth a drink or two, isn't it sheriff? Is there any other reward?"

Bullock ordered two shots for the old man and walked back to his office. He knew what this would mean to Birch if it were true, and he sent a note for Birch to come to his office. An hour later,

Birch stepped in the door, listened to the news, and stepped back outside without a word except "Much obliged."

Amy had caught him looking out the window, planning how to find them, but he didn't know where to start. She knew his best friend and partner, Jed, would help him.

Birch rode over the following day to tell Jed he was ready to go find his brothers.

"About time," Jed said.

The men said goodbye to their women and headed West to an ancient mountain trail that was the quickest way back to the river and down to the small Lakota camp where the boys apparently lived—a trail the *Deadwood Pioneer* newspaper had once called, "The Trail of Death."

BLACK MOON'S REVENGE
September 10, 1879

Black Moon returned to a sacred cliff and looked out over the plains.

Summer has passed, he thought, and the plains are brown and drab, yet still beautiful. He closed his eyes and focused on a far away campfire, small but bright. Soon he slipped into a meditative state with hopes of finding the spirit world.

He had cleansed himself with the cold, pure water from a nearby river. The water was not holy, but it was all he had. Next he cleansed his mind and spirit. The spirit world would only receive him in this purified state.

Soon a lone Lakota chief appeared who proudly wore several eagle feathers from his accomplishments on earth.

"Black Moon, you seek the evil that has invaded our country, and you look for a certain white man who seeks you as well. Take time to rest your mind and spirit on this matter. You may not have the man, but his family is close, faces you have gazed on and walked away from. Look closer to your own brother, Red Hawk, who does not truly know who he protects. They, my brother, are from the loins that produced the man you seek. They are not dangerous and have embraced our ways through their protectors. Now go, my brother, and right this wrong."

Black Moon opened his eyes and was shocked to find that nighttime had fallen.

From the loins, he thought. Those white boys with Red Hawk must be Birch Rose's brothers. I will soon find out, and then there will be Rose blood on mother earth.

Black Moon had ridden his horse around the plains for weeks while trying to decide how to kill Birch Rose after his close call from the knife fight. The Lakota path killer had already lived too long, Black Moon long ago had decided, and it was time for him to die. He rode to a sacred spot in the hills on a different cliff and built a sweat lodge. Outside the lodge he carefully placed rocks in a circle with crosses in the middle, a small medicine wheel. Consulting the spirit world was not a matter to be taken lightly, and he wanted to make sure that everything was correct. Besides, he wanted to see his beautiful spirit helper again.

He stacked many smooth rocks in the fire in his sweat lodge made from an old buffalo hide. The herds were gone, but some of their remains were still used by the Lakota who longed for the big herds to return. Black Moon poured water on the hot rocks and an overwhelming steam rose to purify his earthly body.

Once finished, he stepped back out on the ledge and looked out over a hundred miles of creation. He sat cross legged, closed his eyes and started a trance that some might call meditation. Soon his visions revealed many things that did not benefit his people. He saw more whites taking their country and many less Lakota people walking on the earth.

A smiling face appeared as his spirit helper returned, and Black Moon was happy to see her instead of the old chief who had told him about the boys. He gazed into her dark brown eyes and felt an impossible love.

She smiled with much whiter teeth than life on the plains allowed and spoke, "Black Moon, you have carried on the fight well, and now you must claim the killer of our people. He is a warrior who will not die easily. You must trick him into making a mistake that will allow you to fight him in the hills. I will give you this plan as time passes. Now go back to your life and never forget that you are a proud Lakota warrior."

221

Black Moon's eyes opened and he took a deep breath. He wanted to stay with his fair maiden, but would have to wait until life was gone. For now, he would carry on the fight.

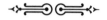

A FAMILY REUNION
September 14, 1879

Several miles away, Birch and Jed guided their mules around large rocks that had remained in the path for several thousands of years. Jed noticed that his partner was quieter than usual, evidence that he was deep in thought. He knew that soon his troubled friend would speak, and he finally did.

"I judge that Bud would be 11 and Benny 10 by now," Birch said. "I wonder how big they are, or by thunder if it is even them."

"We'll see," Jed answered.

"Bud might be big as me. I wonder how they reached those river bottoms by the hills, and not far from that damned path." Birch wondered. "That is not far from where mom was killed."

"A Lakota must have found them and took them there," Jed answered. "Maybe that person who found them will need talking to. I guess we'll see exactly what the situation is when we get there."

This set Birch back to thinking about the boys and what he would do if it was them.

Traveling was slow on the old mountain trail. Both men kept their eyes peeled for Lakota, bear, or other dangers on this ancient trail. Finally they decided to stop and set up a cold camp.

"Chances are Lakota braves already know we are in the area," Jed said. "No use advertising exactly where we are with a fire, though."

The night was uneventful. Birch and Jed started out early the next morning. Sunlight illuminated the eastern horizon with vivid colors of orange and red, and Jed glanced at the colors, happy with the view but not enjoying it as usual. He wondered what they would find at the Lakota camp.

"Do you think they will still want to live in the white way," Birch asked.

"The Lakota way is hard and they will miss the comforts of home," Jed answered. "I think someone has taken them in and taught them. They are lucky to be alive and maybe even more lucky to have been taken in by someone who wanted them. Lakota warriors take great pride in teaching their sons to hunt. But there are Lakota who will kill all whites. Black Moon is one. I wonder how they have survived this long?"

"What will they be like?" Birch asked.

"The same in some ways and different in others," Jed said. "My Cheyenne father taught me, just as Bud and Benny have been taught. They will probably be better men for the experience."

BLACK MOON LEARNS THE TRUTH
September 16, 1879

Red Hawk watched Black Moon approaching the tepee and knew it meant trouble by the look on his face.

His face is cruel. I wonder what he wants, Red Hawk thought.

He quickly found out.

"Where are those two white boys?" Black Moon asked with a fair amount of hatred in his voice.

"Why do you want to know, my brother?" Red Hawk answered.

"Because I want to know where they came from."

"I found them in the Hills," Red Hawk answered, wondering what to do if Black Moon meant to harm the boys.

"No, I mean who is their family?" Black Hawk asked in softer voice, remembering that he was talking to a friend and warrior who had fought many engagements against the whites at his side.

Benny picked that moment to walk around the tepee. He faced a horrible stare from Black Moon.

"What do you want, you dopey old man," he asked in English.

Black Moon did not understand this, but he asked in Lakota, "What is the name of your father, boy, his last name?"

"Rose," Benny answered. "Why do you ask?"

Benny watched Black Moon's face change to hatred and wisely ran back around the tepee. Black Moon started to follow, but was blocked by Red Hawk who received a terrible blow to his head by Black Moon's bow. Red Hawk dropped to the ground.

Black Moon sprinted around the tepee and saw Benny running in the distance. He sat and waited 30 seconds before quietly moving into the woods where he found the boy standing on a log and watching to see if he was being chased. Black Moon grabbed Benny from behind.

"Now boy," he almost whispered. "Let's go find your older brother so you can die together. After that I will find your other brother, and all Rose blood will be wiped off mother earth."

"Let go of me, you son of a dog," Benny unwisely said. "Red Hawk will kill you."

"Shut up, boy," Black Moon said. "Only other plans stop me from cutting your worthless throat right now. I would rather kill you in front of your brother who killed my friend. Start singing your death song. Your life is almost over, and it will soon end on the trail where your brother killed my friend, Red Pony."

Benny shut his eyes and wondered if his life was over.

God, please bring someone to save me he thought, Red Hawk or even Birch if he is still alive. I'm scared.

TIME TO DIE
September 17, 1879

Birch and Jed finally reached the river bottoms and eventually the Lakota camp where they counted 21 rough-looking tepees, meaning that possibly eight well-armed warriors lived there.

Jed decided to ride into camp and ask the first Lakota he encountered about the boys. An old man pointed to Red Hawk's tepee, and it was that simple. Jed walked over and a tall, muscular

Lakota warrior with sharp eyes like a hawk pointed a menacing rifle at his belly. Red Hawk peered over his sights and took a long look at the man he might kill.

"What do you want?" Red Hawk growled.

"I understand you found two boys on the trail between Custer and Deadwood, and I am here to see if they are this man's brothers," Jed answered in Lakota tongue.

Birch heard some rustling in the tepee, and Bud looked at him from behind Red Hawk. Birch immediately knew that he was at the right place and felt a shock at his brother's appearance.

My gosh, look how big Bud is now, and he is dressed like a Lakota, so skinny and dark skinned; he spent all of his time in the sun, Birch thought. He looks well taken care of, except he could use some of Amy's home cooking and a lot of it.

"Hello Bud," he said with a warm smile. Red Hawk looked at Birch and back at Jed to see that he had moved to the side and pointed a pistol at him.

Red Hawk suddenly felt a horrible notion that once again another boy would be taken away.

"Bud, never thought I'd see you again," he said.

"We thought you were dead! Are you taking us home?" Bud asked.

"You bet, brother," Birch answered while returning his deadly gaze towards Red Hawk. "Nothing is going to stop me. Now where is Benny?"

"That damned Black Moon took him yesterday," Bud said. "I found their sign; he took him south. Red Hawk figures he plans to use Benny as bait for you. I was getting ready to go find them and maybe shoot that mangy Black Moon."

"Jed, you stay here with Bud, and I'll go find Benny."

"Now wait Birch, that Black Moon is dangerous. You don't know what he is capable of."

"This is my fight, old friend," Birch answered softly. "Just wait here and see to it that Bud makes it home and back east to college if this does not go well, and thanks for everything. See you later, pard."

Jed tried to argue, but gave up, knowing Rose's stubborn side.

Birch did not have to travel far before finding the first signs that showed a mild struggle and tracks heading south. Black

Moon had indeed taken Benny, and all evidence showed the boy was unhurt with the exception of a bruise or two. He followed the sign until dark, then decided to wait.

Birch broke camp at first light and quickly found the sign. They could not travel far with Benny on foot while Black Moon rode his pony.

Birch remembered Jed's patience while tracking and relentlessly pushed forward, concentrating on the signs. Straining his eyes created a vicious headache, but he dared not avert them for fear of losing tracks that were imprinted in the wet grass. An hour later he found their camp where one small fire had burnt and two bodies had laid as evidenced by crushed prairie grass. They were moving towards the hills where Black Moon would be twice as dangerous.

Birch found the two an hour later while glassing the area with his binoculars and realized that Black Moon had returned to the Trail of Death. They had moved into the hills and were continuing to travel south at the foot of several healthy inclines above the path. He studied the direction they were moving and then made his plan of ambush.

Black Moon and Benny could not hear Birch galloping his horse. He planned to get ahead of Black Moon and ambush him as he had seen groups of Lakota do on several occasions.

He found a perfect place to tether his horse and started climbing to be slightly above Black Moon. He gambled that the two would stay on the course and would end up just under his position.

Birch climbed behind a boulder and waited. It felt like eternity. Soon Benny walked by, followed by Black Moon leading his pony through the rocks. Black Moon did not hear or see what hit him from behind, but only knew it was big, driving his right shoulder painfully into a big rock. He stood up and turned to look in the face of a man he had wanted to kill for a long time.

"Benny, run," Birch yelled.

"Ah, so it is you my cherished enemy," Black Moon said in a soft voice. "Now I am going to kill you in front of your brother and the spirit world. I have waited for this too long."

Birch didn't understand the words, but there was no mistaking Black Moon's intent. He felt the back of his neck turning hot.

"Shut up injun, and fight," Birch answered, not concealing his hate with the memory of his dying father all too fresh in his memory. "Time to die."

Birch pulled out his knife and swiped it at Black Moon who stepped aside, pulled his own knife and cut a chunk out of Birch's ear. Birch answered his cut with another swipe that made a swooshing sound before slicing open the skin over Black Moon's right rib.

The Indian ignored the pain and jumped forward, hoping to drive home a death blow that Birch blocked, dangerously exposing Black Moon's chest to a fatal thrust. The experienced warrior slipped his arm inside the arm that held Birch's knife and knocked the blade harmlessly aside.

Both men bear-hugged, frantically trying to gain an advantage. They fell to the ground, only to roll down a steep hill full of rocks that made painful impressions. The fall allowed each man to recover a knife. Each knew it was only a matter of time before one of them died.

Birch quickly took a swipe and cut Black Moon's wrist that was holding his knife. The startled warrior watched the blade slide down the hill and slip between two rocks. Birch showed little emotion while stepping forward for a better position to drive his knife home and rid the world of his father's killer.

The warrior made an effort not to show emotion, but to find a way to fight—or to die like a warrior. He knew the spirit world was watching and waiting. He knew his spirit helper would be waiting on the other side.

Black Moon took a quick kick at Birch's chin and connected. Birch saw the blue flashing light that meant he was dazed. He did not feel the pain of falling on rocks, only absolute void.

Black Moon raised his hands and yelled to all of his ancestors who had watched this fight between two deadly enemies. A nearby Lakota hunting party heard his victory cry and came running like any group of men who enjoy a good fight. Black Moon still had his hands raised to the sky in gratitude when Birch recovered enough of his senses to soundly kick his enemy in the groin.

Suddenly an arrow slipped through the air, barely missing Birch's head. Birch looked up to see several Lakota standing on a nearby mud bank.

In the meantime, Black Moon fell to the ground in horrible pain; it was a very good kick. His head hit squarely on a rock and his neck cocked in an unnatural direction, indicating that his neck was likely broken.

Birch wanted to make sure of his enemy's death, but knew those few seconds would mean his own death, so he ran down the rocks with the sounds of the screaming war party on his heels.

Occasionally he could hear a rifle bullet scream by or the whoosh of an arrow. He zigged and zagged, maneuvers that saved his life more than once. A running target can be hard to hit when it is moving in directions without rhyme or rhythm. He finally reached his horse, slipped the tether lose and jumped on to start a wild ride out of rifle range while feeling fortunate the Lakota were a hunting party on foot.

He found Benny a half-mile away, hiding behind a big boulder. The young man easily slipped up on Birch's horse, and the two headed back to find Bud and Jed. When they finally reached Red Hawk's tepee, they were not surprised to find Bud hiding there while Red Hawk and Jed stood guard outside.

"What happened pard," Jed asked.

Birch told his story and the condition in which he had left Black Moon.

"But you are not sure he is dead?" Jed persisted.

"No, I didn't take time to ask how he was doing. The arrows and bullets were too close. I had to escape while it was possible. Those guys are good with those bows," Birch answered, slightly irritated.

Jed told Red Hawk about Birch's fight with Black Moon.

"My heart is heavy," Red Hawk said to Jed. "You must take the boys. If Black Moon is still among the living, he will kill them and they still have a lot of life to live. Make it known to all that they will always be our boys, too."

"Let's get out of here," Birch yelled. "Come on boys, time to go to your new home. I'm likely being followed by that hunting party."

Bud and Benny stepped out of the tepee and started to follow Birch and then stopped, turned back and looked at Red Hawk and Yellow Flower, who stepped out of the tepee and stood by her man. Heavy streams of tears flowing down her cheeks. Red Hawk stepped over and slipped his arm around her shoulders. Suddenly, Bud and Benny ran to the couple and hugged them tightly. Jed, not surprised, stepped back over to speak with the grieving couple.

"This is a difficult time," Jed said.

"We once lost our sons to sickness, and the Great Spirit sent us these two boys and now you must take them away," Red Hawk said, his strong voice never wavering.

"Yes, we are taking the boys. This man, their brother, has longed for them. How did you find the boys?"

"I found them on a trail in the hills," Red Hawk said. "They were lost and hungry. We have moved several times to avoid the soldiers, and the boys have learned well."

"What can I do for you?" Jed asked.

"Will we ever see them again?" Yellow Flower asked, tightly clutching the turtle purse against her chest.

Jed motioned for Birch to come close. He spoke quietly to him about Yellow Flower's question. Birch nodded and told Jed what to say.

"Their brother understands what family means, and what it is to suffer loss. He wants them to remain part of your family, too. I will bring them to you every hunting season until they are big enough to make the trips themselves," Jed answered. "But we will have to be cautious of Black Moon or any warrior who thinks like him. We are grateful to you and always will be. The boys would not have survived if not for you."

"There are not many of us left in the hills anymore," Red Hawk said. "Most of our people have gone to the white man's reservations or the spirit world. We know what that means—no longer free to come and go, no longer free to hunt, no longer living as our forefathers did. I have decided that we should live here in Paha Sapa as long as we can. We know how to not be seen. Look for us here next season."

"Goodbye my other father and mother," Bud said. "We will see you before the next snow fall and our rabbits and geese will make Yellow Flower smile again."

"We will hold you in our hearts my sons," Red Hawk answered, not daring to show emotion. There would be plenty of time for that later when he was alone.

Jed had to smile at Bud speaking perfect Lakota tongue. He wrapped his arms around the boys and they turned to leave.

Birch stood back wondering what the conversation was about.

Jed held true to his word, and the boys were reunited with their Lakota family every hunting season until Red Hawk and Yellow Flower became part of the spirit world, horrible days for the boys.

The ride home that day was uneventful until Benny reached in his rock sack and pulled out a smooth creek rock so Bud could take aim at a pine squirrel. Birch glanced over and noticed something shiny on the rocks. He took the rock from Bud and closely examined it to find traces of glittering gold.

"Benny, where did you get these? Do you have any more?" Birch asked.

"Yes sir, I found a whole bunch in the creek when we camped in the hills," Benny answered. "I have a great big sack of them. Ain't they pretty?"

"Yes, brother of mine, you have no idea how pretty," Birch smiled while glancing at Jed who showed a rare smile while shaking his head in disbelief.

"They are just pretty enough to send both of you back east to college someday. But now get ready to meet a very special lady, who happens to cook almost as good as mom. I'm taking the two of you home."

Kenneth L. Kieser

ABOUT THE AUTHOR

Kenneth L. Kieser spent a great deal of his youth riding and falling off horses while playing cowboys and Indians with his cousins on both his dad's and uncle's farms close to Easton, Missouri, just about 12 miles from where the Pony Express started and the house where Jesse James met his demise.

The Rose family, his relatives, took food and other provisions to the Jessie James Gang who always camped in a favorite strip of woods when they passed through the area called Rose Valley in route to various destinations, including an occasional bank robbery.

Kieser watched numerous Western movies with his great grandparents, Milo and Mable Rose (whose family is mentioned in the foreword to *Ride the Trail of Death*) on an old black and white television in the country town of Hemple, Missouri and across the road from the old St. Joseph and Hannibal Railroad spur where the James Gang occasionally passed. He has been a fan of Westerns throughout his life and actually hunted turkeys on a cherished writing assignment with Academy Award winner, Ben Johnson, who starred in numerous Westerns.

Kieser, who resides in the Kansas City area, is a veteran writer with several thousand bylines in both newspapers and magazines. His writing and photos has appeared in many of America's outdoor magazines and several newspapers. He completed a three-year term on the Outdoor Writer's Association of America's Board of Directors in 2002 and is now an active member of the Western Writer's of America, the Southeastern Outdoor Press Association and the Missouri Outdoor Communicators.

Kieser has won several writing awards in competition with other outdoor communicators, mainly in newspaper classes. He won the 2006 Sharon Rushton Award from the Southeastern Outdoor Press Association, for writing about kids in the outdoors, and won the Southeastern Outdoor Press Association's Excellence in Craft, Best Magazine Article or Feature for 2005. He has edited several publications, and once designed a writing program for sophomores at Park Hill High School in Kansas City that was used during a three-year period when several students won writing awards, some in national competition.

Ordering Information

For information on how to purchase copies of Kenneth L. Kieser's *Ride The Trail Of Death*, or for our bulk-purchase discount schedule, call (307) 778-4752 or send an email to: company@lafronterapublishing.com.

About La Frontera Publishing

La frontera is Spanish for "the frontier." Here at La Frontera Publishing, our mission is to be a frontier for new stories and new ideas about the American West.

La Frontera Publishing believes:
- There are more histories to discover
- There are more tales to tell
- There are more stories to write

Visit our Web site for news about upcoming historic fiction or nonfiction books about the American West. We hope you'll join us here — on *la frontera*.

La Frontera Publishing
Bringing You The West In Books
2710 Thomes Ave, Suite 181
Cheyenne, WY 82001
(307) 778-4752
www.lafronterapublishing.com